The hypnotic flames pulled at her, urging her forward. But she couldn't move.

She strained against the pressure of hands encircling her arms. Never taking her gaze from the inferno, Rachel pried frantically at the vise grip. The pain of reliving this nightmare became more than she could bear.

Maggie. Gotta save Maggie.

She had to block out the images.

She felt herself being shaken. "Rachel!" Luke's stern voice catapulted her back to reality. "Let it go!"

Mentally she clawed her way out of the past. Slowly, very slowly, she relaxed. For a long moment she stared at him, trying to rationalize where he'd come from. Then she saw his eyes. Reflected there was regret, pain and something else she couldn't name.

She pressed her face into his chest. She hadn't realized how much she had missed his strength. His arms felt so right, so safe, so secure. His closeness blocked out the memories of the nightmare. If only they'd shared this comfort back then....

Dear Reader,

As a child, my favorite part of the Memorial Day Parade in our small town was always the firemen and the shiny, red fire trucks. I came from a firefighter family and then I married into one. Among my favorite movies are *Backdraft* and *Ladder 49*. Then there was 9/11 and the tragic loss of so many brave men.... Do you see where this is all leading? Writing a book about firemen was inevitable for me.

But *Baptism in Fire* is not only about firemen. It also addresses a subject that has, unfortunately, become a problem of major proportions in my home state of Florida and around the country: the abduction of children. Being a mother and a grandmother, this was the hardest part of the book to write, but a part that my heart told me I had to address.

I hope you enjoy the journey.

Blessings,

Elizabeth Sinclair

ELIZABETH SINCLAIR

BAPTISM IN FIRE

INTIMATE MOMENTS™
Published by Silhouette Books
America's Publisher of Contemporary Romance

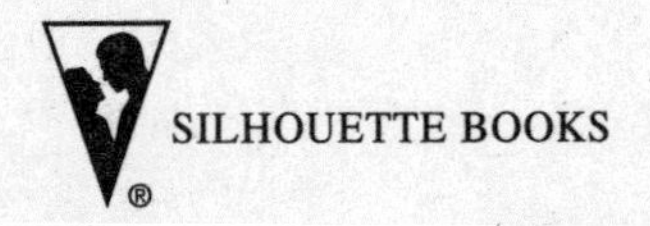

ISBN-13: 978-0-373-27499-4
ISBN-10: 0-373-27499-8

BAPTISM IN FIRE

This edition published by arrangement with Harlequin Books S.A.

Visit Silhouette Books at www.eHarlequin.com

Printed in U.S.A.

Books by Elizabeth Sinclair

Silhouette Intimate Moments

Jenny's Castle #606
Baptism in Fire #1429

Harlequin American Romance

Eight Men and a Lady #677
The Overnight Groom #787
The Pregnancy Clause #827
A Question of Love #916

ELIZABETH SINCLAIR

In 1988, Elizabeth's husband, Bob, dragged her kicking and screaming from her birthplace, the scenic Hudson Valley of upstate New York, to historic St. Augustine, Florida. It took her about three seconds to stop struggling and to fall deeply in love with her adopted hometown. Shortly after their move, at 3:47 p.m. on August 3, 1992, she sold her first romance, *Jenny's Castle,* to Silhouette Intimate Moments®.

Despite the fact that she used to spend hours in the kitchen cooking big meals, Elizabeth's husband, her most ardent supporter, has learned to enjoy hot dogs and delivery pizza as much as he used to enjoy spaghetti sauce from scratch. Oh, and he no longer complains about all the books she spends money on. Bob and Elizabeth have three children, four lovely grandchildren, a rambunctious sheltie, Ripley, and an affectionate adopted beagle, Sammi Girl, they found abandoned along the roadside and took into their home.

For more about Elizabeth, visit her Web site at www.elizabethsinclair.com.

In loving memory of my dad, Preston Charles Ronk,
a thirty-five-year member of the
Walden Hook & Ladder Fire Company, Walden, NY

ACKNOWLEDGMENTS

I would be remiss if I did not express my deepest gratitude to the three men who helped me delve through the world of firefighting and fire forensics and kept me on the authenticity track. Any mistakes or misrepresentations should be attributed to the author.

Ed Sulkowski, Operations Analyst, IFF South Brunswick, has been a fireman for over twenty years with the Highlands Fire Department in Highlands, New Jersey. He is trained in arson investigation, extrusion and fire prevention as well as standard firefighting techniques, and is a member of the ambient IFF industrial firefighters squad.

Wallace Arthur Lind, Senior Crime Scene Analyst (retired), was a police crime scene investigator for seventeen years. In October 1992, he was certified by the International Association for Identification as a Senior Crime Scene Analyst and has processed over 2,000 crime scenes, including homicides; about 1,500 scenes as the lead crime scene investigator; testified as an expert witness in crime scene investigation, bloodstain pattern analysis and scene reconstruction; and trained others in the field.

Dr. Harry R. Carter, a thirty-eight-year veteran in fire and emergency service, is a municipal fire protection consultant, educator and motivational speaker who holds degrees in fire service administration, public policy analysis, fire safety administration, the social sciences and business administration. He currently serves as Chairman of the Board of Fire Commissioners for Howell Township Fire District #2, and is a longtime contributing editor for *Firehouse* magazine and the *Pennsylvania Fireman.* He has authored seven books and more than 1,200 magazine, Web and journal articles.

Prologue

"I'd rather go through root canal without Novocain than go back to Florida," Rachel Lansing said fiercely into the phone. She was unable to believe that a man who professed to be her friend was asking this of her. He knew why she'd left.

"Rachel," A.J. Branson, the Orange Grove Police Department's chief of detectives, sighed. "I know I'm asking a lot—"

"A lot? You have no idea." She swallowed hard and fought for a long time to push back hellish memories of another place, another time, another life. A life she'd believed perfect until— "A.J., I left Orange Grove to put that part of my life to rest, not to mention save my sanity. I have a new life here in Atlanta. Why would I come back?"

"Because this involves kids," A.J. said simply. "No one I know loves kids more than you do and no one I know can profile an arsonist like you."

Kids.

Maggie.

Damn him.

Rachel rose from the couch and paced her small Atlanta apartment's living room. No! She massaged her forehead in an effort to push back the insistent memories rising from the darkest recesses of her mind. But even as she denied them admittance, images of her tall, handsome husband holding their blond little girl as she clutched her worn, patchwork teddy bear seeped into her mind.

Oh, God! Maggie… My sweet baby girl.

Pain sliced through her, nearly drawing her double. Her knees dipped, threatening to collapse completely. She gripped the arm of the couch and took a deep breath.

Her white-knuckled fingers pressed the cordless phone tightly to her ear. "Dammit, A.J., that was a low blow."

"I'm sorry as I can be, Rachel, but in case you haven't figured it out, I'm desperate." A pause. "You know I wouldn't ask you to put yourself through this if I didn't think it was important."

Why hadn't she gone out for dinner instead of coming home? If she had, she would have missed A.J.'s call, missed him stirring up—

"There are other people qualified to do this. Why me?" She tried but failed to keep the anguish out of her voice.

Another pause, then he spoke again, his voice quiet, earnest and firm. "This bastard is about as elusive as any arsonist I've come up against. We've tried for six months to find the answers but we can't. I need an arson profiler who knows the ropes. One who can climb inside the torch's mind. That's you."

A long pause followed, during which Rachel remembered the exhilaration of the hunt, the adrenaline rush of piecing together elusive clues like a giant jigsaw puzzle, and the satisfaction of finally nailing the arsonist and putting him behind bars. Nothing in her present life could compare to the challenge of profiling, of learning the intricacies of how a criminal mind worked and then outthinking him.

All this reminiscing magnified just how much she hated her present job as a secretary in a construction company's office.

However, given the choice, she'd take the boredom of ordering 2x4s any day to reliving the agony of waking up in the middle of the night to find her home going up in flames and her baby gone. When compared to the painful reminders of her only child being kidnapped and probably killed and a husband who no longer loved her, arrogant contractors were infinitely easier to cope with.

"I'm sorry, A.J. You'll have to find yourself another profiler."

"Are you sure?"

A pregnant pause followed his question. Was she sure? Could she turn her back on those kids? Could she step back in time and face everything she'd left behind, step back into a lifestyle filled with memories too brutal to bear? The pain in her heart answered for her.

"Yes. I'm sure," she said, but even she knew her voice lacked conviction. "Find someone else."

Another pause stretched Rachel's nerves to the breaking point. A.J. exhaled a long breath, as if he'd made a decision that didn't sit well with him. "I called you because I need someone with an investment in finding this bastard."

She went stone still. Her fingers tightened on the phone. Sweat broke out on her forehead. "Investment?"

"I didn't want to tell you this over the phone, but this recent series of arsons has some definite similarities to your apartment fire."

An icy chill washed over her from head to toe. "My fire?" She wasn't sure if she'd said it or thought it.

The line remained silent except for her accelerated breathing. Then A.J. cleared his throat as if removing a knot of emotion from it. That didn't surprise her. Maggie's kidnapping and the collapse of Rachel's marriage to Luke had hit A.J. hard.

"There are a lot of similarities, Rachel. I think it's the same arsonist, and I thought you'd want the privilege of helping to collar this creep."

Chapter 1

One Monday morning, after a two-year absence, Rachel walked into the Orange Grove, Florida, police station with a stride that bespoke unmovable determination. If any of the workers knew her, they would have known that look and given her a wide path. But the faces following her progress into the lobby were those of strangers, and instead, they threw casual, unconcerned glances her way and then went back to work.

Rachel surveyed the surroundings and smiled to herself. Maybe the faces didn't ring any bells, but everything else was familiar. The noise level still reminded her of a hive of worker bees, and no matter how hard the cleaning crew tried, the place still reeked of unwashed bodies, stale coffee and cheap floor wax. Forest-green plastic chairs that Rachel wouldn't have given house room bordered one wall and held an assortment of handcuffed suspects awaiting booking. Probably the source of the body odor.

There had been a time when her job as arson investigator

and profiler for Engine 108 and her marriage to Detective Luke Sutherland had brought her here on a fairly regular basis. Back then, she'd always regarded this place as a familiar presence in her life. Now she found herself experiencing a fish-out-of-water sensation.

What difference does it make? You're here to do a job, then leave. You're not here to win friends or settle in permanently.

Rachel walked to the desk and waited while the one familiar person in the room, Desk Sergeant Tony Antola, processed a prisoner being released on bail.

The idle time allowed suppressed doubts to resurface and undermine her resolve. Was she really ready for this? Was she about to jump in over her head emotionally? If she did, was she prepared to face the consequences?

She glanced longingly at the front door and thought about how easy it would be to just slip out, climb into her car and drive back to Georgia. Then images of children without moms, husbands without wives, lives torn to shreds by some crazy bastard who got his rocks off by playing with fire…and her darling little Maggie bombarded her conscience.

Could she handle it? At this very moment, she couldn't answer that, but she knew she had to try, for all those lives and dreams that had gone up in smoke and for herself. She'd never be able to get back what she'd lost, but she'd deal with whatever came her way—one step at a time. For them, for herself and for Maggie.

When Tony finally turned to her, she smiled. "Hi, Tony."

"Rachel!" His eyes widened. He smiled broadly, then seized her hand and pumped it with enthusiasm. "Damn, it's good to see you back here."

"Thanks." She returned his smile and accepted his welcome without explaining that she wasn't really back. "I'm here to see Captain Branson."

"Sergeant."

The one-word command came from Rachel's left and hit her with all the force of a baseball bat being slammed into her middle. It had been eighteen months since she'd last heard it, but she knew that husky voice as surely as she did her own. The owner of that voice had whispered love words to her in the dark of night, read stories to their daughter and promised they would have forever together—then he'd walked out.

Stiffening her back, she turned. Despite her determination not to react, her breath caught in her throat.

Her ex-husband, Luke Sutherland, leaned one broad shoulder against the wall, arms crossed over his wide chest, his hands tucked out of sight beneath his muscular biceps. That purposeful, arrogant stance was also familiar to Rachel. She'd seen it many times, especially in the last six months of their marriage. He'd closed himself off, made it impossible for anyone to see beyond the stern facade he presented to the world. In short, he'd deserted her emotionally and finally physically as well.

That shouldn't have surprised her. Everyone she'd ever cared about had let her down in one way or another: a father who'd left when she was an infant and a mother who'd shut down emotionally and died too young. It was why Rachel had become so good at her job. If you were the best, you didn't have to depend on anyone for anything. Rachel had clung to that independence for years, then she'd made the biggest mistake of her life. She'd met Luke and trusted him to take care of her. In the end, he'd been no better than the two people who had given her life.

Rachel had hoped to never see him again, and now, here they were, face-to-face. She fought to control her breathing, to paint the picture of a calm, in-control woman.

Why hadn't she prepared herself for this? She'd known she'd be running into him. After all, he worked here. Why hadn't she thought of that? But she knew the answer. Catching the arsonist who'd taken Maggie and probably murdered her was all she'd been able to think about from the time A.J. had hung up the phone. Besides, Luke didn't enter into this equation. She had come here for one purpose and one purpose only, and it was not to take up again with the man who had torn out her heart and left it to bleed empty.

Now a whole new set of questions flooded her mind. Had he known she would be coming back? Had A.J. lied to her and orchestrated this to get his two friends to reconcile? No. A.J. wouldn't do that. It just wasn't like him.

Rachel stared at Luke. Words deserted her. Probably because they'd said all they had to say to each other over the deposition table in her divorce lawyer's office. But that didn't mean that his presence didn't spark her pulse to racing. If she hadn't reacted to him at all, she hoped someone had ordered her casket, because surely she'd died. Once he entered a room, Luke was not the kind of man any healthy woman ignored, not even one who had dismissed him from her life months ago.

"Hello, Rachel." His voice was deep, rich and had the effect of silk shimmering over her skin.

He seemed to fill the windowless room. Rachel took a deep breath, hoping to dispel the sudden smothering sensation his presence produced, despite the laboring hum of the AC. "Luke."

He looked past her at Tony. "I'll take Mrs. Sutherland in, Sergeant." Without waiting for a reply, he took Rachel's elbow, but she shrugged him off.

"Lansing. Ms. Lansing." She stared straight ahead, then, when he made no reply, glanced sideways to see if he'd heard her.

One dark eyebrow was raised, but Luke neither looked at her nor said anything. He just led her down the long hall. They stopped in front of a door with a frosted-glass panel embossed with gold letters outlined in black that proclaimed this to be the office of Captain Austin J. Branson, Chief of Detectives.

Luke swung the door wide, and Rachel, careful not to touch him, stepped past him and into the office of the man who had been their closest friend and the best man at their wedding. "A.J.'s at a meeting. He'll be back shortly."

The room thickened with an uncomfortable silence. Her back to him, she felt him move to the side of the room. It surprised Rachel that she could still sense Luke's every movement without looking at him. But, then again, the man did have a presence that permeated all corners of any room.

"What're you doing here, Rachel?"

His question stunned her. She jerked around to look at him. "A.J. didn't tell you I was coming?"

He shook his head. A lock of dark hair slid over his forehead. With a huff of impatience, he pushed it back. "No."

Luke had propped his thigh on the corner of the desk. The bunched muscles beneath the denim fabric brought images to mind of watching him during his daily workout, when sweat coated his tanned body and…

She pushed the thoughts away with both hands.

His dark gaze traveled slowly from her chestnut hair to her gray suit, then downward to her tanned legs, remaining there for a tantalizing moment before moving back to her face. Insanely, she wished she'd worn panty hose.

"You're looking good, Rachel. Georgia agrees with you."

Fighting off the magnetic pull of his gaze, she dropped her briefcase to the floor, then slipped into the chair in front of the desk and pulled her skirt over her knees, effectively cutting short his appraisal.

He smiled knowingly. "You always did have legs that magnetized a man's senses."

She gripped her hands together in her lap to cover their shaking. In an attempt to feed her suddenly starving lungs, she took a deep breath. What the hell was wrong with her? She was over him, over his charismatic ways, over falling victim to his pretty words. Nerves. It had to be nerves. After all, it wasn't every day she embarked on a case that could lead her to the bastard who took Maggie.

Unwilling to prolong this conversation, she glared at him. "I didn't come all this way to discuss my legs. You can leave. I don't need you to babysit me. I'll be fine until A.J. comes back."

"I'll wait," he said and settled his back against the file cabinet beside the desk.

"Suit yourself," she said, then picked up her briefcase and opened it. She glanced at Luke, then quickly averted her gaze to a handful of papers she'd extracted from the open case and attempted to read them. The words swam across the bright white paper. If he would just leave or, at the very least, stop staring at her.

Luke drank in the sight of his former wife. It had been so long. Why was she here? A.J. hadn't mentioned that he'd been expecting her. Had she somehow heard about the arson case they'd been working on and come to offer her help?

If she had, she had a big surprise coming her way. As head of the task force investigating the arsons, he would never agree to having her join the team and, knowing what kind of emotional strain it would put on her, A.J. would never take her up on it. Both he and A.J. knew that Rachel was one of the best arson profilers in the business, but there were too many emotional ties connected to this case, ties she didn't need tearing her apart. So, back to his original question. Why was she here?

She pushed her hair from her face and the light reflected off something at the open neck of her blouse. He waited for a better look, and when she straightened for a second, he saw it. The Oriental necklace he'd given her the week before Maggie was—

He broke the thought off abruptly before it had time to fully form. The last thing he needed right now was to be distracted by the guilt that seemed to ride his back and eat at his belly daily.

The gold necklace winked at him. Given that Rachel had done all she could to cut him out of her life—not that he blamed her—that she was still wearing it shocked him.

His gaze strayed from the necklace to the creamy white skin of her throat, then up to her face. God, she was beautiful. Could have been a model. But she chose to dig through the charred ruins of buildings and the sick minds that started the fires.

Luke drew in a deep breath to steady his libido. A.J.'s office normally smelled of the occasional cigars he indulged in and various other stale odors, but since she'd walked in, he was aware only of the intoxicating scent of her perfume—a scent she had specially made for her, an odd combination of spices and honeysuckle. Seductive and earthy at once, and all Rachel. Despite his efforts, his groin tightened. His pulse quickened. His throat went dry.

How had he ever found the strength to walk away from Rachel? *You found it because she didn't need your guilt hanging around her neck like a dead albatross.* She had her own problems to contend with, and her strength could only support one set of battered emotions. That she had made a new life for herself proved that. Didn't it?

Before he could think about an answer, the door opened and A.J. stepped into the room. His assessing gaze flicked from Luke to Rachel.

Rachel smiled, understandably happy to see her old friend after so long. Older than them by five years, A.J. had Nordic blue eyes and blond good looks that turned the heads of some women, but Rachel had always said she preferred Luke's dark hair and eyes. Still, when she offered his boss the smile Luke craved for himself, he felt the faint stirring of the green-eyed monster. What he wouldn't have given to get that kind of greeting.

She stood and opened her arms. "Hi, A.J."

"Rachel." He engulfed her in a tight embrace, plastering her slight body against his physically fit, six-foot-plus frame. "It's so good to see you. How have you been? It's been way too long."

Gasping for air, she pushed at his broad chest. "I was fine until you did surgery on my rib cage with your belt buckle."

"Sorry." He laughed, then released her immediately. "So, what brings you here?"

Mouth agape, she frowned, then stared first at A.J., then at Luke. "I—"

Luke read the look of puzzlement on Rachel's face. Suddenly, the reason for her presence struck him square in the gut. "Son of a—" Luke rolled to his feet. "Can the act, A.J. I may not be the brightest bulb in the chandelier, but I'm not stupid. You asked her to come, didn't you?"

A.J. shrugged and looked for all the world like a child who had gotten caught drawing on the living-room wall. "Okay, I called her and asked her to consult on the serial arsonist we've been tracking. She said she'd think about it, so I wasn't sure if she was coming or not. Until she made up her mind, I figured I'd keep my mouth shut for a change. I was afraid if I told you, you'd raise hell."

"You got that right." Luke glared at A.J. While his nerves screwed up into tight knots, something akin to panic began forming a ball inside him. He took a step toward his boss. "What the hell were you thinking?"

"Now, wait just a minute, Luke. I'm a big girl and I had the option of saying no." Rachel looked him in the eye, her face grim, her lips set in a tight line. "Luke, I need to do this."

Luke looked from her to A.J., well aware of A.J.'s ability to talk the leaves off a tree, if the need arose. "Like I'm supposed to believe he didn't pressure you into this." Luke stared at her, his jaw clenched so tight his teeth ached. "You *need* to get out of here and go back to Atlanta," he growled, his gaze locked with Rachel's.

His attitude puzzled Rachel. He knew she was a damn good profiler. Why this sudden need to send her packing? It certainly couldn't be because he had any concerns about her personally. The day he'd packed his clothes and walked out of their apartment, he'd given up any right to a say in her life.

"I'm here, and it's a done deal." She snapped her briefcase closed with a decisive click, then turned to A.J. "Can we get started?"

A.J. sighed, his tense expression melting into one of relief. "How long before you have to get back to Atlanta?"

Ignoring Luke's reproachful scrutiny and his presence in the small office as best she could, she said, "I have two weeks of vacation time, so we'd better get to it." Rachel took a pad from her briefcase and clipped a pencil from A.J.'s desk. "Tell me about the fires."

Transforming from concerned friend to hard-nosed cop, A.J. glanced at Luke, then took his place behind the desk. He motioned for Luke to sit in the chair beside Rachel. When he didn't, she glanced around.

"I'll stand, thanks." Luke leaned against the gray file cabinet, which, when she turned to face A.J., would put him just out of her range of vision. His arms were crossed, his flinty gaze silently castigating A.J.

Did his hardened expression mean that he was pissed because A.J. had brought in outside help? Or was it because the outside help was Rachel?

It didn't matter. Either way, she was here and, like it or not, he'd have to learn to live with it.

A.J. waved a dismissive hand at Luke. "Suit yourself." He

opened a file folder and began. "In a nutshell, the three victims are women, one separated and two divorced, single moms living alone, ages twenty-eight to thirty, small children. Two blondes, one brunette. The fires were set at night and when each victim was alone. The kids were with relatives or friends. All were rendered unconscious with a rag soaked in chloroform. The first fire was set about six months ago. Cause of death in all three cases was smoke inhalation."

He took a glossy photo from the folder and tossed it on the desk. "Marsha Adams, married but legally separated, bound with a lamp cord." Other photos taken of the women at the fire scenes followed. "Jane Madison, bound with a lamp cord. Colleen Winston, tied up with duct tape. Both divorced." He wiped a hand over his eyes. "This bastard wanted them to suffer, and they did. One other thing—" He took a deep breath, glanced at Luke, then back to her. "We found all of them in a closet with a Bible beneath them."

Rachel stared at the photos. Instantly she saw the similarities to her own fire, which A.J. had alluded to on the phone. The closet. The lamp cord. The chloroform. The Bible.

The color photos swam before her eyes. Cold sweat broke out on her forehead. She was sure she'd prepared herself for this part. She'd been terribly wrong.

Rachel closed her eyes to shut out the images, but the same frustrating, disjointed memories that had been torturing her for years, memories that she could never put definition to, flitted in and out in snippets like a badly edited movie. No face to put on an arsonist. No one to tell her what happened to Maggie. Just a blur of indistinguishable events.

Sleeping peacefully. Something on her face. A sweet smell filling her nostrils. Sleep. Then waking in a closet.

Her bedroom engulfed in flames. The smoke. Choking.

Closet too small. Can't move.

Hands tied behind her. Bible cutting into her chest.

Helpless to escape.

Helpless to save her baby.

Heat. Intense heat. A voice calling to her.

"Mommy. Mommy?"

Maggie?

Blackness.

Then fresh air seeping into her burning lungs. Wet grass beneath her, soaking into her thin nightgown. A fireman standing over her. Luke, cradling her close to his chest, crying, calling her name and Maggie's.

"Rachel? Rachel? Are you okay?" Luke's voice called her back from that terrible place she'd hidden inside her for so long.

Rachel snapped her eyes open. The images, images that mirrored a periodic dream she'd been having since that night, faded.

She blinked. Luke and A.J. were standing over her, their faces twisted in concern. She searched her mind frantically for something to excuse what had just happened. She knew her ex-husband too well. If she told him the truth, he'd send her back to Atlanta despite what A.J. said. And she made up her mind in that instant that she wasn't going anywhere until she nailed this bastard.

"Yes, yes, I'm fine, just a bit…dizzy. I was so eager to get here that I skipped lunch."

Luke exhaled a huff of air. He crossed his arms over his chest again and glared down at her, eyebrow arched so high it almost disappeared in his hairline. He hadn't believed a word of her explanation.

Determinedly, she squared her shoulders, took a deep breath and forced her gaze toward the photos again. Silently, she employed a system she'd used when she'd started in the firefighters' academy and was confronted with her first horrific fire scene.

You're a professional. Detach yourself. You've got to prove to them that you can do this. If they send you home, you won't be able to help anyone. Detach yourself. This can't *be personal. You are a professional. This is your job.*

Slowly, the tension eased from her body, and her stomach settled. When she felt calm enough, she picked up the pictures. All three women were curled in the fetal position common after exposure to the high temperatures of a fire. Most of their hair had burned off, and the intense heat had split their skin in several places. In all three cases, their arms curled behind them, most of their bonds burned in the fire. Because they had been facedown, the underside of each body had escaped the heat. She could just make out the corner of a book beneath each woman.

She pushed the photos toward A.J. Quickly, he gathered up the pictures and shoved them inside the folder. Instead of handing her the file, he held on to it, glanced at Luke and then to her.

Doubts that hadn't been there before lurked in his eyes and colored his expression. "Maybe this wasn't such a great idea."

"Amen to that," Luke grumbled behind her.

Rachel leaned toward A.J. "If you take me off this case now, I swear I'll stay and work it without the police department. He almost burned me alive, then he took my baby and—" Her voice broke. She glanced at Luke. The concern she'd seen in his expression before had been replaced by a pain she knew well. That of a parent who had lost a child. "And, though we never found her body, it's been almost two years, and I know now that he killed her. I want this sick bastard."

A.J. studied her for a long moment. Her gaze held his without wavering. He nodded and handed her the file folder. "Everything we have is in there—interviews with relatives, spouses, boyfriends, friends. If there's anything else you need, just give a yell."

"How about the arson investigator's photos, the firefighters' narrative reports?"

"They're in there, too. I've designated a room in the annex out back for your office and a place for the task force to meet. The names of the two officers I've assigned to the task force are in the folder."

Stiffening her spine, she clutched the folder. When she looked up, both Luke and A.J. were staring at her.

"What?"

"You okay?" A.J. asked.

Rachel knew she couldn't wiggle out of answering him, but she refused to be treated like a porcelain doll. "Stop worrying about me, dammit." A.J. seemed surprised at her sharp tone, but satisfied. Luke continued to study her. "I told you, I'm fine," she said with much more confidence than she felt.

"Is anyone ever fine with crap like that?" Luke hitched a finger toward her briefcase, where she'd stowed the files.

Was he doubting her or goading her? His complexion seemed to have paled, and she wondered if they were fighting the same demons.

"No, never, but if I'm to do this job right, I need to be able to look at everything as dispassionately as possible." Including you. She swung back to face A.J., who'd been watching them closely. "I'll need to walk the fire scenes."

"When you're ready, I'll walk them with you," Luke said.

Another emotional mountain to climb. "No need. I can do it alone if someone will clear me to enter them."

"I said, I'll go with you." Luke stared unflinchingly at her.

Rachel knew that fixed expression and his adamant tone. There would be no more discussion. She hated that he thought she needed to be babysat, but something deep down inside was glad he'd be with her. "I want to study all the notes and the photos first. I should be ready in a day or two."

Putting off the walk-through was not going to make it any easier, but she swore she would do it before the end of the week. Now that she was here, there was no way in hell she would let Luke see her back down. More important, *she* had to see it through to the end. The time had come to exorcize her demons and what better way than to catch the maniac who was responsible for creating them.

"I'll call you," she said, deliberately leaving it open as to who she was addressing and avoiding eye contact with Luke.

It didn't escape Luke's notice that she conveniently forgot to ask for his phone number, nor that she quite obviously hoped he'd back down from his offer.

Luke knew that she'd envisioned herself and Maggie in those photos and not their victims, just as he had. He'd had to have been blind not to see the way they'd affected her. God knew, he was familiar enough with the sick, helpless feeling, the way it made his gut come up in his throat, the huge empty hole inside him that nothing and no one could fill.

He'd seen those photos innumerable times and still couldn't look at them without seeing his beautiful daughter, without having to fight down the guilt eating a hole in his soul for not being home to stop any of the events that had torn his family and his life apart.

Knowing this could head into territory he faithfully avoided, he closed off that part of his mind. Turning his attention back to Rachel, he watched her closely. Though she hadn't lost one ounce of her beauty, her shoulders didn't seem as square as he remembered them. Her head lacked the proud angle it had always had. Her body had shed a few pounds and appeared, though he knew there was not a delicate bone in Rachel's gorgeous body, almost fragile.

Self-disgust washed over him. Damn A.J. for bringing Rachel here and reminding her. Luke couldn't change the past, but he could and would be there for moral support when she went through the fire scenes. And at the first sign she was breaking under the emotional strain, he'd ship her back to Georgia, kicking and screaming, if necessary.

"What about motive?" Rachel asked.

Luke noted the quiver in her voice. He was sure she'd tried to cover it up, but he'd heard that voice too many times not to be able to read every inflection.

Shaking his head, A.J. leaned back in his chair. "Nothing except the Bible, which points at something religious. Hell, for all we know right now, maybe his mother dropped him on his head at his christening. Who knows? That's your department. Get into his head. Right now, all we have to go on is that the fires are being set by the same torch."

Rachel nodded. "I'll be able to tell you more after I've looked this stuff over."

Luke moved to the side of A.J.'s desk. He knew her caution came as a result of her firefighter training and would keep her from making or voicing premature decisions that she'd have to eat later.

Rachel stood, grabbed her briefcase, clasped A.J.'s outstretched hand, then handed him a slip of paper. "I'll be in touch, but in case you need me, here's my *private* cell-phone number." Offering nothing to Luke but a curt nod, she headed for the door.

"Rachel, one other thing." A.J. looked from Luke to her. "Luke is heading up the task force and will be working closely with you on this. I trust this isn't going to be a problem for either of you?"

"Saving the best till last, right, buddy?" Luke waited, sure she would ask to have him replaced and hoping she'd say she'd go home rather than work with him.

Rachel paused, her back to them. A long moment passed before she turned and looked directly at her ex-husband. "Not if he stays out of my way."

Through A.J.'s open office door, Luke watched Rachel

walk away. His gut instinct was telling him to go after her and do anything he could to convince her to go home. But, stubborn as she could be, he knew it would do no good. It still took everything he could muster not to.

Again, as he watched her disappear around a corner in the long hall, he wondered where he'd found the strength to let her go, to walk out of her life. Maybe because he knew she could make it alone, and she'd be safe without him. Maybe because walking out was easier than looking into her grief-stricken face every day and being reminded of his failure to protect her and Maggie. Maybe, as the days stretched into weeks, then months with no word, he just couldn't face her undying belief that their little girl was still alive. Thank God she seemed to have reconciled herself to Maggie's death.

"Here," A.J. said, ignoring the emphasis Rachel had put on *private,* and copying Rachel's cell number, then handing it to Luke. "If you tell her I gave it to you, I'll say you swiped it."

"Thanks." Luke tucked the paper into his shirt pocket but continued to stare down the empty hall. He knew, if he encouraged A.J., his friend would make it a personal crusade to get him and Rachel back together. Not a good idea.

"Think she still has what it's gonna take to handle this?" A.J. asked from behind him.

Sighing, Luke turned to his boss and friend. "When it comes to expertise and pure guts, I'd put her up against any man in this station." Then he smiled. "But if you tell her I said that, I'll deny every word."

Guts? Yes. He'd stake his life on her courage, and had. But could she withstand the emotional buffeting she'd take investigating the arsonist who had kidnapped and killed their daughter?

Chapter 2

Back in the beach condo A.J. kept for relatives from out of town, Rachel threw her briefcase on the sofa, slipped off her gray suit jacket and shoes, then switched on the TV for background noise. While she unbuttoned the pearl studs on her white silk blouse, she stared at the blond, female news anchor on the screen.

"In local news, the Orange Grove Police Department has confirmed that arson investigator/profiler Rachel Lansing-Sutherland has been called in to consult on the serial arsons that have been plaguing Orange Grove for the last six months. Ms. Lansing's own daughter was abducted two years ago on the night that the Sutherlands' apartment burned down. The case remains officially open, and our sources in the department say that after such a long period of time, abducted children are rarely found alive."

Choking back a sob, Rachel pressed the mute button on the remote. She threw it on the coffee table and headed into the bedroom, leaving the voiceless, female anchor on the TV screen resembling a bad mime.

It had taken Rachel a long time to concede to the belief that her beautiful little girl would never come home again, never laugh at her daddy's silly jokes, never draw those unrecognizable pictures of houses and cows, never drift off to sleep while Rachel sang her favorite lullaby—

Unbidden, the words of the lullaby played through her head. *Hush, little Maggie, don't say a word—*

Grabbing the edge of the dresser, Rachel bent double, clutching her heart. Would the pain never go away? The emptiness never leave her arms or her heart? How does a mother forget a part of her?

Maggie's birth had been the most momentous thing that had ever happened to Rachel. When the nurse laid that tiny being in her arms, their daughter had completed the circle of love she and Luke had found. Rachel had marveled that the fiery passion she and Luke shared could have produced something so small, so perfect, so delicate. Luke adored their baby with the same intensity he applied to his work. Together, the three of them had become a family, sharing their love.

After Maggie's birth, the love Luke and Rachel had for each other had grown by leaps and bounds until she was sure their lives could only get better. But she'd been very wrong. Ironically, all it took to shatter their happiness was a macabre twist of fate and one match.

Exhaustion pressing down on her, Rachel shook loose of the memories and began undressing for a shower. In the mirror above the dresser, she noted that the necklace she wore constantly had snagged in a strand of her chestnut hair. She disentangled the hair and allowed the chain to drop back against her skin. Staring in the mirror, Rachel picked up the medallion hanging from the chain. The artificial light from the bedside lamp caught in the grooves of the Oriental engraving on the gold disk. While in Japan to escort a prisoner back to the States, Luke had bought it for her. He'd told her it was the Chinese symbol for protection and, when she needed him, she had only to rub it and say his name. The whole idea had been foolish fun, but she had never taken the necklace off, not even after the divorce. During the worst times, after she'd ceased opposition to the certainty of Maggie's death, just fingering it had provided her with a small sense of comfort, but no matter how often she had said his name, Luke had never come.

With the pad of her thumb, she stroked the familiar squiggle, noting that the edges of the design had become smooth and rounded, unlike the sharp carving it had been when she first got it. She thought of Luke, his infectious laughter, his charm, his magnetism, and wondered if this little hunk of gold had the power to protect her from him as well.

Showered, shampooed and feeling much better about the job she'd agreed to do, Rachel slipped into jeans and a pale green T-shirt emblazoned with Puppy Love Is Forever, flopped onto the sofa and opened the folder. Turning the victims' photos facedown and moving them to the side, she began to go over the detectives' narrative reports. Using a yellow legal pad she'd pulled from her briefcase, she divided the top sheet into two columns and headed them Similarities and Differences.

Rachel had just gotten started filling in the columns when her cell phone rang. She stiffened, then remembered she hadn't given Luke her number. Digging through the congestion of gas and credit-card receipts, loose change and gum wrappers she'd stuffed into her briefcase during the drive south, she found the cell phone and flipped it open.

"Hello."

"Rachel?" Luke's voice sent a warm ripple through her.

"How did you get my number?" But he didn't need to

answer. She knew. A.J. When she and Luke divorced, it had been as hard on A.J. as it had them. She was sure this was his subtle attempt at mending the relationship.

"I'm sworn to secrecy," he said, a hint of amusement in his tone.

"Well, you can tell A.J. that I'm glad it wasn't my virginity I trusted him to guard."

Once the words were out, Rachel was shocked at how easily she had slipped back into the habit of exchanging quips with Luke.

Would it be just as easy to slip into other things with him? Keeping an emotional distance between herself and the man she'd once loved beyond logic was imperative. She sat straighter.

He laughed. "Yeah. Where we're concerned, he never got high marks for keeping a secret."

An instant replay of the evening A.J. let it slip that Luke had an engagement ring for her crossed her mind. A.J. had waged quite a battle with himself, trying to make up his mind if he should stay and be a part of the big moment or if he should leave them to their privacy. Privacy had finally won out, but not before A.J. had inadvertently blurted out that he couldn't be happier that his two favorite people had decided to tie the knot. She smiled.

A long silence hung on the phone. Why had Luke called? Just to show her he had the number?

"I'm going over the notes A.J. gave me. Was there something you wanted?"

"I just wanted to give you my cell-phone number." He recited the number, and she wrote it across the tope of the legal pad.

"Anything else?" she asked, eager to get him off the phone before she obeyed her urge to see him, to talk to him about this big step she'd taken and ask him to please not fight her on it. Silence. She doodled absently while waiting for him to say something.

Then, "Did you eat dinner yet?"

"No," she blurted a little too sharply, trying to kill the urge to say she'd love to have dinner with him.

He chuckled, deep and sexy. "Even grouches have to eat," he said, reminding her of the first thing he'd ever said to her. She'd gone with him to dinner that night and every night after that. Their entire courtship had been like that, fast, furious and filled with passion and laughter. Then—

No, dammit, she refused to mourn their marriage. She had enough to mourn without adding that. She stiffened her spine.

"I'm not hungry. I'll fix something later." She rarely hungered for anything these days, except what she couldn't have. Like her daughter in her arms.

And Luke? a little voice prompted.

Before he could say anything more, she heard the unmistakable interruption that signaled an incoming call. "I have to take this, Rachel. I'll talk to you later. Don't forget to eat," he admonished, then hung up.

Rachel stared at the dead phone. An acute loneliness washed over her. She folded the phone and laid it on the coffee table. Not until she felt the cold metal on her fingertips did she realize she'd begun stroking the Oriental pendant. When she looked down at the legal pad where she'd written his number, she saw that she had doodled hearts all around it.

Hours passed, and she'd made good progress on assigning the similarities and differences she'd found in the notes. Under the column headed Differences, she'd listed: marital status, hair color and restraints. Under Similarities, she'd written: chloroform, charcoal lighter, victims alone at the time of the fire, all died from smoke inhalation, no signs of sexual assault, one child, each had a Bible placed under her.

Since starting, she'd added a third column to the paper, headed up with one word—Mine. All the similarities she'd listed also appeared under her column. The only differences were that she'd been married and the others had either been separated or divorced at the time of the fires, and she had not been alone.

The common thread that captured her attention was the Bible. Every serial arsonist had a signature. It could be anything from the brand and kind of accelerant they used to the type of incendiary device and where it was planted. This one evidently had religion and, since religious motives were a twisted version of the arsonist's beliefs, it could make him one of the hardest to catch.

She was studying the columns, thinking about the profile of the arsonist, when the cell phone rang again. Rachel jumped.

"Hello," she said, expecting Luke's voice to come back at her through the receiver.

"Rachel, it's A.J. There's another house fire. I'll pick you up in ten minutes."

Adrenaline coursed through her, bringing her to her feet. Blood pumped through her veins at an accelerated rate. "Is it our arsonist?"

"Not sure. We'll know better when we get there. I think it's worth looking into. We've never been on scene while it's happening before. If it is our torch, we might just find him milling around in the gallery enjoying the fruits of his labor."

By the time Rachel arrived with A.J. at the fire site, the south side of the house was a wall of flames. Slowly, she emerged from the car, her gaze locked on the burning wood-frame house. This was her first fire since Maggie's death, and she'd forgotten the sheer power of flames that defied control, the destruction they wreak, the devastation they cause.

Rachel followed A.J. to a position just inside the yellow tape that confined the crowd of curious onlookers to the side-lines. Her training as an arson investigator kicked in, and her gaze automatically scanned the crowd, looking for any sign of someone consumed by sexual excitement, a more-than-helpful bystander, a loner removed from the other gawkers or the deadpan stare of a face transfixed by the flames.

Seeing no one that aroused her suspicions, she turned back to the burning house. The familiar, acrid stink of burning man-made materials filled the air. The sounds of firefighters battling the blaze, yelling orders and calling out words of caution mixed together into an earsplitting cacophony of noise. Then the roar of water leaving a pressurized hose added its voice to the din.

Suddenly, a man screamed a name. Rachel looked toward the voice and saw two firefighters restraining him. The man continued to scream, continued to fight the hands holding him back from running into the building. She stared at him, unable to look away.

"Rachel, I'm going to find the incident commander and see what he knows."

A.J.'s muffled voice seemed to come to her through a thick fog. She nodded but never took her gaze off the distraught man. It brought back vivid reminders of Luke fighting off the firefighters' restraining hands at their fire. Only when the man collapsed to the ground sobbing could she summon the strength to drag her gaze back to the house.

Rachel's nerves began to tighten. She bit down hard on her lip. This is just a fire, she reminded herself. *Any fire. Nothing personal.*

Orange and red flames shot out the windows of one side of the house. Black smoke dotted with tiny glowing embers billowed toward the night sky. Heat waves blurred the outline of the house, twisting its form into a grotesque image of the actual structure. In her mind, as she watched, the image morphed, growing and changing, rising in the sky until it transformed into a high-rise apartment building, the building she, Maggie and Luke had lived in over two years ago.

In mesmerized horror, Rachel watched the flames licking out the windows and up toward the sky. She could hear someone's tormented screams. Her chest tightened. Her vision blurred and time took a sharp nightmarish turn backward. Two-year-old images came rushing at her.

Roaring flames.

Thick, smothering, black smoke.

A hodgepodge of voices.

People running everywhere.

No! Not your fire...different fire...different, she told herself repeatedly, grabbing feverishly at her slipping control.

But the images persisted, growing sharper with each agonizing second. Her palms began to sweat. Her stomach heaved. Her nerves bunched into painful balls of icy fear.

Maggie. Gotta save Maggie.

The hypnotic flames pulled at her, urging her forward. But she couldn't move. Something was holding her back.

Hands.

She strained against the pressure of fingers encircling her arms, but they only tightened. Never taking her gaze from the inferno, Rachel pried frantically at the vise grip of those damn fingers.

"Let go!" She heard her frenzied voice, felt the sweat beading on her forehead. Reality struggled to push through the sharp memories. The pain of reliving this nightmare became more than she could bear.

Can't go there. Can't go back.

God, images won't go away.

She had to block out the images.

Then she felt herself being roughly shaken.

"Rachel!" Luke's stern voice catapulted her over the final edge and back to reality. "Let it go!"

Mentally, she clawed her way out of the mire of the past. Slowly, very slowly, she relaxed.

For a long moment she stared at him, trying to rationalize where he'd come from and why he hadn't been affected as strongly as she had. Then she saw his eyes. Reflected there was regret, pain and something else that she couldn't put a name to.

"I knew A.J. shouldn't have brought you back here," he murmured, pulling her into the shelter of his body and holding her so tight she could barely breathe.

She pressed her face into his chest. She hadn't realized until this very moment how much she had missed his strength. His arms felt so right, so safe, so secure. His closeness blocked out the memories of the nightmare that took their daughter and ultimately their love. If only he'd given her this comfort back then.

Reaching down into her gut, Rachel found the strength to pull away and face him. She tucked her hair behind her ears, then shoved her shaking hands into the pockets of her jeans. "I'm okay."

"Like hell you are. You're shaking like a nervous cat. If I hadn't stopped you, you'd be in there, searching for— " He looked away.

She couldn't deny it. She'd felt an equal pull only once before in her life—two years ago, at their own fire. That night, once she'd been able to breathe again, all she could think of was getting back inside to get Maggie. Little did she know that, by then, Maggie had been long gone, abducted by the arsonist. "I had it under control."

His head snapped around. Disbelief filled his expression. "Bull." His gaze bored into her. "And even if you did, which I don't believe for a minute, what about the next time? What if I'm not around, Rachel?"

In her heart, Rachel knew that any future fires would be different. They wouldn't have the kick in the gut that seeing her first fire in two years, up close and personal, had. Until this day, she'd studiously avoided fires on the TV, in the newspaper, and certainly had not stood in front of a burning building. This was just one more thing in the series of firsts she was facing: first photos, first fire, first death.

This time had been tough. She *would* get stronger.

With shaky hands, she wiped the tears from her cheeks, tears she hadn't been aware she'd shed. "I'm fine now." And deep down, she knew she was or soon would be.

Luke's intense gaze studied her. She met him eye to eye, steady and sure. Irrationally, she was reminded of some of the many reasons she'd fallen in love with Luke Sutherland—his sharp instincts about people and his ability to read them, both of which made him an outstanding cop.

Unfortunately, when it had mattered the most, those same qualities hadn't carried over into his personal life. When the chips were down, what should have drawn them closer drove a wedge between them that neither of them could get past. Luke hadn't seen that she'd needed him desperately to help her withstand the loss of Maggie, to help her hold their life together. He hadn't cared enough about their marriage to help her bind the open wounds and keep their relationship from bleeding to death. He'd thrown away all they had left after losing Maggie…their love. For that, she could never forgive him.

Averting her gaze, she searched the crowd of firefighters for A.J. He was talking to a man Rachel assumed was the fire company's incident commander. After a moment, A.J. turned and walked back to them.

"We might as well get out of here. It's gonna be hours before Rachel can get in there to look around and the fire company can determine if there's another victim to add to our list. Right now, they're classifying it as just another structural fire. Until they can get inside and look around, no one knows for sure." A.J. stared at the blazing structure.

"Rachel's not going in there tomorrow or any other time," Luke said, his face set in determination.

"What?" A.J.'s shocked voice combined with Rachel's.

Luke's expression never wavered. "She's going back to Georgia. We'll find someone else. Someone who—"

"No!" Rachel's fury nearly choked her.

He doubted her ability to come through on the job, all because of what had just happened. But the worst had passed, and she could attack this case with the composed professionalism she'd always shown on her job. His trying to cut her loose before she could prove it infuriated her.

When she spoke again, her tone clearly showed both men just how pissed off she was. Her gaze narrowed on her ex-husband. "Who in hell do you think you are that you can make that decision? I chose to come here from Atlanta to help you. The first time I flinch, you're going to send me home?"

Luke glared back at her. "That was hardly a flinch. And as for who I think I am... I'm the one heading up this task force, and I need people who won't fall apart on me." He stopped, took a deep breath and spoke slowly, as if addressing a child. "I don't want you here."

She did flinch this time.

The flames behind them billowed skyward, their hissing roar a reflection of the anger Rachel felt. She took a step closer to him. "You weren't the one who called me here. And as for me falling apart, I suppose you came to that brilliant conclusion from what happened a few minutes ago."

"What happened?" A.J. asked.

They ignored him.

"Damn straight I did." Luke clenched his fists. "I saw how those crime-scene photos affected you this afternoon, and now the fire. Bringing you here was a huge mistake, but there's still time to fix it before your emotions get you killed."

"What will get me killed is not having my mind on my job because I'm worried that you'll throw me on the next bus home," she shot back at him. "What about you? Are you gonna tell me that your emotions aren't kicking in on this case?"

His whole body stiffened. "We're not talking about me," he said, evading her question. "We're talking about you, and I say you go home."

Rachel faced off with him and gritted her teeth.

"Whether I go or stay is *my* call, and I say I stay."

"You're both wrong," A.J. said, stepping between them. "It's my call." He faced Rachel, his features set in an uncompromising expression. "No one knows if you're up to this better than you do, Rachel. So, I'm only going to ask this once, and I expect you to level with me. Can…you…handle…this?"

"Yes," she said without hesitation. She glared at Luke over A.J.'s shoulder, daring him to argue the point. "Yes, I can."

A.J. looked deep into her eyes, then nodded. "That's good enough for me. I've known you for a long time, and in that time, you've never put yourself or anyone else at risk by taking on a job to prove a point or to feed your own ego. I'm assuming the same still holds true. If you say you can do it, then we'll go for it." He turned to face Luke.

Luke opened his mouth, but before he could say one word, A.J. raised his hand to silence further discussion.

"Meet her here tomorrow to walk this scene. Afterward, you can take her to the others. They've been officially released, so you'll need a warrant to get on the premises. I'll call Judge Hawthorn when I get back to my office and get the necessary paperwork out of the way."

"Thanks, A.J.," Rachel said, breathing a sigh of relief.

"Don't thank me." His demeanor had transformed from her friend, to a hard-nosed cop. "Do your job. If I think for one second that you're giving me less than one hundred percent, I'll replace you faster than my ex-mother-in-law decided she hated my guts." He turned to Luke. "One more thing. Whatever personal issues you two have with each other, settle them on your own time and keep them out of this investigation." He glanced at Rachel. "That means both of you. Am I clear?"

Rachel nodded.

Staring first at A.J., then Rachel, Luke cursed under his breath. "I hope to hell you both know what you're doing," he muttered, and walked away.

Luke ordered another neat scotch, then glanced around the crowded bar. A blonde almost wearing a red minidress made eye contact and smiled. For lack of anything else to do, Luke smiled back. She sauntered toward him, then leaned one forearm on the bar and thrust her ample, man-made chest inches from his nose. The top of her strapless dress nearly lost its precarious hold.

For a second, he imagined Rachel's luscious body filling the flaming red dress, her full breasts overflowing the top. His groin tightened painfully.

"Buy a girl a drink?"

Luke gave her feminine display the once-over. When he was a young stud new to the force and during the two years since he'd last seen Rachel, this woman's barely veiled invitation would have called out to his male libido, but not since Rachel had come back into his life. Since the moment he'd first seen her at headquarters, his head was filled with his ex-wife and that left no room for contemplation of a quick roll in the hay with someone else. He turned away and motioned for the bartender to give the woman whatever she wanted to drink.

A few minutes later, the man behind the bar set a frothy, pink drink in a Manhattan glass in front of her. Instantly Luke thought about Rachel and her favorite drink, gin and tonic. No frills. No pretense. Just like the woman. Suddenly, the all-but-nonexistent interest he'd had in the woman diminished to minus zero, replaced by a soul-deep need for Rachel. Would he ever be able to think of her without that excruciating pain of loss filling him?

"You alone?"

Luke shook his head. "I'm taken," he said, and flashed the ring on the third finger of his right hand, the thin, gold band he'd never been able to bring himself to take off completely.

"Wrong hand," the blonde said, her voice a low purr, her smile seductive and full of unspoken promises.

"I never could tell left from right," Luke said, then downed the last of the scotch and flipped some bills on the bar. "I'm still taken." And probably always will be, he added to himself.

The blonde looked around. "So, where is she?"

He tapped a finger over the left side of his chest. "In here." Then he left the bar.

Outside, he stood on the sidewalk and looked absently up and down the street. The deafening music coming from the bar followed him. He glanced back at the open door and could see the baffled woman at the bar staring at him. He saluted her. She frowned, made a rude hand gesture and turned away.

He probably should have warned her that drinks didn't always come with promises. Hell, little in life did. She'd read more than she should have into a friendly gesture. He could have lied to her, but he hadn't. Rachel was in his heart, as much a part of him as his skin, and had been from the first day he'd seen her with soot on her nose and a determination in her expression that defied explanation. Ever since that day, there hadn't been a night or a day he hadn't thought about her, longed for her, pained for her.

He thought about her at the fire tonight, how scared she'd been, how tortured, and had a sudden need to affirm that she was okay. As he walked toward his car, he obeyed the longing churning inside him and reached for his cell phone, then punched in the numbers he'd memorized off the paper A.J. had given him and pressed it to his ear.

"Hello."

At the sound of his ex-wife's voice, a familiar band of pain tightened around his heart. He forced a lightness into his voice he was far from feeling. "Hey, Rachel. Hope I didn't wake you."

"No. I was just going over the files." Silence. "What did you want?"

"Just to let you know I can meet you at the scene tomorrow around eight. I'll bring the coffee." He waited. "Is that okay?"

"Fine." She sounded preoccupied.

He swallowed. Damn! He didn't want to tell her this, but she'd find out anyway. "Rach, they found another woman in tonight's fire."

Rachel remained silent for a moment or two, then said, "Damn."

"A.J.'ll give you the details tomorrow after we check out the scene." He blew out a long breath. "I'll let you get back to work." While he climbed into his car, he continued to hold the phone to his ear, reluctant to break even this tenuous connection. "So…see you then."

"Luke?"

"Yes."

"Thank you for…for being there tonight."

"No problem." He wanted to add *I'll always be there,* but he knew she had no reason to believe such a promise, coming from him.

Silence.

"'Night." The connection went dead.

"Dream of me," he murmured into the car's dark interior. It was what they'd said to each other every night before dropping off to sleep. It was what he still whispered into the darkness every night from his lonely bed.

He folded the phone and tossed it into the passenger seat. For a long moment, he stared down at the phone, then gripped the steering wheel and rested his forehead against his hands.

He'd lost his precious Maggie to this sick criminal. In his gut, he knew he could lose Rachel, too, if he didn't find a way to protect her from herself. But how did you protect someone who didn't want to be protected? Whose pride was so ironclad, it would take the Jaws of Life to get through it?

The next morning, at precisely eight o'clock, Rachel pulled up her rented Chevy Malibu outside the previous night's fire scene. She refused to give Luke any reason to think she was letting her emotions rule her head. Digging through the burned rubble would be another first for her, another step back into her past, but she'd spent most of last night preparing for it and was determined to do it without any hitches.

She powered down the car window, then shut off the engine. The pungent yet familiar smell of wet, burned wood drifted to her on the humid morning air. A smell she'd never gotten completely out of her nostrils or her blood.

Leaning back, she sipped the coffee she'd picked up at the 7-Eleven and watched a handful of firefighters securing the scene and stamping out flare-ups, their soiled yellow helmets and slickers standing out against the black debris. Their sluggish movements told her they'd pulled an all-nighter, and they were badly in need of sack time.

She checked her watch. Eight-fifteen. Luke, always the prompt one of the two of them, had obviously decided to play with her head. He probably hoped that, if he took long enough, she'd give up and leave, not having the wherewithal to go into the scene alone.

She smiled. Not a chance.

Rachel finished the coffee, put her empty cup in the cup holder, then slipped from the car, making sure to grab the notepad, the pen and the camera she'd brought with her.

As she approached the ruins, firefighter Samantha Ellis came around the side of the fire truck. Rachel and Sam had been friends ever since they'd been the only females in their class of rookie firefighters. When Rachel had left the company to take the ATF arson investigators training program, she'd wanted Sam to come, too, but Sam had been happy to keep hauling hoses, and the lieutenant's insignia on Sam's helmet told Rachel she'd done well.

Over the past two years, Rachel had lost touch with Sam, as she had with most of the people who reminded her of the past.

Sam came toward her, her face set, a stern warning to stay out of the scene hovering on her lips, then recognition washed over her expression.

"Rachel?" Her face broke into a broad grin. "Great to see you." Then she paused, a frown knitting her forehead. "What are you doing here?"

"Hi, Sam. Chief Branson invited me to your…uh…party." She surveyed their surroundings with a critical eye.

Sam cast a quick glance toward the ruins. "Yeah, we've been having a lot of these parties lately."

"So I'm told." Rachel smiled. "Can you loan me some of your turnout gear so I can get started?"

"Sure thing." Sam went to the standby truck and hauled out a helmet, a small shovel, one of the cumbersome jackets and a pair of boots.

Rachel took them, put the jacket aside, then sat on the running board of the truck to exchange her sneakers for the heavy rubber boots. After she'd slipped into the boots, she smiled up at Sam. "I'd forgotten how these things make you feel like you're wearing your big sister's clothes." She stood and grabbed the jacket. "Did you find any trace of an accelerant in there?"

"We won't know until the lab confirms it for sure, but my guess is this torch's choice of fire starter was regulation, backyard charcoal lighter." Sam gave Rachel's clothes the once-over. "Better put on the slicker. You'll trash your clothes in there."

Rachel glanced down at her jeans and snowy-white T-shirt. Then, grinning at Sam, she plopped the helmet on her chestnut curls and shrugged. Having second thoughts, she glanced at the slicker. "These things always made me feel like I had a two-thousand-pound elephant sitting on my back."

Sam sighed tiredly, but managed a grin. "Try carrying it around for eighteen hours."

As she donned the weighty slicker, Rachel noted that Sam's back was slumped with fatigue. Dark smudges rimmed her red eyes. Black soot encrusted the woman's fatigue-lined face.

Under all that grime, it was hard to tell that Sam had once been a Miss Florida finalist. Rachel had never understood why Sam always played down her looks, no makeup, no salon hairdo. Even more, Rachel had wondered why she'd picked firefighting as a career. She'd asked once, but Sam had danced around the subject with all the expertise of a prima ballerina. Sam's blatant avoidance convinced Rachel the subject should be left alone until Sam decided she wanted to discuss it.

"You'll need these, too." Sam handed Rachel a pair of latex gloves, then started toward what was left of the house.

Hauling on the gloves, Rachel sloshed through the wet grass behind Sam. The closer they got to the burned-out structure, the stronger the smell of burned wood and man-made fibers became. Her stomach churned.

Rachel stiffened and reminded herself sternly that she had a job to do. As she prepared to enter the house, determination cloaked any misgivings left over from the previous night.

"We're about done in here," Sam told her as she guided her through the opening where a front door once hung. "Fire's out. Most everything that could burn did, except the woman they took to the morgue about eight hours ago. The closet door was closed—"

"Closed? It was always open with the others."

"We figure the wind currents from the fire either closed it or it swung closed on its own. I doubt our torch did it. This sicko wants these women to see what's coming for them."

Rachel had blanked her actual experience of her apartment fire out of her memory. The doctors called it voluntary amnesia. Whatever it was, until this very moment, Rachel'd had no recollection of the actual fire. Now, as if someone turned a movie projector on and off quickly, a quick flash of the fire eating away at her bedding while she watched it from the floor of her closet, helpless and certain her death was imminent, passed through her mind. Though bits of the panic she'd felt that night and a tiny bit of residual memory remained behind, the image was gone before her mind could register all of it.

Sam continued to brief her while Rachel fought off emotions from scattered memories of the worst night of her life. She pushed them aside. Later. She'd think about it later.

"Just like the other fires, the only thing that managed to survive with just water and smoke damage was the kid's room. A.J. asked that no evidence be gathered until you saw it, so it's all just as we found it." She stepped over a fallen ceiling beam. "At first, we thought this one was different, just a house fire, then we found the woman in the bedroom closet, tied up with lamp cord, a Bible tucked under her." Sam shook her head. "Freaking sicko."

A half hour later, Rachel was squatting in front of the closet. On the floor, a partially unburned area told her where the woman had been lying. Next to that lay the Bible, wet, but, having been sheltered by the woman's body, untouched by the fire. She leafed through the first few pages of the book, observing that the copyright date and the publisher matched those listed in the notes she had back at the condo.

The odor of charcoal lighter still hung heavy in the room. Sam had always been teased that she could outsniff any arson dog, and it seemed she hadn't lost her touch for identifying an accelerant.

Standing, Rachel examined the room. Almost twenty minutes passed before her gaze fastened on what she'd been looking for—the point of origin. A black V started a few inches above the baseboard. The wood strip along the wall looked like the blackened skin of an alligator. The pattern splayed out and up on the wall opposite the closet, and the smell of charcoal lighter was much stronger here.

She glanced back at the closet and shuddered. The cold bastard had set the fire and, judging by the severe burn damage on the inside of the door, left the door open. With her hands tied behind her, he'd left the victim as helpless as a turtle on its back to watch the flames coming to get her. Just like he'd left Rachel. She shuddered but refused to allow her emotions to dampen her resolve to get this job done.

Rachel swung the door closed. The outside was burned, but not nearly as badly as the inside. Sam's conclusions were probably right. The wind currents created by the fire had closed it, but too late to save the woman's life. Methodically, Rachel snapped photos of the inside and outside of the closet, both sides of the door, the Bible, and the point of origin.

"Still have a problem obeying orders, I see."

Luke's deep voice sent shivers down Rachel's spine. She jumped, nearly dropping the camera, then spun toward him. "You're late."

"You didn't wait for me." He strolled past her to look in the closet. "Here's your coffee," he said, holding out one of two cups he'd brought with him.

Grateful that he'd remembered and ready for a second dose of caffeine, she took it and flipped off the plastic lid. The smell of hot coffee wafted up to Rachel. Cautiously, she sipped the steaming liquid.

"Is it okay?"

Oddly enough, it was more than okay. "It's perfect," she said. "I'm surprised you remembered how I take it."

"One sugar and a drop of milk," he recited, then frowned. "I always wondered what difference that drop of milk made."

Rachel set the cup on the edge of the charred dresser. "It's an appeasement."

He frowned. "A what?"

"Appeasement. When I was about sixteen, I started drinking coffee, and my mother said only men drank black coffee, so the drop of milk was an—"

"Appeasement," he finished for her, then laughed.

It had a been a long time since she'd heard Luke really laugh. The sound sent ripples of pleasure shimmering through Rachel.

"Kind of like me suffering through those chick flicks you loved when I would have rather been watching James Bond." He grinned. "But there were compensations."

His words brought to mind what usually happened after they sat through one of those romantic movies. Usually a shower together, soap-slick bodies rubbing against each other, kisses heating blood to boiling, then a quick rush to the bed, if they could make it that far, then—

She glanced at Luke. He was studying her silently. This conservation was getting way too personal for her comfort. She tore her gaze away and dived into relating what she'd found so far.

"Point of origin." She pointed at the baseboard. "Your torch used charcoal lighter."

"Charcoal lighter, huh? Well, he's consistent. Same accelerant used at each scene."

She nodded. "But he brings the Bible with him. It's the same copyright and publisher as the others they found. Can't be a coincidence. Probably symbolic of bringing God into the lives of his victims."

"Why in there?" Luke motioned toward the empty closet.

Rachel stopped in the process of turning over a charred shoe with the point of the shovel. "I'm not sure yet, but offhand I'd say it plays a significant part in the religious fire ritual."

Luke ran his fingers through his mane of black curls. "The religious fanatics are always the hardest to nail down."

"Not necessarily a fanatic, but don't rule it out. This is definitely someone with strong religious ties. This guy has it in his twisted mind that he's carrying out some kind of holy punishment. Question is, what? And why these particular women?" *And why include me in the count?* "There must be something these women had in common beyond being single mothers, alone at night. When we figure that out, we'll be on our way to catching whoever it is. I'd like to meet with the task force tomorrow."

"No need."

She started and turned to him. "I disagree. I need to meet with them ASAP."

Luke leveled a stare at her. "You won't be here."

She knew in her gut what he was about to say. "What the hell is your problem, Luke? Why do you keep telling me to go home?"

"Dammit, Rachel. I won't let you do this."

"You won't let..." She laughed. "Why this sudden concern about me?" When he didn't answer, she planted her hands on her hips and faced him squarely. "Let's get this out of the way so I can get on with my job. Do I threaten your—"

Before she could finish, Luke took a step forward and grabbed her arm with his free hand. "I know what this is going to resurrect for you, and I don't want to put you through it."

"Why?"

"Because I've given you enough to bear."

Rachel frowned. The words were spoken so softly, she could barely hear them. That's the closest he'd ever come to admitting he'd destroyed their marriage. But she didn't want to discuss it. Not now. Maybe not ever. "We've been through all this. Bottom line is, A.J. wants me here, and I want to be here. End of story."

"Then you plan on seeing this through?"

"Come hell, high water or Luke Sutherland," she said.

Moments later, Luke watched Rachel drive off. No matter how much she denied it, he was certain this whole thing was ripping her gut apart a piece at a time. He wondered how long she'd be able to stand up to it.

Logically, he knew if they were going to nail this bastard, she was their best hope. He'd never met another investigator who could profile an arsonist the way she could. She seemed to have an inborn sense that led her to the torch, a way of putting herself in their heads. But this time was different from all the rest. This time she had a personal stake in finding the arsonist. Which was exactly why he worried that she was not emotionally equipped to see the job through without falling apart.

The Rachel he'd married had been strong, but that was before they'd lost Maggie. Afterward, he'd been so buried in his own guilt, he hadn't seen her falling apart until it was too late. By then, he was trying to hold the pieces of himself together. He wouldn't make that mistake again.

The flaw in Rachel's armor had always been her pride. She took pride in her work and pride in her abilities. And this time, if he didn't find a way to stop her, that same pride could very well lead her into a place from which he'd never be able to bring her back.

Chapter 3

After leaving Luke, Rachel decided she could use some downtime, free from reminders of arsonists or Luke Sutherland, before going home to pore over case files again. What she needed, she decided, was a relaxing cup of coffee, with no one to bother her.

The smell of smoke still clung to her hair and skin. Though she'd worn the protective gear Sam had given her, a few black smudges of soot had managed to find their way onto her jeans. Oddly, she didn't care. In fact, it brought with it a sense of having come home.

Determined to find the solitude she sought, she pulled into a parking space in front of the Latte Factory, a quaint little coffee shop nestled in a strip mall between a supermarket and a toy store, two blocks from her condo.

Purposefully, she turned off the engine, then switched off her cell phone, locked the car and headed for the front door.

She had barely settled at one of the wooden trestle tables facing the rest of the shop when Luke's face appeared in her mind as clear as if he were sitting across from her. So much for forgetting. Instead of pushing the images away as she normally did, she allowed them to remain, to study him without him making assumptions about her inquisitiveness.

Time seemed to have ignored his craggy features and mesmerizing brown eyes. He had the same devil-may-care look about him as he'd had the day they'd met. Her heart had stopped then, just as it threatened to do now. Why couldn't she look at him dispassionately, as she would any man on the street? Why did he have this tantalizing effect on her? The very last thing she wanted was to be affected by him in any way, and certainly not with the growing need she felt at each meeting.

She closed her eyes tight to erase his image.

"May I help you?"

Rachel jumped. Her eyes flew open.

A young waitress dressed in a cute French peasant's outfit, the flouncy skirt short enough to be dangerous to bend over in and a name tag that proclaimed her to be Nina, stood beside her table and grinned down at her. "Sorry. Didn't mean to scare you."

"No problem. I was just daydreaming." Day-nightmaring was more like it.

"What can I get for you?"

"A café au lait, please."

"Foam or whipped cream?"

Though Rachel knew she could use a few calories to help replace the ten or so pounds she'd lost after Maggie's kidnapping and never gained back, right now, after inhaling smoke all day, the idea of the sweet cream didn't sit well with her empty stomach.

Rachel shook her head. "Foam, please."

"You got it," Nina said, and hurried back behind the counter.

Rachel glanced around the shop. The interior was warm

and decorated to resemble an outside patio in the French countryside. Silk roses and plastic bunches of grapes hung from the fake-brick walls. Trestle tables nestled behind dividers that looked like garden planters, overflowing with greenery. The fragrant aroma of freshly ground coffee beans perfumed the air, along with the smell of the croissants that a sign proclaimed were *baked on the premises.* Next to it hung a picture of a mountain range advertising gourmet coffee.

Four other customers occupied the room. Two women sat at separate tables, both sipping large coffees. One of them had her head bent over a magazine, her long, chestnut hair falling forward to conceal most of her face. The other, a pretty, middle-aged blonde, stared out the large, plate-glass window, her expression vacant. A man sat in a corner pounding away on the keyboard of a small laptop and another man sat at the counter, his large beefy arms folded across his barrel chest, his gaze on Rachel.

Something about the way he locked his gaze with hers made Rachel cringe. Hoping to communicate her lack of interest, she quickly looked away.

It took a few moments before the unmistakable crawling sensation on her neck told her the man had not gotten the message. From the corner of her eye, she checked to see if she was right or just being paranoid. She was right. She twisted uncomfortably in the seat, turning half away from the counter and his piercing gaze.

Absently, she watched a gang of teenage boys pass in front of the window. One of the boys wiped a half-eaten apple over the hood of the car parked beside Rachel's. She shook her head.

Nina returned with Rachel's café au lait and placed the bill on the corner of the table. She reached for the slip of paper and in doing so was able to once more check on the man at the counter. He was still looking in her direction, his expression communicating his unmistakable interest.

For a time, Rachel stared at her coffee cup, absently tracing the logo of mountains with a coffee bean superimposed over it with the tip of her nail, hoping that if she ignored him, he'd lose interest. When she could stand it no longer, she glanced up to find him still staring at her. Just before she averted her gaze, she noted his sweeping inventory of her body. The jerk was trying to hit on her. A creepy chill shivered up her spine.

Unable to stand his appraisal any longer, she grabbed the bill and her coffee mug and made her way to the cash register. After Nina had transferred her coffee to a to-go cup, she paid her bill, then went to the ladies' room to splash cold water on her face. Feeling more relaxed, she made her way back to the front section of the shop, noting as she did that everyone had left, except for the waitress washing cups behind the counter.

A relieved sigh escaped her. She was not normally a paranoid person, but there was something about that guy that made her skin crawl.

As she exited, the tiny bell over the door jingled. She walked toward her car and saw that a piece of paper had been tucked under the windshield wiper. Probably an advertisement for a local business.

Taking out her keys, she leaned over the hood and pulled the paper free, then unlocked the car and climbed inside. About to lay the advertisement on the passenger seat, she stopped dead. This was no advertisement. The letters on the paper were handwritten.

Leeve now…while you still can!

The misspelled words and the undisciplined scrawl shouted *kid.* The teenagers she'd seen with the apple maybe? They'd think something like this was very funny.

Tearing her gaze from the message, she twisted first left then right, checking every corner of the lot for any sign of them. If this was their idea of a joke, it was not funny and in her present mood, she was just the one to explain that to them.

Her hand had automatically gone to the pendant hanging outside her T-shirt. As she fingered the gold disk, her gaze swept the lot once more. No sign of the teens.

Grabbing her keys from the ignition, she got out of the car and went back into the coffee shop. The waitress looked up as the tiny bell announced Rachel's arrival.

Nina smiled broadly. "Hi again. Forget something?"

"No. I was wondering if you saw anyone near my car while I was in the restroom." Rachel pointed to her parked car.

Nina looked where Rachel pointed, then shook her head. "Nope. Sorry. I was washing dishes. Is there something wrong?"

"No. Nothing's wrong. Thanks." No sense getting the girl upset over what was probably a kid's prank. Rachel turned to go, then stopped and swung back to face the girl. "That man who was sitting here at the end of the counter. Do you know him?"

The waitress shuddered and curled her nose as if she smelled something offensive. "Freaky, isn't he? I've seen him go into that rooming house down the block from here. Mabel's B&B, I think it's called. I wish he'd find another place to get his coffee. He comes in here every afternoon and really creeps me out."

Mabel's was right across the street from where Rachel was staying. With that realization the chills returned, this time raising gooseflesh on her arms. Great! Just what she needed, a voyeur virtually living on her doorstep. She made a mental note to make sure her blinds were closed.

"Should I be worried?"

Nina shook her head, her long brown hair swishing across her shoulders. "No, I don't think so. He's never said anything to me except 'Coffee, black.' I think he's just a looker who gets his kicks checking out all the ladies."

Having worked with the police for a lot of years, Rachel knew the type well. They weren't breaking any laws, but they made their share of women very uncomfortable.

"Thanks," she said, and headed back to the car.

Before getting into the driver's seat, she slid the note into her briefcase. Since Luke would use any excuse to be rid of her, he didn't need to know about this. He'd have her on Interstate 95 heading back to Atlanta before she could freshen her lipstick. And that was *not* going to happen just because some kids thought it would be funny to rattle her.

She drove the short distance to her condo, got out and locked the car. Out of the corner of her eye, she noted a newer-model, green sedan had pulled into a space a little way away from her. No driver emerged from the car. Rachel shrugged and headed for the condo complex's front door. As she was closing the door, the green sedan backed up and left the parking area.

Showered and shampooed, Rachel stretched out on the couch with her notes from last night's fire. She'd barely gotten started when a knock sounded on the door.

Preoccupied with her thoughts, notes still clutched in her hand, she continued reading them as she wandered to the door and opened it.

Luke shifted one of the three large, white bags he held marked Wong's Market. "Bad habit, not finding out who's on the other side of your door before opening it."

After the incident at the Latte Factory earlier, she couldn't agree more, but she would never admit it to him. Then again, had she known it was him, she would have played possum and hoped he'd think she wasn't home.

"Wouldn't have worked," he said, his lips curling in a heart-stopping smile. "I saw your car."

That he still had the ability to guess what she was thinking before she said it unnerved her so much, she could only watch helplessly as he stepped inside and closed the door behind him.

By the time she'd recovered, Luke was in the kitchen unloading the bags. She joined him and began inspecting the items he'd lined up on the counter: boneless chicken breasts, soy sauce, sesame seeds, rice, broccoli, scallions.

"What's all this?" She picked up a bottle of wine and read the label. White zinfandel. Her favorite.

"From experience, I know that eating alone is not all it's cracked up to be, so I thought, why not eat together?" He grinned at her. "Get out the wok. You can stir-fry and I'll chop." When she didn't move, he said, "You do have a wok, don't you?"

Rachel shook herself loose of the web of his smile. "I…I don't know. I have no idea what A.J. keeps around here." She turned to the bank of floor-to-ceiling cabinets. "I've either been eating out or having something delivered."

"Or not eating at all," he added, doing a once-over of her body. "You've lost weight, Rach. You need a little more meat on those gorgeous bones of yours."

His words brought on an involuntary shiver of awareness. God, she didn't want him here, didn't want to feel anything for him, didn't want to react to his charm, his smile, his voice. But what her head wanted and what her body wanted seemed to be on opposing sides.

With an effort, she tamped down the wave of excitement building inside her, then covered it with an indignant huff. "I don't see how my weight or my eating habits should concern you," she snapped coldly.

He studied her for a moment, then turned back to cutting the boneless chicken breasts into narrow strips, but not before she noted the flash of pain resulting from her sharp tone and thoughtless words.

"It does when you're working for me, and I need you to be one hundred percent on," he finally said, his tone low and controlled.

She *had* lost weight. She was not eating well, and she'd noticed the difference in her stamina.

Damn! She hated when he was right.

Throwing a scathing glare at his back, she began searching the cabinets for a wok. Three cabinets and a lot of noisy banging of pots and pans later, she found one hiding under a colander.

When she spun around to place it on the stove, she almost ran straight into Luke's wide, hard chest. Her pulse picked up speed. Her senses swirled like fallen leaves caught in an autumn wind. Slowly, she raised her head to find him staring down at her, his eyes filled with desire.

Before she could do something she'd live to regret, she moved quickly to one side in an effort to put space between them and lost her balance. He grasped her upper arms. A current of acute sexual tension shivered over her.

"This isn't going to work," she mumbled, referring to the limited space of the small kitchen. Her blue-eyed gaze lifted to lock with Luke's.

Acutely aware of her silky skin against his palms, Luke had to fight to keep a coherent thought in his brain. "It will if we give it a chance," he said, unsure if he meant the cooking arrangement or something neither of them seemed ready to address.

To avoid the off-limits thoughts chasing around his mind, Luke let her go, then surveyed the cramped kitchen. "I'll move to the other side of the counter. You stay here and man the stove." Quickly, he gathered the vegetables, meat, chopping board and knife and scooted around to the other side.

He'd just started working on the scallions, when the sound of the wok dropping against the glass cooktop drew his attention.

"Slipped," Rachel said with a sheepish grin.

A wave of intense longing crashed over him. If this had been two years ago, that grin would have ignited a delay in supper and a quick trip to the bedroom. Food would have been forgotten.

But it wasn't two years ago. It was here and now, and all they had between them was a tenuous, barely civil working relationship. He knew, better than anyone, that the chances of Rachel and him finding what they'd lost were zero to nothing.

As if this admission had opened a floodgate in his mind, the guilt and second guesses poured in. What if he'd handled Maggie's disappearance better? What if he'd tried to understand more of what Rachel had been going through? What if, when Maggie had been declared *probably deceased,* instead of pulling away, he'd gathered Rachel to him and they'd lived out their grief together?

And the biggie... What if he hadn't decided to work overtime that night and had been home where he should have been, protecting his family?

Luke had been beating himself up for two long years over the bad decisions he'd made, but none more than working that night. Rachel's birthday had been a few weeks away, and he'd wanted to get some overtime in to take her to the Bahamas on the honeymoon they'd never had. As a result of his decision, a stranger had invaded their home, set fire to it, nearly burned Rachel alive and snatched Maggie.

Anger, hot and destructive as a raging forest fire, seared through him. His hand tightened on the handle of the knife. He sliced through the meat as if it were the throat of the person who had stolen their daughter and shattered their happiness.

Not until he heard Rachel's gasp and looked down at where her gaze was fixed, did he realize that he'd cut his finger. She rushed around the counter and took his hand.

"Come with me, and we'll get it cleaned out and bandaged."

"No need to fuss," he said, grabbing a dish towel on his way past the counter and pressing it against the cut.

She stopped abruptly. He ran into her back. For a moment he forgot his injured finger and was conscious only of her slim curves pressed against him. She stepped away quickly and spun to face him.

"Everyone knows that chicken blood carries a host of bacteria. When you contract lockjaw and your finger falls off, I don't want anyone blaming me. We *are* going to clean this cut, so stop acting like a baby and move your butt into the bathroom."

Wordlessly, and suppressing a smile at her commanding tone, he followed her into the guest bathroom. This room was much smaller than the kitchen, and he had to sit on the closed toilet seat with her positioned between his spread legs. His forehead beaded with sweat that had nothing to do with the cut finger. This was as intimate as he'd been with Rachel in over two years, and he wasn't sure he could survive it.

In an effort to harness his raging libido, he reached for something that would take his mind off her body so close, her legs pressing his, her special spiced-honeysuckle scent filling his nostrils.

He smiled. Maggie used to cuddle into Rachel's neck, take a deep breath and say, "Mommy smells like apple pie." Then she'd kiss her mother's neck, and Rachel would giggle. It had become a nightly ritual when Rachel carried her to bed and then sang her to sleep. Maggie never cared that Rachel couldn't carry a tune in a basket. All she cared about was that her mommy and daddy loved her and would protect her.

Luke pushed the pain away and thought instead about the investigation. Much safer territory than memories of Maggie or Rachel's nearness. "Have you done the profile on the arsonist?"

"A partial."

She opened a bottle of peroxide, held his finger over the sink and poured out a liberal amount, watching as foam bubbled from the cut. When it stopped foaming, she poured more over it.

He gritted his teeth against the sharp sting and seriously believed she was enjoying this torture. "And?"

"And I haven't finished yet." Grabbing a guest towel, she dabbed at the cut.

"So what do you have so far?' Why was she making him drag this out of her? He shifted slightly, unintentionally bringing his leg in direct contact with the back of her knee.

Rachel caught her breath. Damn him. He knew how sensitive she was there. These quarters were too close as it was. Why was he making this even more difficult? She moved away and sat on the edge of the tub, placing the gauze and adhesive in her lap. This put her at eye level with him. She wasn't sure that looking directly into those dark, sensuous eyes of his was any better than feeling his leg against hers.

Quickly, she averted her gaze to the roll of gauze and focused on something less personal. "The arsonist probably works during the day, since all the fires occurred at night. He's either an acquaintance of all the victims, which, given their diversified standard of living, is highly unlikely, or he stalks them, picking and choosing which woman he will go after next. I vote for the latter."

She paused, applied antiseptic cream, then wound the gauze around his finger. "Hold this," she instructed.

He placed his free finger over the end of the gauze. The gold wedding band on his right hand twinkled in the bathroom light. Rachel swallowed and averted her attention, glad when he asked another question.

"If he works a day job, when does he have time to stalk them?"

"Weekends. The long periods between fires tells me he is not in a hurry. He takes his time choosing his victim." She applied the adhesive and then looked Luke directly in the eye. "Don't underestimate this guy. Though these fires are not sophisticated and use no fancy incendiary devices, they are extremely well planned and carefully orchestrated. So, I'd say, the arsonist is a detailed planner with a basic college education and not in anything technical or chemical."

"Why not technical or chemical?"

"The lack of sophistication. If he had any knowledge of electronics or explosives, he wouldn't have used charcoal lighter."

Her stomach growled, the sound magnified in the small room.

They both laughed.

"Guess we'd better finish cooking and feed you."

They stood at the same time. Rachel found herself plastered against Luke's chest with the door to her back. Finding herself in the same position for the third time that night, she began to wonder. Accidental? Had he planned it?

Before she had time to really think about that possibility, her senses began to swirl. She could feel his breath fanning her face, smell his masculine scent, count the accelerated beats of his heart against her breasts.

Unable to stop herself, she slowly raised her face to his. He was staring down at her, his gaze taking in every detail of her face. He cupped her jaw in his callused hand. His thumb skimmed over her cheek.

Her knees weakened. Her heart beat out a frantic rhythm in her ears. Helplessness invaded her senses. She wanted Luke as she'd never wanted anything in the last two, empty, lonely years. She wanted him to scoop her into his arms and carry her to the bedroom and make love to her into the night. She wanted him to erase all the pain and bring back the joy of love.

Her gaze met his, and his head began to lower. His lips parted a fraction. His breath whispered over her hot skin. She closed her eyes and waited for his kiss.

Chapter 4

As Luke's mouth hovered over Rachel's, the air in the condo bathroom seemed to grow thinner, her breathing more labored. She waited for Luke's kiss. Waited for the touch of his lips on hers for the first time in two years. Anticipation ballooned inside her.

Then she felt him slip past her, leaving her alone—and humiliated.

It took a few moments to get her senses under control and allow embarrassed anger to burn off the desire. When she'd stabilized her emotions, she followed him back to the kitchen where she found him calmly breaking a sprig of broccoli into bite-size florets, as if the scene in the bathroom had been a figment of her imagination.

"What the hell was that all about?" she demanded, hands on hips.

He glanced up at her, his gaze brimming with the innocence of a child. "What?"

"That…that…what just happened in there," she said, hitching her thumb toward the bathroom door, reluctant to put the incident into specific words.

He laid down the knife and leaned his forearms casually on the countertop. "Am I to take it from your indignation that you wanted to continue?"

Damn him! He was acting as if it were her idea, as if it meant nothing to him. Well, it hadn't meant anything to her either. Nothing at all.

She glowered at him. "In your dreams, Sutherland."

He laughed, loud and long. The sound trickled over her like rain on a windowpane, saturating her very soul. "You never were a good liar, Rach."

Arrogant son of—

Rather than looking even more foolish, she fumed silently and continued to glare at Luke.

It was taking every bit of Luke's control to put up this devil-may-care front. What he wanted, what he'd wanted in the bathroom, was to grab her, kiss her until she melted in his arms and then carry her off for a night of passion. But he knew that wouldn't exorcize any of their ghosts. In the morning, she would still be the woman who could not forget or forgive him for letting her down, and he'd still be a man shouldering more guilt than any one human should have to carry.

He straightened, picked up the knife and took out his sexual frustration on the unsuspecting vegetables that still needed to be chopped for the stir-fry. "Come on, Rach, get over here and man that wok. I'm about done with this stuff." If they couldn't make love, he was damn well gonna see to it that she put some weight back on her. A sad substitute, and it spoke volumes about how far their relationship had deteriorated.

He didn't look up to see if she'd moved. He didn't dare. One more longing look from her and all his good resolutions would go down the drain. Instead, he concentrated on moving the prepared vegetables and chicken to her side of the counter. He felt the movement of the air and got a whiff of her spicy perfume as she passed by him and then stationed herself at the stove.

Thirty minutes later they sat at the table looking down at their empty plates.

"That was the best Chinese I've had in ages," Rachel said, leaning back and sighing, her anger forgotten under the weight of a good meal. She'd eaten more than she had in as long as she could remember. Why? Because Luke sat across the table from her?

Luke stacked their plates and carried them to the sink, poured coffee for each of them and brought the thick, ceramic mugs back to the table, but he didn't put them down. "The sun is going to be setting in a few minutes, and there's an ocean breeze to cool things off. Why don't we go out on the balcony and have our coffee."

Rachel took her cup and followed him to the two lounge chairs facing the Atlantic Ocean. She settled into the chaise and stared out at the whitecaps tracing long lines across the deep blue water beyond the deserted beach. The light breeze carried the unique smell of the sea and a fine spray of saltwater. The silence between Luke and Rachel was broken only by the squawk of a gull searching for dinner and the rhythmic pounding of the waves hitting the beach. Luke sighed, drawing her attention.

Eyes closed, he'd stretched out on the lounge chair, his ankles crossed, his big hands cupping the mug on his flat stomach. This was the most peaceful evening they'd spent together since before the fire. It was almost as if the last two years had never happened, and any minute Maggie would come racing through the door and launch herself onto her unsuspecting daddy.

But Maggie wouldn't come through any door ever again, never cuddle her freshly bathed body close to Rachel as she sang her to sleep. Maggie was gone, and it had taken Rachel a long time to come to terms with that admission.

"Rach?"

She smiled. Only he had ever called her by that shortened version of her name. "Yes?"

For a moment, he didn't answer, as if trying to find words. "Do you remember anything from the night the apartment burned?"

At first, she wanted to tell him she didn't want to talk about it. Then she decided it was time. How would she purge her demons once and for all unless she faced them? "Just bits and pieces." She didn't go into the flash of memory she'd had at the fire site. Besides, that had happened so fast, it hadn't told her much.

"Haven't you ever wondered about the details?"

She took a deep breath. "Every day."

Silence again.

"Me, too."

That surprised her. She'd always believed that Luke had gotten the full story from the police and the firefighters. "But, I thought—"

He turned to face her. "A.J. put Johnson on it and kept me away from the case as much as he could. That was fine with me. I never saw the files, and I never asked. Never wanted to hear it. All I wanted to know was where Maggie was, and no one could tell me that." His voice cracked. He blinked and turned away to stare out at the rolling surf. "Just before he called you here, A.J. realized the connection between the arsons and our fire. He briefed me on the bare bones. I guess he figured we could get into it more deeply when you got here."

For a long time, they remained silent, both staring out at an empty ocean, as empty as her heart, and kept the counsel of their own thoughts. Finally she found the courage to voice what she'd been thinking since she'd come back to Orange Grove.

"Maybe A.J.'s been protecting you for too long, and maybe I've been running for too long. Maybe it's time we found out what's in those fire reports. And not just for the sake of the case."

He didn't speak for a while, then finally, just nodded his agreement.

"Luke?"

He turned to her. "What?"

"I'm glad you came by tonight." And she really was. She'd needed a night of normal activity before she jumped into the investigation with the task force.

This was the first civilized conversation they'd had in two years. She wasn't naive enough to believe it would last beyond this night or that it meant they would ever get back together again. With her volatile temper and Luke's sarcastic nature, Rachel was certain they'd go head to head again before this case was solved. Their relationship had been battered and beaten beyond resurrection. But for now, they at least had a tentative peace between them.

He smiled. "I'm glad I came by, too."

Silence again.

"Luke?"

"Yes."

"Do you ever think about her?"

He remained quiet for long moments, his gaze fastened on the horizon. "Every night and every day, every time I see a kid with blond curls—" His voice broke.

She touched his arm and without looking at her, he covered her hand with his.

The silence returned, this time comfortable and warm.

What had happened tonight was not momentous, but it was a start toward healing both their wounds.

Rachel laid her head back against the chaise and closed her eyes. She wasn't sure if she'd slept, but Luke's sudden movement brought her alert.

Standing, he stretched his hands above his head. Muscles rippled across his chest and shoulders. A strip of bare skin came into view below the hem of his baby-blue golf shirt. "You look beat. I think I'm going to get out of here so you can get some sleep. You'll need all your wits about you for the meeting with the task force tomorrow."

Rachel barely heard him. Her attention was still riveted on his body. She shook herself. She had to stop this crazy reaction to him.

Tearing her gaze away, she stood and gathered their mugs. "I'll be there as soon as I drop by the firehouse and pick up the reports...*all* of them."

He gave a brief inclination of his head, then walked inside. "Want me to help you clean up?" he asked, surveying the clutter in the kitchen.

"No. It'll only take me a few minutes. Go home and get some rest." She walked him to the door. "I'll see you in the morning."

At the door, he opened it and then turned back to her. Before she could stop him, he placed a fleeting kiss on her mouth. "Thanks...for everything."

Long after he'd disappeared from sight, Rachel stood in the open doorway, her fingers pressed to her lips, her other hand clutching the pendant.

The dream came that night.

Maggie, alone, sobbing, searching hopelessly for someone to help her. But everyone she met turned away.

Then she came to Rachel.

"Mommy?"

But the smoke thickened, the heat grew more intense, and Rachel turned away, too.

"Mommy! Mooommmy!"

Maggie's screams jolted Rachel awake. Sweat soaked her nightgown, plastering it to her cold, damp skin. Her hands shook. She searched the corners of the darkened room for a small, lost girl. But all she found were shadows. Tears cascaded down her hot cheeks.

"Maggie. Baby." Her anguished cry echoed around the room.

Loss, intense and searing, burned through her. Rachel lay back, her wide-eyed gaze on the ceiling. Tears trickled unheeded from the corners of her eyes to gather on her pillow. Inside her, the worst kind of loneliness any woman can ever know churned and rolled. She wrapped her arms around her body, as if filling them with herself would ease the ache of not having her baby to hold. But the ache was almost beyond bearing and she rolled to her side to reach for the phone.

When she realized that she'd been about to call Luke, something she hadn't thought about doing in two years, she yanked her hand back.

No. She'd weathered this alone before, and she could do it now. One night of easy conversation did not convince her that he'd be any more supportive than he'd been two years ago. Of all the people in this nutty world she would not trust with her peace of mind, it was Luke Sutherland.

Twenty minutes later, cried out, wide awake and back in control, Rachel carried a fresh cup of coffee to the balcony, stretched out on the chaise and watched the moonlight play over the waves. Though she felt bone tired, she was afraid to close her eyes again…afraid the dream would come back. And why had it come back at all?

Right after Maggie's kidnapping, she'd had the same dream every night, but in the last few months, after she'd come to terms with the realization that Maggie would not be coming home alive, the dream had ceased.

Why had it returned? Why now when she was trying to prove to Luke and A.J. that she had everything under control?

It had to be Luke. His presence tonight had brought back too many memories of a time they could never recapture. It was her own fault. She'd allowed him to come in, fix dinner, arouse her sleeping senses, get too close. It couldn't happen again.

As Rachel sat there, sipping her coffee, her attention was caught by a lone figure coming down the beach. It was impossible in this light to tell clearly if it was a man or woman. The person stopped in front of Rachel's condo and appeared to be looking out to sea, then turned and faced Rachel's building. After staring at the building for a long time, he or she moved back up the beach.

Dread oozed over Rachel. She had a vivid image of the man in the Latte Factory. She'd forgotten about him. Even though her building had a guard stationed in the lobby, and he checked everyone coming and going, admitting no one without the tenant's say-so, she still felt uneasy. Getting up, she went inside and closed and locked the sliding glass doors. She watched from behind the glass until the figure disappeared from sight, then she closed every blind in the place.

As Rachel scanned her notes and sipped her morning coffee, she found something she had overlooked in the photos. Before she presented it to the task force, she wanted another look at the last fire scene to make sure it was consistent with all the others.

Quickly gathering up her notes, she stuffed them in the briefcase, grabbed her keys and locked the door behind her. In the parking lot, she climbed into her car, started it, then checked the rearview mirror before putting the car in reverse.

Her gaze froze on the image projected there. Standing on the other side of the street was the man from the coffee shop. He stared fixedly in her direction. Unwilling to pass him, she stalled by pretending to be looking for something in her pocket. She told herself that it was a public street. The man lived nearby and had every right to be here. That didn't stop the gooseflesh from sprouting on her arms.

Chapter 5

When Rachel walked into the annex where A.J. had set up the task force headquarters behind the police-department building, Luke was already there. No one else had shown up yet. The empty room suddenly took on intimate proportions.

"Morning, Rach."

Her determination to keep him at arm's length firmly in place, she nodded at him, said, "Morning," then deposited her briefcase on the table at the front of the room.

To keep her mind off how the black sports shirt accentuated his dark good looks, she began preparing for the meeting. A large corkboard holding a street map of Orange Grove sat on an easel. An open box of multicolored pushpins rested on the thin ledge at the bottom. Next to it was a dry-wipe board with several colored pens and an eraser in its tray. Two long tables had been arranged classroom style in front of the table at which she stood. Each table provided seating room for two to three people.

Then she grinned. In the corner of the room, a small, metal

table held a coffeemaker, dry creamer, disposable cups, plastic spoons and a box of sugar packets. A.J. had thought of everything, even feeding her insatiable need for caffeine.

Luke came to stand beside her. "Sleep well?" he asked.

"Fine," she answer stiffly, erecting a wall of formality between them.

He glanced at her, his brow furrowed in question. Then he shrugged his broad shoulders. "Did you stop at the firehouse?"

She nodded, then dug a file out of her briefcase and handed it to him. The flap, printed in black letters, read Sutherland. She hadn't opened it. She'd tried once she got back to her car, but she found she couldn't do it.

Luke laid it aside. It looked as though he was no more eager to delve into that time in their lives than she was.

Rachel checked her watch, then, wanting to be ready to start as soon as the rest of the task force arrived, she began pinning the photos of the victims and the scenes from each of their fires on the corkboard. Then she divided the dry-wipe board into columns and began transferring the information from her legal pad to the board, including the information she'd listed from her own fire.

She heard the scratch of a chair on the floor and turned to see the other members of the task force arrive, two detectives and Samantha Ellis, who had been added at Rachel's request.

"Hi, Rachel. Thanks for asking them to include me on this. After that last fire, I want to see this guy fry."

"No problem. I wanted an accelerant expert and a seasoned firefighter on the task force. I can't think of anyone more qualified than you are to be my second set of eyes."

Sam's complexion grew slightly pink under Rachel's praise. She smiled and took her seat.

When everyone had arrived, Luke closed the door and walked to the front of the room to stand beside her.

"Some of you may know this lady," he said, half turning

toward her, "but for those of you who don't, she's Rachel Suth…Lansing. Rachel is a trained arson profiler, and Captain Branson has asked her to help us work up a profile for our torch. Listen to her closely. Take notes. While Rachel is a part of this task force, she will be my closest assistant, so if she gives you an order, consider it coming from me as well."

Though she'd heard them before, long ago, Luke's words took Rachel by surprise. He was, in effect, making her his partner. He'd done this on other cases they'd worked together while they were married, but she hadn't expected it this time, especially in light of how eager he was to send her home. Had he changed his mind about her leaving?

Before she could give the possibility much thought, he stepped back and gave her the floor. "Okay, Rachel, let's hear what you have so far."

Luke moved to the back of the room, giving her the floor to address the task force. Rachel stepped in front of the corkboard and faced the gathered members. Slowly, she began filling them in on what she had put together on the arsonist so far.

"The simplicity of the incendiary device," she started, pointing to a picture of what was left of a pile of newspapers that had almost totally burned to black flakes, "tells us that this arsonist probably does not have the technical education to devise something more complicated. So, we're talking high-school education, some college, but nothing higher than an Associate's degree."

One of the detectives, Juan Montoya, spoke up. "Couldn't it also mean that he just didn't bring anything with him to set the fire and grabbed whatever was available, or that he was in a hurry, maybe even that the fires were random?"

Rachel smiled. "It could, Detective. We know that the accelerant at each scene was charcoal lighter. Given that none of the victims even owned a barbecue grill, the chances of him finding it on the scene were unlikely. Therefore, it's safe to assume he brought it with him. If he was smart enough to build a more sophisticated device, chances are he would have, something with a timer or a slow fuse that would provide getaway time. And finally, because the victims all have these connections—" she pointed at the list on the dry-wipe board "—it's safe to assume that these arsons are not random."

The detective nodded thoughtfully.

Rachel glanced at Luke, who was wearing a broad smile. Was it pride? Oddly, that pleased her.

"As for him being in a hurry, that would mean he would have had to find the accelerant on the scene. As I've already said, there was nothing that would lead me to make a reasonable assumption that the victims, who didn't have grills in their homes, would have had charcoal lighter lying around, just waiting for someone to set fire to their homes." Rachel pointed to the next picture—a Bible.

"Each victim was found with a Bible beneath her. Each Bible had the same copyright date and publisher. It's extremely unlikely that all the victims happened to have the same book by accident. Therefore, he must have brought one to each fire scene. This torch had religious motivation and more than likely positioned the Bible as a way to bring his victims to a meeting with God. Perhaps a meeting in which they would find forgiveness. Our arsonist is on a mission to purify these women by fire. A baptism in fire, if you will."

"Forgiveness for what?" Sam asked, leaning her chin in her palm and studying the list intently.

Rachel crossed her arms and leaned against the table. "Forgiveness for whatever the arsonist perceived to be her sin." She left the photo display, walked closer to the front of the group and frowned. "This is where it gets sticky. Religious-based fires can be motivated by anything from an objection to a neighbor's faith to excommunication from a church. We have to think with the twisted reasoning of the arsonist. When we find out what the *sin* is, then we can zero in more closely on who's setting the fires."

"What about your fire? Captain Branson said there was a connection to you. What was your sin? Being married to Sutherland?" The questioner was the heavyset detective with a sarcastic grin curling his lips and mustard stains on his tie.

A soft chuckle passed through the room. Feeling some of the blood drain from her face, Rachel glanced at Luke. His smile had disappeared. He opened his mouth, she presumed, to reprimand the detective for his misplaced humor. She shook her head to ward him off. She could handle this and without help from Luke.

She held his gaze for a moment more, her hand clutching the pendant. He nodded almost imperceptibly.

Rachel turned toward the dry-wipe board and indicated the list marked Mine. "Since I was the only one in the apartment at the time of the fire, and my memory of the event is still fairly fuzzy, I've had to rely mainly on the little I can recall and the information the police gave me." She pointed at each of the photos in turn. "The Bible. The lamp-cord ties. The chloroform. The victim positioned in the closet."

"Too many coincidences to be a coincidence," Sam said, quoting a cliché that authorities used often.

Rachel nodded. "Exactly. Hopefully, after I read the firefighters' narrative reports, I'll remember more."

"You sure the torch used chloroform? It's a controlled substance." Again, the goading question came from the fat cop with the mustard stain. He seemed intent on catching her on her facts.

She struggled to recall his name. Herb…Donaldson.

"First, Detective Donaldson, I smelled the sweet odor that identifies the substance. It *was* chloroform. As for how it was obtained, I know that the average Joe on the street shouldn't be able to get it, but I'm sure if you can buy Viagra over the Internet, you can also buy chloroform."

A red hue colored Detective Donaldson's pudgy cheeks. "Right. The Internet."

Rachel finished by going over the columns of similarities and differences, then thanked them for their attentiveness and turned the meeting over to Luke.

Luke picked up the pile of case files off the table. "I want you to go over these. Find any connections, no matter how vague. Got it?" He looked around. Everyone nodded except Montoya, who rolled his eyes and shook his head. "You got a problem with this, Montoya?"

"We've already been over these, Luke. There's nothing else to find."

"Then go over them again and again. There's gotta be something we're missing. We looked at most of them individually. This time I want you to compare them against each other. Find the similarities, just like Rachel did with the fire scenes. If they talked to the same person on the phone, I want to know who it was. If they buy the same brand of toilet paper, I want to know what kind it is and what supermarket they bought it in. See if any of the victims had a criminal record that can tie them to someone with an ax to grind. Have your findings back here tomorrow morning."

Amid grumbles and groans, the room cleared slowly, leaving Rachel and Luke alone. Rachel watched the fat detective leave. His sneering smile made her think of the man from the Latte Factory. A chill ran down her spine. If for no other reason than a little peace of mind, she needed to talk to someone about this.

Making a sudden decision, she turned to her ex. "Wanna buy a girl lunch?"

She had no idea why she'd decided to discuss this with Luke of all people. Logically, she could have gone to A.J., but she didn't want to. It had to be Luke. She waited for his reply.

Her question seemed to shock him, but he recovered fast. "You're on," he finally said.

They left the annex together, entered the back door of police headquarters, made their way through a back corridor and ended up in the entrance lobby. As they headed toward the front door, a blond woman wearing a bright yellow dress and carrying a very large, straw tote bag passed them.

"Hi, Detective Sutherland," she said, flashing a smile at Luke.

"Hey there, Hannah. What are you doing here today?"

The woman shrugged. "I'm checking on a kid they just picked up. They think he might be one of our runaways." She glanced at Rachel, then at the line of empty plastic chairs. "Anything on those fires yet?"

Luke shook his head. "We're working on it." He gathered Rachel's elbow in his hand and urged her forward. "This is Rachel Lansing. She's a special arson profiler we've called in on the case. Rach, this is Hannah Daniels, my favorite social worker."

"Hi." The woman smiled at Luke, then shook Rachel's hand. "Didn't I see you on TV?"

Rachel smiled stiffly. "Yes." The woman looked familiar, but no more so than all the other blondes who had made a play for Luke.

"Well, I have to go check that runaway."

Rachel stared at the woman, hating her instantly for her pert smile, luscious curves and flowing blond curls, and for the way Luke smiled at her. Rachel suddenly felt scrawny and plain in her navy suit. Maybe telling Luke about the man from the Latte Factory wasn't such a great idea after all. Maybe he wouldn't care.

"Check with Tony." Luke looked at his watch. "The shift is changing, so you may have trouble finding anyone to ask. They're probably keeping him in one of the interrogation rooms in the back. You know the way there, right?"

"In my sleep. Thanks." The woman flashed another

winning smile at Luke, waved, and then walked down the hall. "Good luck on the case," she called over her shoulder.

Luke took Rachel's arm and led her out into the growing heat of the Florida afternoon. A black cloud hung on the horizon, forecasting the appearance of an afternoon thunderstorm. The wisps swirling around the cloud's boiling center resembled the battle growing inside Rachel.

Should she confide in him about the man? Was this woman more important to him than the paranoia of an ex-wife? She decided to test the waters.

"Girlfriend?" she asked, tamping down the unreasonable jealousy threatening to make itself evident in her tone of voice.

Luke arched an eyebrow. "No. Social worker. She comes here all the time to pick up runaways and kids going into the system." He looked at her and grinned devilishly. "Why? Jealous?"

Rachel forced a laugh. "In your dreams, Sutherland."

She thought she saw disappointment on his face, but a honking car horn alerted her to the oncoming traffic. When she looked back, the expression was gone.

"Okay, why the lunch invitation?" Luke liberally peppered his roast-beef sandwich while munching on a potato chip.

The early-bird diners having already come and gone, the small sandwich shop was nearly deserted. A few latecomers, like themselves, occupied tables far enough from Luke and Rachel that their conversation would not be overheard.

Rachel paused, her iced tea midway to her mouth. "Why do I need a reason? We're coworkers, this would be a great time to discuss what took place at the meeting this morning."

"That's BS, Rach. I got the feeling from the cold shoulder I got this morning that you're regretting last night, and the last place you wanted to be was in that task force room with me.

So why beg me to take you to lunch, unless you had something else in mind?"

"I did *not* beg. I merely…suggested."

"Right." His full, tempting lips tilted up on one side. "Now, stop evading the issue. What's up?"

He knew her too well. For a while, she concentrated on her BLT, toying with the lettuce peeking from beneath the toasted bread. The smell of bacon grease drifted up to her, making her nervous stomach churn even more. Why was it she could go toe-to-toe with someone like an arsonist or Detective Donaldson and not flinch, but, for some reason, when it came to Luke, her backbone turned to jelly?

It wasn't that she didn't want to tell him. It was just that the whole thing with the man from the coffee shop suddenly seemed silly. Besides, what did she expect Luke to do about it? The guy hadn't broken any laws, unless, while she'd been living in Atlanta, making a woman's skin crawl had become illegal in Florida. She tore off a piece of lettuce and rolled it between her thumb and forefinger.

"Rach?" He'd laid his hand on hers, stilling the nervous movements. "Spit it out."

Obviously, he was not going to drop it. "Okay." Sighing heavily, she looked Luke in the eye. "There's this guy—"

Luke stilled. She couldn't tell what he was thinking.

"Well, he's been hanging around, watching me." She laughed nervously. "Now that I've said it, it sounds even more silly." She waved her hand. "Never mind. It's probably nothing."

Luke leaned forward. "If there's someone stalking you, it's not nothing."

"Well," she said, "that's the problem. I don't know if he *is* stalking me or if he just happens to be around when I am. I saw him in the Latte Factory and on the beach outside the condo. I mean he's not there all the time, just sometimes, and he does live in the neighborhood—"

"Do you hear yourself? You're making excuses for a man who may be stalking you."

"I just don't want to sound like a hysterical, female alarmist."

"There are a lot of women who didn't sound the alarm in time that are now residents of Greenlawn Cemetery. Do you want me to check him out?"

"No, just forget it." Rachel looked at Luke. She could read his expression. He was going to confront the man. "Luke—"

"What's this guy look like?"

She tried to avoid telling him any more, but his glaring expression said he wasn't going to let go until she'd complied. She gave him a quick thumbnail description. "That's all I remember. Luke, please don't—"

His ringing cell phone cut her protest short.

"Sutherland," he barked impatiently into the phone. "What? When?" He listened, his gaze going to Rachel. "Right." He folded the phone and tucked it back in his khaki-pants pocket, then stood and threw some bills on the table. "We have to get back to headquarters. There's been an incident."

Luke had filled Rachel in on the call from A.J. in the car, but even that hadn't prepared her for what met her gaze when they walked into the task force annex. The photos she'd left tacked to the corkboard lay on the table in ashes, along with her notes and the map of Orange Grove. The smell of smoke and something else hung in the air.

Sam turned as Rachel and Luke came deeper into the room. "Charcoal lighter."

"What?" Rachel picked up a small unburned corner of a photo and sniffed it, confirming Sam's statement. "Are you telling me our torch got in here and set fire to the evidence?'

Sam nodded. "Sure looks that way. You know my philosophy...in our business, coincidences don't just happen. They're planned."

"Damn!" Luke slammed his balled fist against the table. The pile of ashes scattered in a wider circle. "How in hell did he get in here?"

Sam looked from Luke to Rachel. "The door was unlocked."

Rachel sighed. They'd been in such a hurry to leave, neither of them had thought to lock the door behind them. Now, all their evidence photos were gone.

"This puts us below square one." Rachel collapsed into a nearby chair.

"Not necessarily." A.J. stepped forward. "Being the anal person that I am, a personality trait that I have suffered much ribbing for, I never give out the original photos or evidence files. I'll have copies made." He started to walk away, but stopped and turned back to level a censorious glare at Rachel and Luke. "If this door is left unlocked again, I'm not going to be such a nice guy. Am I clear?"

Both of them nodded.

Once everyone had cleared out, Rachel and Luke left the annex, being careful to lock the door behind them.

"I'll follow you home," Luke said as they walked to their cars.

"No need."

He stopped and turned to her. "I said, I'll follow you home."

Though she protested and lost the argument, the idea that he cared about her safety pleased her much more than it should have and sent a warm, secure sensation rushing through her. This was the man she'd met a long time ago. But that man had changed to an uncaring, cold stranger. What guarantee did she have that this one wouldn't, too?

Traffic had been light, and they arrived at her condo fifteen minutes later. She plucked her briefcase off the front seat, then got out of her car and walked over to his. He rolled down his window.

"Want some coffee?" she asked, more because she needed to fill the awkward silence than because she really wanted to tempt fate again by spending more time with him in the condo. What she needed was time alone to think.

"No. Thanks. I'll take a rain check. I have something I need to do."

She nodded then walked toward the condo, breathing a sigh of relief. But she was aware that Luke's car did not move until she was safe inside. She stood at the window and watched until Luke pulled out of sight. Then she headed out to the balcony, suddenly aware that she still carried her briefcase. She dropped it to the floor and collapsed on the chaise. Her mind swirled with questions about the day that had just passed.

Had telling Luke about the man in the coffee shop been smart? Had she made a mountain out of a molehill and just read more into the man's interest than was really there? After all, he hadn't even spoken to her, and it could have been anyone on the beach that night. More important, would Luke read it as a weakness and add it to his list of reasons to send her back to Georgia?

And as far as the incident in the task force room went, it was definitely unnerving, but A.J. would replace the burned documents and photos and both she and Luke would make sure the door was locked from now on. It did not bring them any closer to catching Maggie's abductor. The only info they had gathered from the vandalism was that the person who'd burned the evidence had used the same accelerant as their torch. The shift had been changing and with all that confusion, no one had noticed anyone loitering in the back halls that wasn't supposed to be there.

She ran the questions through her mind over and over, until her brain refused to process anything beyond the idea of a good night's sleep. But would she sleep?

She sighed heavily and glanced at her watch. She had to

relax. She needed an early start tomorrow to get the room back in shape before the rest of the task force arrived. Maybe a hot shower would help. She gathered up her briefcase and dragged her tired, aching body through the open French doors leading into the bedroom. As she passed through the doors, she dropped the briefcase and continued toward the bathroom, shedding her clothes as she walked.

As she'd hoped, the shower did the trick, and she was soon crawling into bed while fighting to keep her eyes open. Her head had barely hit the pillow when her eyes drifted closed.

Then the dream came again.

Luke had parked a few spots away from the front of the Latte Factory. His patience was rewarded within the hour when a man matching Rachel's description entered the café. He waited five more minutes. Inside the small coffee shop, Luke spotted the man at the counter, ogling a woman near the front window. Heavyset, badly groomed, dirty work clothes. Unobtrusively, he sauntered to the counter and lowered himself onto the empty stool beside the man.

"Excuse me." He waited for the man to turn to him. When he did, Luke smiled. "You and I need to talk."

"Buzz off. I don't know you, and I got nuttin' to say to you," the man growled, then started to turn his back to Luke, who stopped him with a forceful hand on his arm.

Reaching into his hip pocket, Luke pulled out his badge case, opened it and laid it on the Formica top, near the man's coffee cup. "You're right. You don't have anything to say, but you *are* going to listen to what I have to say. I'm sorry, I missed your name."

The shiny badge caught the fluorescent light. The guy looked down at it, then at Luke. Wariness glimmered in his eyes. "George. George Jackson. But I ain't done nuttin'."

"On the contrary, George," Luke said, plastering a smile

on his lips for the sake of the other customers. "It's pretty obvious you're a ladies' man." The man began to squirm on the stool. He tugged at the hold Luke had on his arm, but Luke only dug in his fingers. "I think you *have* done something, George, something we need to discuss."

He leaned closer to the man so he couldn't be overheard. Acrid body odor made Luke pull back a few inches. The thought of this scum coming within fifty feet of Rachel inflamed his temper, but he kept it in check.

"There was a woman in here a few days ago, pretty, chestnut hair. She says you were showing an undue interest in her, and you're making her nervous, George," Luke murmured, intentionally repeating the man's name to let him know he would not forget it soon.

"I don't know who you're talking about. It wasn't me." Luke noted that George fingered a gold cross hanging around his neck.

Again Luke tightened his hold. The man grunted with suppressed pain and stopped struggling for his freedom. "Oh, but I think you do know who I'm talking about, and it *was* you, George. You see, she gave me a very thorough description of you, and this particular lady doesn't make mistakes about people. People are her business." He looked down at the man's filthy clothes. "Yeah, it's definitely you."

When Jackson would have denied it again, Luke shushed him.

"Now, George, I told her she was probably imagining things, and I was sure it would never happen again." He tightened his hold fractionally, and the man grunted in pain. "You're not going to make me out a liar, are you, George? You see, this particular lady is very important to me, and I wouldn't want her to think I was not telling her the truth. I can count on you to help me out here, can't I, George?" he asked in a forced whisper and another fractional tightening of his grip.

The man nodded vigorously.

"That's good to hear, George, because our prisons are full enough, and I'm sure you wouldn't want to add to the overpopulation."

Luke let go of the man's arm, and instantly, the guy was off the stool and out the door. Luke watched him until he disappeared from sight between the cars in the parking lot.

He looked at the girl behind the counter and smiled as if nothing had happened. "I'll have a black coffee, please."

She poured it for him and, when he tried to pay her, she slid his money back at him. "This is on me. Nina," she said, pointing to her name tag. "Anyone that can chase off that creep deserves a cup of free coffee."

Luke smiled, but inside he was wondering if George was truly gone. "Thanks. How about a piece of the blueberry coffee cake to go with it?"

Nina grinned. "You got it."

An hour later, the coffee cake eaten, Luke was working on his fifth cup of coffee and thinking over the day's events. How had the torch gotten into the annex without being seen? All right, he'd left the door unlocked. Very stupid on his part. Even so, the torch would have had to go through the lobby, past the desk and through several halls where someone was bound to notice anyone who didn't belong there.

"Refill?"

Luke looked up to see Nina standing in front of him, coffeepot at the ready. "No. I've probably put away enough coffee tonight to keep me awake for a month." Not that he'd been sleeping all that well since Rachel came back. "I think I'll just go on home."

He started to get up, when he heard the pulsating *whoop whoop* of a fire engine's horn. Before he could see where the fire truck was headed, his cell phone rang. He glanced at the caller ID. It was A.J.

Chapter 6

Rachel's dream was different this time…but the same.

Smothering smoke. Blazing heat.

Someone by the bed…

Maggie? No. Too tall.

A sickly-sweet odor. Chloroform!

No! *Can't sleep. Must find Maggie.*

Won't leave her this time.

"Maggie?"

Rachel fought her way through the blinding smoke. Her hands grasped at air. Her eyes burned.

"Maggie?" Oh, God, where was she? She'd always been there before. She has to be here. "Maggie, baby, answer Mommy."

Silence, except for the howling flames. Too hot. Thick smoke. She choked on the acrid air, deep, wracking coughs tore at her burning lungs.

Can't give up. Can't.

"Maggie!"

Her own scream still ringing in her ears, Rachel sat upright in bed. Her widened eyes raked the room. A barrier of orange and yellow flames blocked out the wall at the foot of her bed and the doorway into the living room. Was she still dreaming? Was this real?

Intense, searing heat bit at her face. Smoke curled up her nose with each breath. Tears blurred her vision. She blinked rapidly. The sleepy fog cleared. Instantly, reality flooded her brain.

Flames, actual flames, were engulfing her bedroom.

Her mind whirled. She had to get out. But how?

Calm down. Think, Rachel! Think!

Unbearable heat bombarded her. Her exposed flesh stung painfully. She could smell the stench of her singed hair.

Protect yourself.

Jumping out of bed, she yanked the quilt along with her. She threw it around her head and body to block out the horrendous heat of the fire. Now she had to get out. Her gaze flew around the room. The French doors onto the balcony.

Dropping to all fours, she began to crawl toward the doors. The blanket tangled around her, hampering her movements. Digging her nails into the carpet's nap, she pulled herself along, fighting for every inch of her slow progress.

Closer to the floor the air was fractionally cooler, but still hot enough to feel like her skin was cooking. The smoke was beginning to drop lower and lower. Her throat felt as if the fire itself had crept down it. She gulped air and held it. When her lungs felt as if they'd burst, she began emergency skip-breathing—a survival lesson from her academy days she had hoped to never use.

Inhale. Hold. Inhale. Hold. Exhale.

Poking her head from beneath the quilt, she prayed she was still heading toward the balcony. Smoke hampered her view.

Panic began to build in her. Would she make it? Was she destined to meet her end this way? She didn't want to die. Too much yet to do. Determinedly, she dug her nails into the rug and pulled herself forward, praying it was the right direction. She concentrated on breathing and inched toward escape.

Inhale. Hold. Inhale. Hold. Exhale.

Behind her, she could hear the faint clamor of the firefighters' heavy boots as the men poured off the elevator and hurried toward her condo. As they knocked down her door, the sound of splintering wood rose above the growl of the fire. Then the deafening eruption of flames devouring a chair in the corner of the room blotted out all other noises.

She glanced over her shoulder. Long fingers of flame were climbing the wall. Oh God, what if there was a flashover? She'd die.

Stop it! Stop thinking! Just crawl. Crawl and breathe.

Biting down on her tongue, she forced herself forward.

Inhale. Hold. Inhale. Hold. Exhale.

Despite herself, she looked back. An organized line of flame worked its way toward the foot of the bed. Instantly, the dust ruffle blazed like a million matches. Then the bed became a pool of fire.

She shuddered, trying not to think about what would have happened if her dream hadn't woken her up. Pulling the quilt back over her head, Rachel pushed her screaming body toward the doors and escape. Wisps of cooler air touched her heated skin.

Almost there. Just a little farther.

Behind her, the firefighters' voices grew louder, but still barely audible over the rolling thunder of the flames. Hope swelled in her. Then died a quick death. They would never get through the blaze blocking the doorway in time. She was on her own.

Inhale. Hold. Inhale. Hold. Exhale.

Near the door to the balcony, her knee hit something sharp and pointed. Looking down, she found her briefcase right where she'd dropped it on her way in from the balcony earlier. The evidence had burned up once today. It wasn't going to happen again. She grabbed it and held it close to her chest with one hand, while she pulled herself onto the concrete floor of the balcony and then upright next to the railing with the other.

Air. Blessed air. Thank goodness the flames had only come at her from one direction, not like before, not from three…

Her mind closed off the thought. Gulping large quantities of air into her searing lungs, she peered over the edge. She could make out two engine companies, Truck Company 79 and Engine Company 108; at least a dozen police cars; and an anthill of firefighters scurrying in and out of a web of hoses.

Frantically, she searched for one face, certain he'd be there. She found Luke, and waved wildly, her gaze fastened on him alone.

When Rachel appeared on the balcony, Luke whispered a brief prayer of thanks. Behind her he could see the dancing flames coming closer and closer. Black smoke poured from the doors and curled upward. His blood ran cold. He could not…*would not* lose Rachel, too. Luke waved to her.

The night they'd lost Maggie played through his mind like a horror movie. Flames, smoke, water, confusion, Rachel curled in a ball on the lawn on a plastic sheet, a blanket thrown over her. Tears, whispered words of love. Then the final blow when the firefighters found no sign of their lovely little girl.

Cupping his hands to be heard over the chaos around him, he shouted, "Hang on, honey. We're coming."

Quickly, he turned to the incident commander. Luke might as well have been invisible. The IC concentrated unerringly on directing the driver of Truck 79 to a right-angle position that would make it easy to pluck Rachel from the balcony with the folded tower ladder that lay accordion-like along the top of the truck, a platform at the end.

"Ellis! Get over here," the IC yelled.

Luke had a glimpse of Sam running toward them, then divided his attention between the fire truck and Rachel. She looked over her shoulder. Luke followed her gaze. The flames licked hungrily at the opening of the French doors. It wouldn't be long before they spread to the balcony.

He grabbed the IC's arm. "Get her down, now!"

Tearing his arm from Luke's grasp, the IC glared at him. "You need to stay out of the way. Ellis is going up to get her."

Luke stepped forward. "I'm going with her."

"No you're not," the IC snapped impatiently.

"That's my wife, and I'm—" A hand on his arm stopped him.

"You know that's against regs. No civilians allowed on the platform." Sam, her face serious, looked him in the eye. "Trust me. I *promise* to bring her down."

He hesitated, then ran his fingers through his hair and nodded. "I'm going to hold you to it."

Sam climbed onto the truck, then mounted the platform, and the IC signaled the driver to raise the ladder. The hydraulics hummed as the tower ladder slowly unfolded. Luke watched it inch its way heavenward at a snail's pace.

Faster, dammit! Move faster!

The ladder continued its agonizingly slow ascent.

His gaze darted to Rachel, still huddled against the balcony railing. The flames oozed around the edges of the door, their long orange fingers reaching out, as if to snag her and pull her into their grasp.

Hang on, Rach. Hang on.

"Please, God, I can't lose her, too." Not until he heard his own whispered voice did Luke realize he'd been praying.

Pain brought Luke out of his hypnotic fear. He looked down to find his nails digging into the palms of his hands. He tried to relax, but the higher up the platform inched and the more flames shot out the French doors, the tighter his nerves coiled. When the ladder reached the fourth-floor balcony, it swung closer to the building and swayed for a moment, like a cobra ready to strike.

Rachel dropped the quilt she had covering her head and back, handed Sam something, then started to climb over the railing and onto the platform. Just then, wind gusted off the ocean. As they reached for this new supply of oxygen, menacing flames grew and billowed out the doors. Her nightgown made it difficult to straddle the railing. She made a couple of attempts before she finally hiked the material up around her thighs and climbed over. Rachel barely made it onto the platform before the fire engulfed the balcony, lapping over the sides like an overflowing bathtub.

As the ladder began its snail-paced descent, Luke released the air from his straining lungs. When the ladder folded and once more came to rest on the truck, Rachel scrambled over the side and straight into his arms.

"Thank God," he repeated over and over against her hair. He smiled a *thank-you* over her head to Sam. Sam patted Rachel's back then hurried to assist a group of firefighters holding a hose on the building.

Rachel clung to Luke. Her body shook uncontrollably.

"Let's get you checked out."

Luke draped a blanket the IC handed him around Rachel's nightgown-clad body, then led her through a group of people in nightwear, huddled together, watching their homes go up in flames. Like animated statues, the crowd parted to allow Luke and Rachel an open path to the EMTs waiting on the edge of the fire perimeter.

Just before they ducked beneath the yellow scene tape, A.J. called to them, his hair showing definite signs of bed head and his baby-blue shirt looking suspiciously like a pajamas top. Luke waited impatiently for his boss to catch up to them.

"Are you okay?" As he searched Rachel's soot-streaked face, A.J.'s eyes mirrored his deep concern.

Rachel nodded. "Fine," she croaked out, her voice rough.

"We're gonna need your statement." A.J. glanced from her to Luke.

"She can't talk now. I'm taking her home," Luke said, his arms still encircling Rachel's waist, her head resting against his shoulder. "When she's had a chance to rest, we'll talk." He left no room for argument. He looked down at her. "First we have to let the EMTs check you over." He guided her toward the ambulance parked a few feet away.

"She's lucky," the EMT told Luke and A.J. a few minutes later. "Nothing worse than she'd suffer from a long day at the beach—no burns to amount to anything, very slight dehydration and a sore throat. Could have been a lot worse if she hadn't woken up and got out of there as fast as she did." He pulled the blanket back in place around her shoulders while he listed instructions for her care. "Make sure she drinks a lot. It'll help ease her throat and replace some of the moisture she's lost."

Someone called to Rachel. They all turned toward Sam, who was holding out the briefcase Rachel had saved from the fire. "Don't forget this."

Luke stared at the briefcase, then down at the woman he'd pulled back into his arms. "You rescued your briefcase?"

She smiled wanly and shrugged. "What can I say? I'm a woman."

A.J.'s sober expression melted into a smile. "Now I know she's okay."

Luke muttered an expletive under his breath and helped Rachel into his car. When he'd settled himself behind the wheel, he turned to her. "You're going home with me. Is that a problem?"

For a moment, she stared at him. She must know as well as

he did without saying the words that their torch was probably the one responsible for tonight's fire. Either that, or it was one hell of a coincidence. Her face had been splashed all over the TV. It was common knowledge by now that she was looking for the arsonist who had taken and probably killed their daughter. It made perfect sense that he'd want to stop her. Hadn't he already tried with the fire in the task force room?

Luke exhaled when she shook her head. "No, no problem." She paused and swallowed. "I have…something important…to tell you."

Rachel lurched in surprise when he turned the car down Hypolita Street, and gave an openmouthed gasp when he pulled into the driveway of the small house they'd been planning to buy before their family had fallen apart. They'd decided that, with its location just steps from the beach and with a school a block and a half away, it would be the perfect place for Maggie to grow up.

Before she could say anything, he turned to her. "I found out last year that no one had bought it yet, so I did."

"Guess it'd…been waiting…for you." Rachel smiled, but there was a sadness in her heart. She'd hoped it had been waiting for *them.*

"Well, let's get you inside." He climbed out, came around to her side, then helped her out. Together they walked toward the three-bedroom, beige-stucco house they should have shared as a happy family.

Inside, Rachel glanced around. Instantly, she recalled the night they'd lain in bed until the wee hours of the morning, planning how they would decorate the house once it was theirs. Glancing around, she could see that Luke had remembered everything, from the white wainscoting around the bottom of the walls topped off with federal-blue paint to the two chairs and the round table positioned in the bay window.

She studied one of the chairs, a bell going off in her head. Walking deeper into the cozy living room, she took a closer look at the chair on the right. It had been the one they'd kept in Maggie's room. The nick in the wooden arm, a result of Maggie having banged a wooden spoon against it, was still visible. She ran a loving finger over the indentation.

"Drum, Momma!" The echo of Maggie's happy voice reverberated in her ears.

Rachel's throat closed off on a suppressed sob. She swallowed hard, wincing against the burning pain.

"It was one of the only things to survive the fire." Luke stood close behind her, close enough that she could feel the warmth of his presence.

"You had it reupholstered," she said in a strangled voice as she caressed the baby-blue brocade, her favorite color.

"Had to," he said, "what with the fire and water damage, not to mention the stains Mag—" It sounded as if his breathing had been cut off. He turned away. "Can I get you something to drink?"

"Please," she croaked past the tears clogging her throat.

A few minutes later, they were settled in the kitchen's breakfast nook, another of their plans for the large kitchen, sipping cold drinks. Rachel took her third long swallow of ice water, luxuriating in the coolness against her parched throat. When she set the glass down, she found Luke watching her intently.

"What?"

"I just remembered that you had something you wanted to talk about. Is your throat up to it?"

"Yes. It's feeling better all the time." She raised the glass to him. "This helped. Thanks."

"My pleasure," he said, his grin widening. "So, what was it you wanted to tell me?"

"The fire was set by our arsonist."

Luke studied her for a time. “That already crossed my mind, but I’d like your take on it. Why do you think it’s our torch?”

“Logic.”

“Logic doesn’t play well in court without solid evidence to back it up.” He sipped his soda and watched her over the rim of the glass. “Besides, it’s a secure building with a doorman on duty 24/7.”

“I haven’t figured out the doorman part.” She took another drink to ease her throat so she could talk. “As for the cause of the fire, think about it, Luke. I don’t smoke, so it removes that possibility. A.J. just had the entire condo refurbished and rewired. Unless he hired an incompetent electrician, which I can’t see Mr. Efficiency doing, the chances of the wiring being the cause are zero to none, not to mention the fire was in the doorway. Electrical fires usually start near an outlet or ceiling fixture.” She shrugged and emptied her glass. “What’s left?”

Luke rose and got another bottle of water for her. Then he sat and leaned his forearms on the table. “I agree, but I also get the feeling you think there’s more.”

Rachel spun the glass, watching the drops of moisture form a perfect circle around the base. “When I was escaping the fire, I suddenly thought that it was a good thing the fire seemed to have only one point of origin.” She stopped spinning the glass and looked at him. “Not like the other fire I was in, which had three.”

His dark brows furrowed. “Three?”

She leaned forward, her face alight, eager. “I distinctly recall now that the fire came at me from three separate points.”

“So what does that mean?”

She took a sip of water, then leaned back. “It means we’re going to call A.J. in the morning and have him get us another warrant for each of the fire scenes. I want to walk them again and see if I missed additional points of origin and if they’re the same as our fire.” She swallowed more of the icy drink. “We’re also going to need to go over the photos and reports from our fire for comparison and…" Her voice, which had become progressively scratchier with each word, faded on a painful croak.

Luke stood. "We can do all that tomorrow. Right now, you're going to take a shower while I make you hot tea and honey to ease that throat, and then you're going to get some sleep." He stood over her waiting for her to get up. He was hovering, and she loved it. "I put one of my shirts on the bed in the guest room." He pointed at her soot-smeared, pink nylon nightie and curled his nose. "That's sexy as hell, but quite frankly, Rach, it stinks."

They laughed for the first time that night. The rich, happy sound was just what Rachel needed to ease the tension of her brush with death and being alone with Luke.

Luke had just forced himself to stop thinking about the thin wall separating him from Rachel and started to drift off when her wail jarred him out his half sleep. Throwing back the blankets, he bolted from the bed and ran down the hall to the guest room, impervious to the fact that he wore only Jockey shorts.

Before he even made it as far as the door, her voice rang out.

"Maggie!"

He'd been afraid of this. Her experience tonight had brought back memories of their apartment fire, and they were haunting her dreams.

Inside, he found Rachel thrashing about, imprisoned in the sheets. The pillow and blankets lay on the floor; the sheets were twisted around her ankles; the dress shirt was bunched around her waist. Hurrying to the bed, he turned on the lamp, then sat on the edge of the mattress. He grabbed Rachel's shoulders and gently shook her.

"Rach, wake up. You're dreaming, honey. Wake up."

She fought against his hands for a moment before her eyes popped open. Frantically, she looked past him, her gaze darting around the illuminated room. "I thought—" Then she stared sightlessly at him, as if not seeing him at all. Slowly, the glazed expression cleared, and she sat up.

Rachel slid her hands over her face. "It was so real." She looked at him. Terror still stained her eyes. "The room was burning again. I couldn't find Maggie. She was—"

Tears leaked from her eyes, then ran in steady rivulets down her cheeks. Soon her entire body dissolved into soul-wrenching sobs, each one lacerating his heart.

He gathered her into his arms. "I know, baby, but it's okay. It was just a dream." She buried her face against his chest.

As he listened to the gut-wrenching sobs emitting from her, guilt enclosed Luke like an iron fist. Then the what-ifs rained down on him. What if he'd been home that night? What if he hadn't insisted on working overtime to earn extra? What if he—

He stopped himself. This was not about him. It was about helping Rachel live through the terror the arsonist had brought down on them again. And deep in his gut, where his hunches came from, he was certain the arsonist was the one who had set this fire tonight, and he was almost sure he knew who it was. But that would have to wait until tomorrow. Tonight, he'd hold Rachel and chase away the demons.

He shifted his position so his back was against the headboard, then cradled her across his chest. Holding her tightly, he buried his face in her hair and fought back his own tears. Despite the faint smell of smoke that still clung to her, he thought he could detect the fragrance of spicy honeysuckle that was Rachel's alone. Since she'd shampooed her hair, it was probably nothing more than his vivid imagination. As Rachel continued to weep uncontrollably, he felt as if a hand had reached into his chest and was squeezing the life from his soul.

Long agonizing moments passed before her sobs died to intermittent hiccups.

"Feeling better?" he asked against her hair.

She nodded, her cheek smearing her tears across his bare chest. Then she shifted her body to loop her leg across his thighs and slip her arm around his waist.

Luke inhaled sharply. His bare thigh was now cradled in the V of her legs. Her intimate heat warmed his skin and sent his libido off the charts. He took a deep breath and tried to concentrate on anything but what was happening below his waist.

"Uh...I should probably go back to my own room," he said, his voice sounding a little too high to be his.

As if his words had burned her, she drew away instantly, putting a lot of space between them. He suddenly felt colder than he ever had in his life. Slowly, he rose from the bed and made his way toward the door.

"Luke?"

He turned back to her.

"Please, don't go."

Chapter 7

For a long time Luke stood in the bedroom doorway, staring at Rachel, trying to decide if going back to her bed was the wisest thing he could do.

She already hated him for walking out on her. The fire tonight hadn't changed that. All it had done was hide it behind a fog of vulnerability. In the morning, when the fog had cleared, he'd hate himself for taking advantage of that vulnerability, and she'd hate him for using her to ease his loneliness.

When they'd lost Maggie, they'd also lost each other. He would not sully Maggie's memory by using it as leverage to get into Rachel's bed. A night of lovemaking could not bridge that gap that yawned between them. Nothing could. And right now, he didn't need any more guilt to carry around.

"Do you really want me to come back there, Rachel?"

Her puzzled expression spoke of the indecision his question had created in her mind. And her silence spoke louder than any words could. A twinge of regret stabbed him in the heart. Why had he allowed himself to hope that she'd tell him it *was* what she wanted?

Needing to get out of there before he changed his mind, he walked back to the bed, leaned down and kissed her lips briefly. "I'll be right down the hall. Call if you need me."

Before she could say anything, he slipped out, pulling the door behind him, leaving it open a crack so he could hear her if she awoke again.

In his bedroom, he collapsed onto the bed, knowing the night's sleep he'd looked forward to was lost. This chivalry crap really sucked. He hoped Rachel understood the sacrifice he'd just made for her.

He closed his eyes in the vain hope that sleep would come, but all that came were images of Rachel, images he'd been too worried to register when he'd first entered her room. Rachel with his shirt hiked high on her thighs, exposing her long, curvy legs. Rachel pressed against him, her breasts lush and inviting. Rachel begging him to stay.

"Oh, hell."

He grabbed the remote off the night table and aimed it at the darkened TV screen. Instantly, a late-night talk-show host appeared with a dog who was supposed to be able to talk. Luke stared blindly at the screen, willing away the images of Rachel that pushed at his mind.

Rachel stared at the door, her fingers pressed to her lips, and bit back the tears. Luke had walked out on her again. Why did that surprise her? Deep down, though she hated admitting it, she knew. She'd started to trust him again. Whenever she'd reached out to him in the last few days, he'd been there for her. But once more, when it was important, when she needed him most, he walked away.

Had she read his attention wrong? Had he just been giving her the same comfort he would anyone who had gone through what she had, been there for her the way he'd be there for anyone in need of a cop?

Call if you need me, he'd said. Well, she did need him. She'd needed him two years ago, and God help her, she needed him now. She needed to feel the security of his arms around her, the substance of his existence beside her, the warmth of his love surrounding her.

You're a fool, Rachel. He'll just walk away again. Face it. When it really counts, he's not someone you can count on. Running is all he knows.

She was not up to the chase, and it would be a cold day in hell before she'd ask him again.

Buying Rachel jeans, T-shirt, shoes and panties to replace what she'd lost in the fire and then taking them back to the house had taken longer than Luke had expected. Checking his watch, he hurried up the front stairs of the ill-kept rooming house where Nina had told him George lived.

With a severe lack of possibilities as to who had tried to burn Rachel up, but certain it tied into the arson case, Luke was going to pay a visit to the guy from the Latte Factory. Retribution was a hell of a motivator.

Now he knocked on the door and waited for someone to answer. Luke hoped to catch George at home, but if, as he suspected, the jerk was responsible for the fire either in retribution for Luke's threats or because he was their torch, he might have played it smart and moved on.

A few minutes later, the door opened to reveal a woman in her mid-fifties with bleached hair wound haphazardly around pink foam rollers and wearing a soiled, flowered bathrobe.

"Yeah?"

Luke flashed his badge. "I'm looking for George Jackson. Do you know if he's in?"

The woman made a face, then uttered a rude expletive. "He's

gone. Left last night around midnight or so. Bag and baggage. No notice, but good riddance, I say. Nothing but trouble."

Luke's interest peaked. "What kind of trouble?"

"Had the cops here once before looking for him." She leaned closer to Luke and lowered her voice to a stage whisper. "Wouldn't tell me why they wanted him, but I had a good idea. Some woman probably filed a complaint against him. George likes the ladies. Leered at all the women, including me." Luke backed away from her wine-drenched breath. She spread her arms above her head, and the torn seam in her armpit gaped open. "I ask you, do I look like the type who would give a man wet dreams?"

Opting not to answer that question, Luke cleared his throat and shifted his gaze to the pot of half-dead petunias hanging from the edge of the porch roof. "Uh…did he say where he was going?"

She dropped her arms and glared at Luke. "Nope. Don't know. Don't care." She slammed the door.

Heaving a deep sigh, Luke went back to his car and headed toward Hypolita Street to check on Rachel and put out an APB on George.

Rachel entered the empty task force room, her briefcase clutched to her chest, feeling slightly self-conscious. She didn't normally go braless, but since there had been no bra among the clothes Luke had left for her while she slept, she'd had no choice. By the time she'd taken a cab to the condo to pick up her car then driven to headquarters, she'd still felt naked.

Thank goodness, it was too soon for anyone else to be there. That gave her a few minutes to get used to the idea that beneath the aqua and white Miami Dolphins T-shirt was nothing but Rachel Sutherland.

Rachel Sutherland? She hadn't thought of herself in terms

of her married name since her divorce from Luke had become final. Why now? It unnerved her that the name had come so readily to mind.

"Morning, Rachel."

Thankfully, A.J.'s arrival prevented further thoughts on that subject. "Morning."

"How're you feeling?" He helped himself to a cup of coffee, then sat down across from her.

"Fine," she finally said. "My throat is still a little scratchy, but nothing like last time. I consider myself lucky. If you recall, after the apartment fire, I couldn't utter a word or eat solid food for almost a week." She met his gaze. "A.J., I'm so sorry about the condo."

"Why? You didn't set the fire, and I do have insurance. Thankfully, my condo was the only one damaged. I'm just thankful you're okay. That's what's important." He grew quiet, then tapped the manila file folder he'd laid on the table. "Fire investigators just called me. They're sure the condo was arson. Charcoal lighter poured on the bedroom rug. Near as they can figure, it went across the bedroom door and then another line straight to the bed."

Rachel fought down the chill brought on by the memory of the fire line she'd seen edge across the floor and ignite the bed.

"I talked to the doorman at the condo complex. A couple of the condo residents told us that he's a college kid, and whenever he parties hardy, he takes a nap in the back room and leaves the front door unlocked so no one will disturb him. That also leaves the master-key board open to be picked clean. Each one has the apartment number and the present occupant's name on the tag." He sipped his coffee.

"Well, that explains a lot. All our arsonist would have had to do was watch and wait until the kid went to take his nap, then grab the keys." She glanced at A.J. "So what's being done about it?"

"The owner fired him last night and is having a locked case made for the master keys."

"A little late, but a good move," Rachel said, shaking her head. She thought for a moment, then couldn't resist asking, "Have you heard from Luke this morning?"

"A little while ago. Why?"

She was sure he'd sneaked out before she'd have a chance to talk to him about the night before. She scrambled to cover her real reason for wondering about Luke's whereabouts. "He was supposed to ask you for new warrants for the other fire scenes."

"It's already in the works. He said something about additional points of origin."

Rachel told him about her flash of memory.

"I should have them for you as soon as Judge Hawthorn is in his office." A.J. stood, then paused. "Since Luke said he was going by the house to check on you, I take it he doesn't know you're here." She shook her head. "Then you don't know that he checked on some guy he thought might be a lead. Name's George Jackson. Says he hangs out in a coffee shop down the street from the condo. He'd already skipped out. The landlady said he'd had other run-ins with the police, so Luke's coming in to check his rap sheet." A.J. finished his coffee, stood, stretched and made a hook shot with the cup into the trash can across the room.

Rachel's temper began to heat. "He checked on George? Why?"

"Luke says he chewed him a new one yesterday for harassing you, and he thought it might be a retribution fire."

Anger boiled up inside her hot enough to rival last night's inferno. How dare he do exactly what she'd asked him *not* to? She knew it had been a mistake to tell him. Damn him! She didn't need Luke Sutherland or anyone else to fight her battles. When she saw Luke again, she'd—

A noise behind her drew her attention. She swung around,

ready to chew Luke out. But it was Sam. Rachel watched the interchange between A.J. and Sam as he walked past her toward the door.

A.J. left the annex, but the sound of him whistling as he crossed the courtyard carried back inside. Rachel smiled. She'd never heard A.J. whistle before.

Sam noted Rachel's perusal of the situation. Her face flushed slightly, then she took A.J.'s empty seat and looked at Rachel. "What?"

"Is there something happening with A.J.?" she asked, grinning, her anger at Luke pushed to the back of her mind for later.

"Happening? Of course not. I was just saying good morning to him, and he filled me in on what they found at last night's fire." Sam busied herself with the folders she'd carried into the room. "The chief sent these over. They're the narratives from your fire."

"Thanks." Rachel took them, slid them to the side, then centered her gaze back on Sam.

"Aren't you going to look at them?"

Rachel's grin widened. "In a minute. First I want to hear more about you and A.J."

"There is no me and A.J." Making a face at Rachel, Sam stood. "You want some coffee? It'll give you something to occupy your mind besides your way too vivid imagination."

Rachel continued to study her friend. Was she so desperate to find happiness herself that she had started manufacturing it for others? And what if Sam and A.J. did have something going? It was none of her business.

"Okay, point taken, but I'd better be the first in line when you get ready to confide in someone."

Sam turned back with a steaming disposable cup in each hand. "Promise," she said. She handed Rachel her cup then sat again. "You went home with Luke last night, right?

Rachel froze, with the cup halfway to her mouth. "Yes."

Slowly, Rachel lowered the cup back to the table. Now that her anger no longer colored her thoughts, she was able to answer without wanting to strangle Luke for his visit to George after she'd specifically told him to stay away.

"And…?"

"*And* nothing." Not because Rachel hadn't wanted to. Hell, she'd all but turned back the covers and moved over to make room for him. But when he'd asked if it was what she really wanted…

Sam cocked her head. "You sound disappointed."

Hesitation made her remain silent. Could she confide in Sam? Though they'd been friends in the academy and afterward, she hadn't really talked to Sam in years. Then she remembered how closemouthed Sam was about her own past, and she knew in her gut telling Sam would be like locking her words in Fort Knox.

One corner of Rachel's mouth curled up in a cynical smile. "Disappointed? Maybe. Confused? Yes."

Sam remained silent, as if sensing Rachel's fight to find the words to explain her dilemma. Finally, Rachel just started talking. By the time she'd finished, she'd told Sam everything that had happened after she got to Luke's house.

Sam shifted in the chair, then crossed her legs. "Maybe you're jumping to conclusions about why he wouldn't stay with you."

"Jumping to…" Rachel sputtered. "There were no conclusions to jump to. Rejection is rejection." Rachel tapped her fingertips nervously on the tabletop. "What would *you* conclude?"

Thirty minutes later, alone with the echo of Sam's promise to keep their conversation confidential still ringing in her ears, Rachel was no closer to an answer about the night before with Luke than she had been that morning. Her head had begun to throb.

She opened the briefcase and began rummaging around for the bottle of aspirin she always carried, but what she discovered made her forget Luke and her headache.

Lying at the bottom of the briefcase was a brand-new Bible, exactly like the ones found at all the fire scenes. Exactly like the one they'd found under her at the apartment fire.

A chill ran over her. She reached out to pick it up, but stopped and slipped on a pair of the latex gloves she kept in the briefcase. She reached for it again and stopped, but this time because her fingers had curled into a ball, as if touching it would somehow bring back that terrible night two years ago when she'd lost everything in the world that mattered to her.

She took a deep breath, opened her fingers and forced herself to pick it up. A pink sticky note protruded from the pages. Carefully, Rachel opened the book to the marked page. On the sticky note was written: *Leeve while you can.*

Not only was the same word spelled wrong, it was also in the same childish scrawl as the note that had been left on her windshield. She searched through the briefcase for the note. Spreading the Bible on the table, she held the note next to the sticky note. The writing was identical and so was the message.

Oh my God!

Until now, she'd only guessed that the arsonist had set last night's fire. This was absolute, tangible proof. Suddenly, she felt as if she were touching the person who had invaded her home and left it for her to find. She shuddered, as if a stranger's cold hand slid over her flesh. Invasion.

She dropped the book. It hit the table with a dull *thud.* For a long moment, she stared at it, then she shook away her crazy thoughts and got down to the business of figuring out why, when she could have died in the fire and never read it, the arsonist had gone to the trouble of leaving her a note.

Then it struck her full in the face. Last night's fire was not intended to kill her, just scare her away from Orange Grove.

That would explain why the accelerant was only on one side of the room. With that realization, all aversion to touching the Bible fled. Determination replaced it. This bastard had no idea who he was dealing with. He was not going to scare her off. Not until she finished what he'd started.

Then she noticed the highlighted passage.

Vengeance is mine sayeth the Lord.

"You think so, do you, you sick son of a—"

"What's that?"

Rachel jumped. She hadn't heard Luke come in. "A message from the arsonist." She handed it to him and explained about where both notes had come from.

"You got this," Luke asked heatedly, holding the first note by the very corner and waving it at her, "and never told anyone?"

"I thought it was from a bunch of kids who were messing with the cars."

He paced the room. "Dammit, Rach. You trust people too easily."

Everyone but you.

She stared at him. "It's a gift," she said sarcastically, trying to cover her anger with herself for trusting and him for being right.

He glared at her, picked up the phone and punched in a series of numbers from memory. "I need someone at the annex right away to pick up some items for fingerprinting." Then he replaced the receiver. "They have our prints on file, so they can eliminate them from any others they find." He began muttering to himself, a sure sign he was upset and using great control to keep his anger in check.

She picked up the papers he'd tossed on the table. Warrants for the fire scenes. "While that stuff's being processed, we should take another look at these." She waved the warrants at him.

"You up to climbing through burned-out buildings?"

Relieved that he hadn't demanded she go back to Georgia

as she'd expected him to, Rachel jumped up before he got any ideas about leaving her behind. "It was my throat that got singed not my legs. Let's go." When he didn't move, she glanced at him.

A smile teased at the corners of his mouth. "Nice shirt."

All his attention was centered on her braless chest. She'd seen that look before, and it usually preceded a hot night of lovemaking. Her stomach did a funny little flip.

Two hours later, they were headed to the fifth fire scene. Luke could tell by the downward curve of her mouth that Rachel was feeling discouraged. The first three scenes had been razed, and new buildings were already rising out of the ashes. Hopefully, the owner of the fifth, the small house fire where Rachel had freaked out, was not quite as efficient as the other four.

As he drove, she scanned the photos of the other fires. Over and over she flipped through them. Finally, she sighed and shoved them into her briefcase.

"Don't you want to look through them just one more time?" he teased, trying to lighten her mood and keep his mind off the fact that beneath that Miami Dolphins T-shirt was naked flesh.

"Do you know how demoralizing it is to think you may have missed an important part of a crime scene? Good grief, Luke, I'm trained to do this. I've never missed evidence before." She gazed out the window, a hard set to her full lips.

He had the sudden urge to stop the car and kiss them until her tight mouth relaxed, and she put her damn pride in her pocket. His hands tightened on the steering wheel, and he willed his foot to remain on the accelerator.

"Don't forget, the investigators on the first scenes, before you came on board, also missed them. So, you're last man in a line of screwups." He grinned and glanced sideways at her.

"Rach, give yourself a break. We all make mistakes. You move on and make sure you don't repeat them."

Her mouth twitched. Then she turned to him and smiled. "I know. I'm taking myself too seriously."

How many times had he said that to her? When she'd give anyone else the benefit of the doubt, she left no such wiggle room for herself. One misstep and she'd beat herself up for days.

"First of all, you walked all the scenes months after the fires. Anyone could have been in there moving things, destroying evidence. And that last one was a bit traumatic for you."

Her sigh drew his attention. "I guess I do need to give myself a break now and then."

Rachel's admission damn near made him drive into the trunk of a Mercedes that had stopped for a red light. Never before had he ever heard Rachel admit that it was okay not to be professionally perfect.

He knew the prejudice that abounded in what had always been a man's occupation, but she'd exceeded any barriers long ago. The woman was the best at what she did. Now, if he could just get her to stop feeling that she had to prove it day after day.

"We're here," he said, pulling the car up in front of the blackened skeleton of the house. Nothing had changed since the last time they'd been here, except the No Trespassing sign. "And it looks like you're in luck. Let's go see if your extra points of origin are a figment of your dreams or are really there."

"Oh, they're there," Rachel said, her voice confident. "They are definitely there."

Chapter 8

Knowing better than to offer any assistance, Luke stood back and watched as Rachel began her methodical search of the burned-out house's bedroom. Since this was the last victim they'd added to their growing list and only a few days old, the ruins were pretty much the way the fire company had left them.

He'd seen her do this a number of times, and that she could find the smallest clue in so much unrecognizable, charred chaos fascinated him. A half hour passed. Forty-five minutes, then an hour. Very slowly and systematically, she searched, stumbling over scattered debris, pulling up floorboards, digging into piles of blackened materials with her shovel, shifting half-burned furniture out of her way and examining the smallest pieces of ashes.

When she'd inspected everything in plain sight, she began looking under, behind and above things. Then she dropped to her knees and looked beneath the badly burned bed frame. As she stretched her arm under the bed, he saw a smile curve her lips. For a moment, she struggled, then she pulled out an old brass table lamp. It looked very heavy and, although he was no authority on home furnishings, very much like one his grandmother had had in her living room when he was a kid.

Protected no doubt by the shade's frame, the light bulb had survived the fall off the nightstand as well as the fire. The only damage appeared to be to the covering of the shade, the half-melted remains of the shade's metal framework and a bulbous swelling of the glass on one side of the bulb. It was that spot where Rachel centered all her attention.

Luke straightened, alerted by her close inspection of the light bulb. "Did you find something?"

Rachel shook her head. "Not sure," she murmured.

As she redirected her attention to the partially burned nightstand, Luke went to stand beside her. Holding the lamp in one hand, she ran the latex-gloved fingers of her free hand over the surface of the nightstand. Oddly, despite one charred, broken leg, the surface of the table seemed to have sustained little damage.

Rachel brushed away dust and ash, pieces of scorched plaster and soot to reveal four indentations in the soft wood. Sitting the footed, brass base of the lamp on the table, she spun it slowly until each of the brass feet fit snugly into its own indentation. Then she inspected the side of the table and peeked behind a piece of singed Sheetrock propped against the wall.

Luke leaned forward to see what she was looking at. To him, the table's charred side looked more like blackened alligator skin than wood, and told his untrained eye exactly nothing. The same was not true for Rachel. She looked as though she'd just discovered the mother lode.

Suddenly, she straightened, nearly knocking him over, threw her arms around his neck and planted a long kiss directly on his lips.

"We got it." A wide grin curved her tempting lips.

Luke barely heard her words. He was too busy catching his breath. He knew excitement spurred her reaction, but that kiss came closer to heaven than anything he'd experienced in over two, very long years. Right at the moment, he could have cared less about points of origin or fire, except for the one burning below his waist.

Despite his growing arousal, her smile of triumph was infectious, and he couldn't help grinning back at her, his arms still holding her close against him. For him, however, his pride in her far exceeded her joy in the discovery.

"Okay, explain it to this dumb cop," he said, trying to get his mind off the blatant sexual images swamping it.

As if she'd just realized where she was and what she'd just done, Rachel pulled away and turned her back to him. Luke's heart twisted painfully in his chest.

"Yes. Uh… See this?" She pointed at the bubbled side of the bulb. "That only happens when the heat is intense enough to heat the gases inside the bulb. The bubble points toward the most intense heat source. The alligatoring of the wood on the side of the table happens for the same reason. Since they both point in the same direction—" she shouldered the piece of Sheetrock aside "—this is one of the missing points of origin," she said triumphantly, indicating a blackened spot on the floor. "The pictures taken at this fire are in my briefcase. Can you get them for me?"

Thankful to get away from her before he embarrassed himself further, Luke hurried out, leaving Rachel to begin her search for the third point of origin.

When Luke was out of sight, Rachel collapsed onto a fallen ceiling beam that lay propped against the wall. She took a deep breath and tried to gather her wits. What had made her throw herself at Luke and kiss him? Had she been temporarily insane? But what really rattled her was the physical evidence that said he would have been more than happy to take it to the next level. And, God help her, she would have, too.

Determinedly, she pulled her concentration off her growing attraction for her ex-husband and back to her investigation. Taking several cleansing breaths, Rachel stood on wobbly legs and resumed her search for the third point of origin. As she waited for her composure to return, she checked the location of the two known points with respect to the closet. The one they found on the first walk-through was directly opposite the closet and because the charring was more intense, she knew it had been lit before the one she'd just found.

Mentally she drew a line to connect the points. The one she'd just found was to the side at a right angle to the line that connected the closet and the first fire. She drew mental lines that connected them several different ways before she settled on the only one that, given the religious nature of aspects of these crimes, made perfect sense. But it would only work if she could find the third point of origin.

By the time Luke came back with the folders, she had located the last initial fire site, directly across from the one beside the nightstand. It completed the cross she had drawn in her mind.

"You have it, don't you?" Luke said, staring at her from the doorway.

"Yes. It's over there." She pointed to the far side of the room. "All three points, and the closet, form a cross. The victim was put in the closet at the foot of the cross, a form of submission, of being brought before her Maker for judgment." She sighed. "Now we have to figure out what they were being judged for." She took the folders and sat on the beam again.

"I brought this in case you wanted to record the new evidence." Luke held out a camera.

"Thanks." She started to get up, but his smile drained all strength from her knees. What was wrong with her? She knew his charm for the lethal trap it was. But her body paid no attention to her mind. Not trusting her legs to support her, she smiled at Luke. "Would you mind shooting some pictures of both points?"

He frowned at her, then nodded. "Sure."

To get her mind off him, she opened the folders and checked the pictures that were taken of this fire, the only one she had attended and seen firsthand. There were no photos of the specific spots she'd found, but some of the shots included those areas and a pile of burned material. It could have easily been overlooked as nothing more than another pile of ashes.

However, that simple explanation did not sit well with someone who prided herself on her thoroughness. How had she missed this?

"Do you need pictures of anything else?" Luke asked, coming to stand beside her and set her nerves on edge again.

Her question was instantly answered. The last time she was here, Luke and she had been arguing about him sending her home. One thing she'd learned at the ATF training program was that investigating a fire scene was a gear-grinding, snail-paced, meticulous process that required undivided, intense concentration. Normally, she didn't speak to anyone once she'd entered the fire scene. Not so that time.

The argument had caused enough distraction that she had not given her full concentration to her investigation. She had screwed up. As she recalled, she could not wait to get away from him and had hurried out. She should have stayed longer, been more meticulous.

"Rach?"

She glanced up to find Luke waiting for an answer.

"Do you want any other photos?"

"No. Thanks." She dragged her thoughts back to the scene and what she'd discovered.

Luke set the camera in her open briefcase and took a seat on the beam right next to her. "So, now that we know there was more than one point of origin, what does that tells us that we didn't know before about the arsonist?"

Rachel tucked the photos back in the folder and in doing so, managed to put a bit of distance between them. "Something very important. The arsonist is a woman."

Luke started. "A woman? Are you sure?"

Slightly ticked that he'd question her expertise, she frowned at him. "Typically, when a man sets a fire, it's very haphazard. Fuel is scattered. Accelerants are splashed over a wide area. When a woman sets a deliberate fire, she *arranges* it. Fuel is confined neatly in a specific area. Accelerant is applied just to the fuel and not randomly over the scene." She continued quickly before he could voice the question she saw lurking in his eyes. "Yes, there are exceptions, but for the most part, that's proven to be the case." Taking a deep breath, she surveyed the room. "I'd stake my reputation on our arsonist being a woman."

As soon as Luke and Rachel entered the task force room, the noise came to an abrupt halt. All eyes turned to them. He gave them a quick rundown on the notes Rachel had received. He'd leave it to Rachel to tell them about the points of origin and her suspicions as to the gender of the arsonist.

Luke still wasn't sure he went along with Rachel's hypothesis of a female arsonist, but, since he'd known her, she'd rarely been wrong, so he was more than willing to give her the benefit of the doubt—for now. However, George still headed up Luke's personal suspect list.

On the table he found a report from the Fingerprint Division. "The only prints they found on the notes were Rachel's and mine. None on the Bible," Luke said, giving the team an oral summary of the information in the report. He studied the report silently for a moment. "They found a substance on the Bible that they sent for analysis." He handed Rachel the report.

"Rachel has new information on the fires, so give her your attention, then we'll go over anything you've found." He stepped aside, leaving the front of the room to Rachel.

Rachel took a deep breath, then told them about the additional points of origin and her conclusion that the arsonist was a female.

"Now, wait a minute..." Donaldson leaned forward, resting his pudgy arms on the table. This morning his tie had no mustard stains, but it looked as though he'd slept with it under him, along with his shirt and suit. "You're telling us that, because of the way the fire was arranged, you can tell it was a broad...uh...woman?"

Bracing for another go-round with his sarcasm, Rachel raised an eyebrow and leveled her gaze on him. "That's exactly what I'm saying, Detective."

Rather than argue the point, as she'd expected, he surprised her by saying, "Damn. Who would have thought? Makes sense though. A woman can drive a guy nuts with her neat-freak ways."

Rachel wondered if Donaldson was married, and if he was, she decided his wife must be a candidate for the funny farm or the Congressional Medal of Freedom. She glanced at Luke, who, from the smirk on his face and his obvious struggle not to laugh, must have been having similar thoughts.

She smiled.

He winked.

Her stomach flipped.

Damn!

She cleared her throat. "Okay, what connections between the victims did any of you find?" Rachel asked the members of the task force.

Montoya shook his head. "Since we've seen the police reports a million times and Sam's seen the fire reports just as often, we worked on the theory that fresh eyes might find something new. Donaldson and I took the firefighters' narrative reports. Nothing beyond what you've already outlined."

Rachel fought off a wave of disappointment.

"Dead end." Donaldson sighed, his large chest heaving until his shirt buttons strained the material. "We'd hoped maybe they'd seen something we didn't know about. We even checked the videos."

Rachel glanced at Sam. She was studying her notes. "I took the police reports." She looked up. "It occurred to me that, aside from you, Rachel, these women were all single mothers, probably on fixed incomes, possibly on welfare. So I called the DCS."

"And?" Rachel asked, hoping the Department of Child Services would have a lead for them.

"One of them was getting assistance, but the others had jobs." When Rachel would have spoken, Sam stopped her again. "But there is a connection that stitches them all together like a neatly made patchwork quilt. All of the victims were under investigation by the DCS for child abuse."

Progress at last. "Good work, Sam. We'll need a list of all their relatives, friends and co-workers to interview, even if we've already talked to them."

Out of the corner of her eye, Rachel noted that Donaldson was staring at her, his brows knitted in thought. She waited for him to comment. When he didn't, Rachel turned to Montoya. "Were you able to get any fire department records of fires in surrounding areas that resemble these?"

Donaldson's stare remained centered on Rachel. Her skin began to crawl much like it had under the stare of the guy in the coffee shop.

Montoya didn't see his partner's expression. "We requested anything that comes close to our arsons in any way from every fire company within a fifty-mile radius of here."

Trying to ignore Donaldson, she concentrated on the

young, Hispanic detective. "Good. I want to see them as soon as they come in."

Rachel shook loose of the discomfort of the detective's intense gaze, a gaze that had turned almost angry. What had she done now to set him off?

Occupying herself by collecting the reports from Montoya and Sam, she tried to push the detective from her thoughts. She glanced at Luke. He, too, had noted Donaldson's strange behavior. When she sent Luke a questioning glance, he shrugged, evidently as much at a loss to explain it as she was.

A noise brought her head around. Detective Donaldson had pushed his chair back, his usually ruddy face redder. His expression had changed from one of scrutiny to one of accusation.

"Detective?" Rachel glared into the face of the man who had drawn the attention of everyone in the task force room.

Donaldson folded his arms across his barrel chest and met her gaze. "We've been busting our butts looking for a connection with these fires, including the one that burned down your apartment two years ago. Seems that Ellis's report left something out."

A tense hush fell over the room. Fighting to retain her composure, Rachel stared back at the detective. "And your point is?"

"My point is that your kid went missing right after the fire. Could that be the connection to your apartment fire, too?"

Chapter 9

Rachel felt as if she'd been hit in the gut with a boulder. It didn't take much imagination to figure out what Donaldson's thinly veiled insinuation meant. He was accusing her of child abuse.

Out of the corner of her eye, she saw Luke bolt to his feet. His expression had turned as menacing as a vicious storm cloud. Fists clenched at his sides, he stalked across the room toward Donaldson. The detective stood and backed away.

"You son of a…" Luke drew back his fist.

Without thinking, she threw herself between Luke and the detective.

Anger replaced shock. She and Donaldson hadn't liked each other from day one, but not only to accuse her of child abuse, but also to intimate that she might be responsible for Maggie's disappearance went beyond inexcusable.

Glaring at Donaldson, she whispered through clenched

teeth, "I'll forget you asked that if you put in a request for an immediate transfer off this task force."

Donaldson glanced from Rachel to Luke. His face lost some color, but he held his ground. "You didn't answer my question. Could the child abuse factor be the connection to your fire?"

Luke swore and stepped around Rachel, then lunged for the detective.

Rachel grabbed Luke's arm, struggling with all her strength to hold him back. "He's not worth you losing your badge or getting a visit from Internal Affairs." Then she turned and glared at Donaldson. "I find your attitude and tone uncalled for and intolerable. Get out of here before I call someone to remove you."

The detective seemed to realize the prudence of making himself scarce. Careful not to take his eyes off Luke, Donaldson skirted the edge of the room and hurried out the door.

Rachel looked around. The air in the room could have been sliced like a roasted chicken. "Detective Donaldson had every right to raise that question. For the record, my answer would have been absolutely not. I never abused my child. Now, does anyone else have a similar question?"

Montoya lowered his gaze and became very busy rearranging the papers scattered over the table in front of him.

Sam flashed her a wide smile in combination with a high sign and mouthed, "You go, girl!"

Rachel turned back to Luke. Swallowing her need to defend herself against Donaldson's accusations, she put everything she had into controlling her voice. "We'll need a subpoena to get the DCS records. Can you ask A.J. to get that in the works ASAP? And tell him we're going to need a replacement for Donaldson on the task force."

Luke studied her for a long time. She touched his forearm and squeezed it. "I'm fine." He paused, then nodded stiffly and left the room.

She watched him leave, wishing she could go with him to

escape the thick blanket of discomfort left by Donaldson's unanswered question that hung over the room. Instead, she turned back to Montoya. "Make sure I get those fire reports as soon as they come in."

He nodded. "You'll be the first to know."

Rachel put her notes and files back in her briefcase. "We meet back here tomorrow."

Without looking around her, she made her way to the door, but before she stepped through it, she called to Sam to lock the door behind them, then hurried from the building.

A large knot formed in her belly. Logically, she knew that child abuse could not be the connection they'd been searching for between her and the other victims. Never in this lifetime could she even consider abusing her beautiful daughter in any way, unless loving her too much could be considered abuse.

But Sam had not said all of the victims *except you* were under investigation. She'd said *all* of the victims. Did that include her, or had it just been a poor choice of words?

Though, in her heart, she knew it didn't, in her fevered thoughts every interaction she'd ever had with Maggie began to magnify out of proportion. Suddenly every swat Rachel had ever delivered to Maggie's behind magnified in her mind to a beating, every time she'd raised her voice became a tirade of angry words, every time she'd punished her with a time-out turned into imprisonment.

She rushed through the building, eager to reach her car and escape everyone. She avoided eye contact with anyone, afraid she would see the accusation in their eyes.

"Rachel."

She heard Luke calling her but she paid no attention. She couldn't face him. She wasn't sure who she hated more, Donaldson for his unfounded accusations or herself for second-guessing what kind of mother she'd been to her dead child.

* * *

Luke walked into his house fifteen minutes after Rachel. Despite repeated knocks on her closed bedroom door, he got no response. Finally, though very worried about the aftereffects of her run-in with Donaldson, he gave up and trudged back to the kitchen. Taking a cold beer from the fridge, his gaze fell on the Next Day UPS package that he'd brought in from the front porch and which now lay on the counter. It was addressed to him. He checked the return address and smiled.

Taking a step toward the guest bedroom, he stopped. Instinctively, he knew Rachel needed this time to herself. He replaced the package on the counter, then began rummaging through the fridge for the makings of supper, but he couldn't take his mind off the woman behind that bedroom door.

He didn't have to be a nuclear physicist to know what was going through Rachel's mind. He should have ripped out Donaldson's tongue then broken every bone in his body when he had the chance. Luke couldn't remember the last time he'd actually seen that particular shade of bloodred. It was a good thing Rachel had headed him off or he'd have smeared Donaldson's cocky, insensitive face all over the floor.

Rachel had been the best mom any kid could ask for. That anyone would even hint that she was abusive was worse than ludicrous. It was insane and insulting. But to confront her, a woman who had lost her child to a deranged arsonist and in front of the task force—

A sudden cold wetness on his leg drew Luke from his raging thoughts. He looked down to discover he'd squeezed the tomato he'd just taken from the crisper until it had popped, spewing seeds, pulp and juice all over his pant leg, the floor and the refrigerator.

Throwing out a long string of expletives, he cleaned up the mess, washed his hands, then dropped into a chair and sipped his beer while he waited for his rage to abate.

* * *

Rachel paced the bedroom, the only sound that of her breathing and the occasional scuff of her bare feet against the pale green carpeting. Hours ago, Luke had called to her that dinner was ready, but she'd opted to remain in her room, her appetite nonexistent, her ability to keep food down questionable. Since then, the house had grown silent, telling her Luke had probably gone to bed.

When he'd knocked earlier, she'd wanted to fling open the door, throw herself in his arms and beg him for reassurances that she had never hurt their baby. Somehow she needed to hear it from him. Never in her life had Rachel felt less certain of who she was. How she hated Donaldson for making her feel like this, and how she hated herself for allowing him this power over her.

She sat on the edge of the bed, ran her fingers through her hair, then stood again and resumed pacing. Stopping in front of the mirror, she gazed at her reflection. There were no words written across her forehead that proclaimed her an unfit mother, but then, having seen the seamy side of people far too often, she knew better than most that looks were not always indicative of what was hidden inside.

As she stared at herself, her gaze fell on the pendant lying against her nightgown. She reached for it and curled her fingers around it. Softly, she said his name.

"Luke."

He didn't magically appear. But then she knew he wouldn't. She knew that this time, she would have to go to him. He was respecting her right to work this out alone, but she couldn't, and she desperately needed him to hold her.

Without hesitating, Rachel wrenched open the door and padded down the hall to Luke's room. As she made her way toward his room, the AC kicked in and blew cold air over her scantily clad body. She shivered and wrapped her arms around herself for warmth. His door stood slightly ajar, as if he'd left it that way on purpose so he could hear her call.

Slowly, she walked to the bedside and looked down at him. In the dim light spilling in through the drapes from the street lamp, she could see him staring back at her.

"Hey, sweetheart. Can't sleep?" His voice was husky and deep.

Rachel shook her head.

He rolled to his side, then threw back the blankets. "Come here." He patted the bed beside him.

Rachel climbed in next to him. He threw the blankets over her, then gathered her in his arms and held her chilled body against his.

"Wanna talk about it?" He kissed her head.

She wasn't sure. Now that she was here, it all sounded so ludicrous.

"It's what Donaldson said in the task force room, right?"

She nodded.

Luke shifted her body so that they were lying face-to-face. "Don't even waste your time thinking about it. I don't know what the connection between our fire and all these other fires is, but it sure as hell isn't that." He framed her face with both hands and looked deep into her eyes. "Rach, no kid ever had a better mother than you were to Maggie and no matter what anyone says, you can't believe otherwise. Okay?"

Rachel nodded, afraid to speak. Even if she still had her doubts, she'd needed to hear that from him. As long as he believed that, she could.

She stared at Luke. Her heart ached. This was the man she'd married, the man who had always been there to listen to her, to help her sort out her problems, to understand, to love her. Heaven help her, she needed him now, needed the haven of his arms.

"Can I stay here with you tonight?"

* * *

He knew that this was probably a very bad idea, one they would both regret in the light of day, but he couldn't turn her away. In the aftermath of Donaldson's accusation, his guilt about his part in that terrible night had risen to the surface, and he needed her right now as much as she needed him.

"If you promise to stay on your own side of the bed and not steal all the covers," he said, trying to make light of a situation that was as weighty with tension as a blacksmith's anvil.

Rachel flashed him a watery smile. "Thanks." She started to turn away to her own side of the bed, but he stopped her.

"I forgot to add that you have to let me hold you." His voice was soft, a mere whisper.

She considered it for a scant moment, then snuggled down in his arms. It wasn't long before he felt the rhythmic rise and fall of her chest against his. Despite holding his near-naked ex-wife in his arms, Luke felt a peace flow over him that had been missing from his life for some time.

Though Rachel fell asleep quickly, as Luke became increasingly aware of the body beside him, he was sure this would be one night when he wouldn't get a moment's rest. However, to his surprise, he found himself relaxing and his eyelids growing heavy.

The sound of his blood being pushed through his veins by his racing heart brought Luke awake with a jolt. His breathing came fast and jerky. He lay there, trying to understand what was happening. Then a soft hand caressed his chest and stomach. Almost at the same moment, he became aware of a warm leg slipping across his thighs.

He was still attempting to get his bearings when warm breath filled his ear and a tongue traced the edge. The painful throb of his swelling arousal brought him fully awake. He pulled back slightly and looked down into Rachel's face. Her eyes were closed.

"Rach, are you awake?" he whispered.

"Uh-huh."

Her tongue snaked inside his ear.

Chills prickled his flesh.

"Do you know what you're doing?'

"Uh-huh."

Her hand dropped down to encircle his arousal.

He sucked his breath in sharply.

"Do you know what's going to happen if you keep doing it?'

"Uh-huh."

"Do you want it to happen?" His voice had become hoarse with growing desire.

She slid over him and stared down into his eyes. "You ask far too many questions, Detective."

The tips of her breasts skimmed his chest, sending little arrows of heat shooting over his flesh. Then she leaned forward, allowing her hair to cascade around them, and buried her mouth against his. She swirled her tongue around his, instantly recalling all the nuances that aroused him. Slowly, she rotated her hips against his thighs. Only the thin fabric of her flimsy nightgown separated their skin.

Luke groaned deep in his throat and grabbed her hips, stopping their tantalizing motions. "You don't know what you're doing."

Rachel knew exactly what she was doing, and she also knew that there probably would come a time when she'd kick herself around the block for doing it, but, right now, she didn't care. The Luke she'd married had come out of hiding, understanding, warm, loving and secure. She could not—would not—let go of him, at least for this one night.

Luke pulled her nightgown over her head, then discarded it over the side of the bed. Just as quickly, he wriggled out of his Jockey shorts and tossed them to join her nightgown on the floor. He looked into her eyes as if searching for something, then ran his hand down her spine. Rachel arched her back. His arousal burned into her thigh. Reveling in the sensations racing through her at the touch of his skin on hers, she pressed against him in a silent plea for more.

Luke rolled her to her back and stared down into her eyes. His gaze was dark with desire. "Oh no. Not yet. I've waited too long for this to hurry through it."

Burying his face in her neck, he nibbled her skin, then bathed it with his tongue, exploring the crevices behind her ears and in the indentation above her collarbone. Shivers rippled down her body. She dug her nails into his shoulders and held her breath in anticipation of what she knew was to come.

Slowly, Luke's mouth moved over her skin until he reached the valley between her breasts. He trailed a chain of kisses to her navel, then moved back to capture one swollen nub between his teeth. Gently, he tugged on her, then suckled, laving the nipple at the same time. He repeated the motion several times, moving from one breast to the other.

Rachel squirmed beneath him, the need to stop the teasing sensations and at the same time prolong them driving her.

Then his hand slid between her thighs, and she felt his fingers pressing for entrance into her heat. Rachel's insides swelled with the pleasure coursing through her until she was sure she'd burst with wanting Luke.

"Now," she whispered. "Please, now."

But he continued to deny her and himself from the thing they both wanted most. Instead, he slipped his finger inside her and imitated the act that she begged for. She arched her hips, driving his finger deeper, seeking the satisfaction he refused her.

Luke struggled for breath. She was hot inside, hotter than he could ever recall her being before. He felt his control slipping out of his grasp. Desperately, Luke hung on to the fraying edges. It had been so long since he'd held her, touched, tasted her. He wanted this to last because he knew that, for whatever reasons she had sought him out tonight, in the morning those reasons would be gone and there would be no more nights like this. Never again would he hold Rachel and love her.

The thought fired his desperation, tearing his control from his tenuous grasp. He slipped between her legs. She opened for him, willingly, eagerly. Her hands anchored his hips, her nails digging into his flesh, claiming him.

He entered her slowly, trying to allow her time to get used to him. Rachel was not one to wait for anything and now proved to be no different. She raised her hips, driving the length of him deep inside her.

Luke's world threatened to explode. A rush of sensation so strong careened through him, he had to hold on to Rachel's shoulders to steady himself. Biting down on his lip, he stopped her movements by pinning her hips to the mattress, knowing that, if he didn't, this would end before it began.

"Not so fast, sweetheart," he gasped against her neck. "It's been two years, and I don't want to shortchange you."

She must have understood because she lay very still, her hands splayed on his back, her breath coming in short gasps. He could feel her heart pounding against his chest.

As they lay there waiting for control to return, Luke felt more content that he had in years. He was home, if only for tonight. He refused to lament that. Instead, he absorbed the feel of Rachel pulsing tightly around, her body pressed to his, the smell and touch of her skin, the taste of her lips.

When Rachel grew restless, Luke began to move. Gently he made love to her with all the care and consideration he could. But tonight, she didn't seem to want him to be gentle or careful. They made love with a wild abandon that rocked both their worlds right off their axis.

The fuse that had been smoldering inside him for days burned bright and hot, sending desire raging through him. It felt like the first time they'd made love, insatiable and close to savage. Beneath him, her hips began to move faster and faster.

The pressure grew and grew until releasing it was all that he could think of. She cried out his name and held him to her. Then came the explosion, the lights, the endless tunnel of sheer pleasure. Holding her as close as he could, Luke rode out the storm that showered down on them.

After their breathing had eased and they could speak, Luke turned to her. "Rach—"

Rachel placed her fingers over his lips. "No. Let's not analyze it. It happened, and we both needed it. Let's leave it at that."

Pain squeezed Luke's heart. Even though he'd told himself differently, he'd been unable to keep a small glimmer of hope from forming that this might be a new beginning for them. Reluctantly, he nodded his agreement.

Rachel was right. What had just happened hadn't changed anything. He'd let down his family in the worst possible way, and she still hated him for walking out. In the end, the only possible outcome to all this would be that they'd solve their case or relegate it to the cold-case files and move on in their own directions. The realization that he would never have a future with Rachel created a chasm of emptiness and despair inside Luke that he knew would never be filled.

"I'd better go back to my own room," she finally said, slipping from his arms and retrieving her nightgown from the floor. Quickly, she pulled it over her head and then stood. For a moment, she stared down at him. Then she bent down and kissed him briefly and smiled. "Thank you."

"My pleasure," he said with a lightness he was far from feeling. Then he remembered. "Wait. Don't go yet. I have something for you."

Chapter 10

"You have something for me?" Rachel asked, stepping back so Luke could get out of bed. The night's silence outside the window was broken only by the waves hitting the beach just beyond the sand dunes.

She held her breath as he flipped on a bedside lamp then walked naked to the dresser, his muscles undulating beneath his tanned skin, and picked up a small blue box. Physically fighting the urge to push him down on the mattress and prolong this night of lovemaking, she moved warily away from the bed as if it were a predatory animal ready to pounce on her.

"Here." He handed her the box.

She glanced at him, then waited while he sat on the edge of the bed and pulled the sheet over his hips. Deprived of the distraction of his nakedness, she gazed down at the box.

Now that she could see it close up, she recognized the box. "Is this..."

Luke smiled secretively. "If I wanted to tell you, I would have before I gave it to you. Open it."

She sat beside him and lifted the lid. Inside was a familiar crystal bottle with a stopper shaped like a hummingbird. An amber liquid filled the bottle. "My perfume," she whispered.

With her fingertip, she traced the delicately carved hummingbird and tried not to cry. Only Luke would understand the special connection to Maggie that this scent represented.

"I know you lost yours in the fire at the condo, so I called the place in Atlanta where you have it blended and had them ship some here."

Rachel didn't know what to say. She'd forgotten about the perfume, but Luke had remembered. The gesture touched her more deeply than anything he'd ever done for her.

Taking out the stopper, she dabbed a spot of it on her wrist, inhaled deeply. Maggie's little voice played in her head. *Mommy smells like apple pie.*

Fighting back the tears, Rachel replaced the stopper.

"Thank you." She blinked, leaned closer and kissed his cheek.

If Luke had hoped for a more profuse outpouring of gratitude, he didn't show it.

She stood and cradled the bottle close to her chest. "Good night, Luke."

"Good night, Rach."

He said nothing further, but she felt his eyes watch her as she left.

When Rachel opted to drive herself to headquarters the next morning so she could buy a few clothes on her way to work to replace those she'd lost in the condo fire, Luke heaved a sigh of relief. Added to his bad mood, a product of less than two hours' sleep, was the suspicion that she was just avoiding him, but he really didn't need to be stuck in a car with her in rush-hour traffic for thirty minutes today. Not after last night.

He didn't bother with coffee at the house. Instead, he picked up a cup at the Latte Factory and checked to see if George Jackson had showed up in the past few days. Nina assured him, making no effort to disguise her intense gratitude, that he hadn't.

By the time Luke walked into the task force room, Rachel was poring over a pile of papers. Since she hadn't noted his presence, he observed her for a moment.

God, she was gorgeous. Every movement she made was graceful and sure. Her hands, fine-boned and fragile, had comforted their child with a strength and love that had often amazed him. Even in fashionably faded new jeans and a pink T-shirt with a little donkey on the front, she was one classy lady…one *sexy* lady.

Vivid memories of the night before seeped into his thoughts. He shook them away.

"What's all that?" he asked, coming to stand beside her and gesturing to the array of papers spread over the table.

"The reports Montoya got from the fire companies in the outlying areas."

"Any luck?"

Without looking up, she shook her head. "Not yet. Where have you been?"

He sat down across from her. "I went by the Latte Factory to see if Jackson had showed up in the past couple of days."

Rachel sighed and lowered the report she'd been reading. "Luke, you're wasting your time looking at him. We need to concentrate on the arsonist being a woman."

Luke leaned forward. "How can you be so positive? Just because the fire was what you call *neat?* He lived across the street from you. The man stalked you. By your own admission, he made you uncomfortable enough to confide in me about it. I confronted him, and that night your condo was torched." He counted his points off on his fingers. "Motive. Opportunity. How the hell much more proof do you need?"

She tapped the stack of papers with the tip of her pen. "Show me proof that ties him to us two years ago, and to the other victims." She paused, giving him time to speak. When he didn't, she went on. "You can't, because so far there is none, and I don't believe any exists. Until that day in the coffee shop, I had never seen Jackson before in my life, and I'd bet my savings that he never saw me before either. Yes, perhaps he was a stalker. But that does not make him a serial arsonist. Under normal conditions, you'd see that, too."

His head snapped up. His eyes grew dark. "Normal conditions? What's that supposed to mean?"

Rachel hesitated, then threw his own words back at him. "It means that you're too emotionally connected to this case and you're letting it interfere with your judgment."

Luke didn't miss the tie-in to what he'd told her when she'd first arrived in Orange Grove. "Do you think turning the tables on me will explain everything?"

"I never denied that I had an emotional connection. However, I've learned to keep it out of my work. Answer this for me. In any other case, would you have confronted a suspect the way you confronted Jackson?"

Knowing Rachel was right, he refrained from replying. He'd only gone after Jackson initially because he'd wanted to protect Rachel. Under normal circumstances, until the proof was there, he'd have watched from afar, knowing that by confronting the suspect he'd take the chance of scaring him away, just as he'd done with Jackson.

To avoid her censuring gaze, Luke went to the coffeepot and poured himself his second cup of coffee of the day and hoped that it would work better than the first one had to calm his raw, sleep-deprived nerves.

If he wanted to look the truth in the eye, he knew that as long as Rachel was working this case with him, his emotions would be bleeding all over it. The cop in him knew that was wrong and dangerous for both of them, and that he should be able to control himself, to separate work and emotion.

Bottom line was, as much as he loved Rachel and wanted her back, he'd failed her and Maggie once. He'd lost Maggie and nearly killed Rachel. He had to isolate his emotions, or he took the chance of failing her again.

He turned back to Rachel. "So is there anything in those fire reports that's gonna shed some light on this case or are we chasing our tails again?"

Drawn by his formal tone of voice, Rachel raised her head and looked at him. He'd sidestepped that part about his emotions nicely. Gone was the man who had made love to her last night. In his place was Detective Luke Sutherland, all business. She wished she could turn her emotions on and off as easily as he could.

Following his lead, she adopted the same unemotional tone. "No. Nothing so far."

Unfortunately, adjusting her tone of voice did nothing to stop the continuing resurgence of memories of the night before, memories of his touch, his tenderness, his compassion, his lovemaking, his…

For sanity's sake, Rachel had to let go of that. She concentrated on the reports and tried to read. It took a moment before she could focus on the words stretched across the paper. Finally, her emotions abated and her brain kicked in, and she finished the report, then set it aside with the others that had proven to be of no help.

Expecting to find another report that offered nothing of substance, she scanned the next sheet. Then she stopped. A name jumped out at her. The hairs on her nape stood on end. Rachel had learned long ago not to ignore her instincts.

She read on carefully before saying anything. The awareness increased with every word she read. She looked across the table at Luke, who was quietly sipping his coffee and staring off into space.

"What's the name of that woman you introduced me to the other day, the social worker?"

For a moment, she thought he hadn't heard her. "Hannah Daniels." He frowned. "Why?"

"This report is on a fire that killed a woman named Charlene Daniels in Henderson, a whistle-stop town about an hour south of here."

"Could be coincidence. Daniels is a pretty common name."

"I agree, but how coincidental is it that her daughter's name is Hannah?"

He looked more interested, but not convinced. "So, Hannah's mother died in a fire? It can still be chalked up to coincidence."

Rachel read on, then smiled. "Well, how's this for another coincidence? The firefighters who removed her found a burned Bible under the body." She leaned back, waiting for his reaction.

Luke sat up as if someone had poured ice water down his back. "Okay, you've got my attention now. Any other similarities to our fires?"

As she read the rest of the report, she was aware that he had moved from the other side of the table to sit beside her. "No. Just the Bible. But that doesn't mean much. Serial criminals often start simple then escalate as they gain confidence."

"What about cause of death?"

"Cause of death was ruled smoke inhalation by the coroner. No autopsy. The body was removed from the scene and taken directly to a funeral home. Henderson's coroner was probably a local doctor, elected to the position because everyone in town liked him and not because he knew beans about forensics."

Both Rachel and Luke knew that this lack of attention to cause of death sometimes happened in towns with strained budgets that couldn't begin to support a forensics lab or the salary of a trained medical examiner and a team of forensics specialists. The local general practitioner often held the position of coroner, and unless there were definitive signs of foul play, the bodies went straight to embalming and totally bypassed the autopsy procedure.

"Damn!" Luke reached for the phone. "We're going to need to talk to him. What's his name? I'll call records and see if they have an address on him."

"Dr. Ralph Clark," she read from the report.

Luke dialed a number from memory. "It's Luke Sutherland, Jack. I need the address and phone number of the coroner in Henderson, Dr. Ralph Clark." He waited.

For the next few minutes, his expression went from hopeful, to angry, then to resigned.

"What?" Then he swore. "Figures. Thanks." He hung up. "Dr. Clark died about a year ago."

Recalling Hannah's come-hither smile and the invitation in her eyes when she'd looked at Luke that day, Rachel fought down a stab of jealousy and stood. "Well, then, let's go talk to your girlfriend at the DCS," she said, grabbing her briefcase and heading for the door.

"She's *not* my girlfriend," he protested vehemently, hot on her heels.

"Right," she said aloud, her tone disbelieving.

Inside, she knew Luke had no romantic feelings toward the woman. He could never have made love to her last night if he was in a relationship with another woman. Whatever else Luke Sutherland was, he was not a cheat. But deep down, she almost wished he was. At least then she would stop hanging on to this futile hope that she and Luke could ever find a life together again.

If Rachel thought the Orange Grove police station's outer office was busy, she quickly changed her mind after walking through the doors of the Department of Children's Services. In front of them was the DCS receptionist's desk, occupied by a decidedly bored-looking woman in her early twenties.

Behind the desk an assortment of cubicles formed a mouse maze at the center of the large room. A variety of people, ranging from small children to the elderly, moved among the cubicles, attempting to reach their assigned social worker. Printers hummed as they printed out the required forms for each need. Low and muted voices filled the air and furthered the room's likeness to a hive of worker bees. Over it all hovered the stench of defeated humanity.

"We're here to see Hannah Daniels," Luke announced to the gum-chewing receptionist.

"Do you have an appointment?" The bottle redhead never looked up from the fashion magazine she was reading. Her jaw continued to work, tirelessly mutilating the gum. Periodically a *crack* could be heard emitting from the vicinity of her mouth.

Good grief, Rachel thought. How very professional. But she knew that these unskilled positions were often filled out of necessity, and qualifications sometimes fell by the wayside for lack of applicants.

Impatient to be heard and fed up with the attitude she was getting, Rachel reached across the desk and snatched the magazine from the woman's grasp.

"Hey!" she squeaked and sat up straighter, glaring at Rachel. "Gimme back my magazine. No appointment. No admittance. Those are my orders."

Had she not heard a word they'd said? Rachel raised her voice a notch. "We are not going to make an appointment, and we still want to see Hannah Daniels."

"Well—" the woman smiled sweetly at them, the humor never reaching her pursed lips "—yelling at me isn't gonna help. Without an appointment, you aren't going to see anybody here unless I say so." She glowered at Rachel and grabbed the magazine back. "And I don't say so." Her attention immediately veered back to the glossy pages. "Take a seat and if we have an opening, I'll call you."

Luke huffed and dug into his jeans pocket. This time *he* grabbed the magazine from her hands and replaced it with his open badge case. "Is this enough of an appointment?"

The redhead sat straighter. "Why didn't you say you were cops?" She picked up the receiver and hit one of the buttons on the array of numbers and letters covering the phone base. "Ms. Daniels, there's two co...er...police officers here to see you." She listened for a moment, all the time continuing to torture her gum, then said, "I'll send them back." She hung up the phone and looked up at Luke, then pointed over her shoulder with one of her bright red-tipped fingers. "Her office is in the back, right corner."

As Rachel glanced back over her shoulder, she caught the receptionist checking out Luke's posterior. A wave of possessiveness bubbled up in Rachel. Without thinking, she placed her palm against the small of his back. Out of the corner of her eye, she saw him turn to stare at her in question. She kept her eyes forward and continued to wend her way through the maze of cubicles beside him.

At the back of the room they found a glassed-in office. Sitting behind a desk piled high with papers and file folders was the blond woman Rachel remembered meeting at police headquarters, Hannah Daniels. The same inexplicable feeling of familiarity she'd experienced then, overcame her again.

Luke peeked his head around the door and smiled. "Hi, there. Got a minute?"

Hannah glanced up, then, seeing who it was, returned his smile. "Luke! If I'd known what *cop* to expect, I would have primped a bit." She patted her blond hair, then laughed lightly. "Come on in."

Rachel grimaced and mimicked Hannah's words behind

Luke's back. Jealousy was not a normal part of her makeup, but this woman just brought the green-eyed monster to life in Rachel. Then Rachel thought about it. Was what she was feeling really jealousy?

She decided it was nothing like what the receptionist's ogling of Luke's behind had made her feel. In fact, this had nothing to do with Luke. Not one to make snap decisions about people, Rachel was shocked to find that despite knowing nothing about Hannah, she flat out disliked the woman.

Still unable to rationalize her assessment of Hannah, Rachel followed Luke into the small, stuffy office and slipped into one of the two seats facing Hannah's desk.

"So," Hannah said, folding her hands on the desk and looking from Luke to Rachel, "what can I do for you?"

Luke looked decidedly uncomfortable, as if searching for an approach that wouldn't offend Hannah. What had ever happened to his people-reading skills? She cautioned herself to stow the judgmental attitude and listen to what the woman had to say.

"Did you ever live in Henderson?" Rachel asked, not having the same problem confronting Hannah as Luke apparently had.

An instant of shock flashed over Hannah's face before she rearranged her expression. "Why, yes, I did. I lived there until I moved here almost five years ago. Why?"

"You know we've been investigating the arsons that have been taking place in Orange Grove," Luke began.

"Yes," Hannah said.

"Well, we've also been looking at fires that happened in the surrounding communities and—"

"Oh." Hannah nodded. "Don't tell me you think the fire that killed my mother is connected?" She stared at Luke, her hand over her heart.

"Suppose you tell us about it and let us decide," Rachel said, hoping her tone of voice sounded encouraging. "Just start anywhere," she added.

Hannah shifted some of the folders to the side. Rachel could tell that thoughts of this event were not sitting well with Hannah. She continued to move the folders around, eventually making an opening between her and Rachel and Luke.

Rachel had just started to settle back in her chair when she noticed a to-go coffee container on Hannah's desk that hadn't been visible before. On its side was a picture of a mountain with a coffee bean superimposed over it. Across the side of the cup, block letters spelled out the Latte Factory.

Chapter 11

Instantly Rachel recalled why Hannah Daniels looked familiar to her. She'd been in the Latte Factory the day George Jackson had been ogling her. Rachel had been so distracted by him that she'd taken only cursory notice of the other customers. Before she could think any more about it, Hannah began to speak.

"I've tried so hard to forget the fire that killed Momma, that I'm not sure how much I can recall." Hannah leaned back in her chair and gazed out the only window in her tiny DCS office.

While Rachel waited for Hannah to go on, images of all the destitute people who might have sat here before her filled Rachel's mind: mothers needing milk for their babies, women left to fend for themselves and feed their families, and the down-and-out who sought a helping hand to get their lives back.

"Just think about it for a minute and try your best." Luke's conciliatory tone was gentle and patient.

Rachel fumed silently. Okay, he wanted to play good cop/bad cop. Fine with her. She had no problem being the one to push Hannah to tell them what they needed to know.

"Surely something this important hasn't been wiped totally from your memory." Rachel's voice was sharper than she'd intended and held a distinct hint of disbelief.

Luke glared at her.

Hannah swung sharply to stare at Rachel. "Not wiped out, just…dimmed."

Her tone was defensive, as if Rachel didn't believe her. And she didn't. Despite the fact that until recently, Rachel had blocked out details of the fire in her own apartment, she felt sure that if her parent had died in a fire, she would remember every detail of that horrible day. Besides, the report had said that Hannah wasn't home. Therefore, she hadn't had the added trauma of waking up to find her world burning around her.

"Fine. Dimmed then." Hannah was obviously not going to willingly share what she knew of the Henderson fire. "Tell us what your *dimmed* memory can recall."

"Rachel," Luke whispered reprovingly, shifting in his chair to frown at her. "Her mother died."

Rachel glared back at him, outraged that he didn't understand her need to know, even in the face of Hannah's loss. "And five years later, *our* child died in a fire very much like the one that killed her mother. Is it unreasonable that I want to know the details?" she hissed in a stage whisper.

He turned his back totally to Hannah. "Not unreasonable at all. Just have a little respect for her grief."

Rachel backed away. The anger drained out of her. She had done exactly what she'd accused Luke of earlier, let her emotions rule her head, and as a result been too rough and maybe shut Hannah down as a result. After all, it wasn't Hannah's fault that Maggie was gone.

"Sorry," she said to Hannah.

Hannah had obviously heard every word of the low-toned argument. Now, totally ignoring Rachel's apology, she looked from one to the other. "*Your* child? You two are married?"

"*Were* married." Luke cleared his throat. "We're divorced."

"Now, about the fire..." Rachel prompted.

Hannah looked strange...crestfallen? No, she looked off balance. Why? Then it came to her. Having an ex-wife around had to be awkward when you were attracted to a man.

"Hannah?" Luke prompted.

She roused from her thoughts. "Oh. Sorry. You wanted to know about the fire." She paused and began to fidget with a pencil, weaving it in and out of her fingers. "I wasn't home, but the firefighters told me that the fire started in the living room."

"Where were you?" Rachel asked.

"At a friend's, I think." She shrugged. "Anyway, Momma often lay on the couch, watched TV and smoked. I'm assuming that she fell asleep, and her cigarette set fire to the house. When I got home, the house was ablaze and the firefighter told me my mother was inside. It took a long time to put the fire out, then they found her on the couch." Hannah caught a sob in her throat, stood and walked to the window.

"The fire report said they found a Bible under her," Luke said, his voice soft.

Hannah turned back from the window and nodded. "Yes, I'm not surprised. She was a very spiritual woman, always reading the Bible and quoting from it." She drew a small, square box from one of the desk draws, extracted a tissue and wiped at the tears running down her cheeks. "Never missed a Sunday at church."

Rachel was beginning to feel like a rat for being so rough on her. Obviously, her mother's death still affected Hannah strongly.

The phone on Hannah's desk rang. "Excuse me." She picked up the receiver and spoke into it. After a moment, her eyes widened, then she looked at her watch. "Thanks." She hung up and turned to Rachel and Luke. "I'm so sorry. I have an appointment on the other side of town in ten minutes. I have to leave now to make it. These people don't hang around if I'm not there on time. If you have any more questions, just give me a call."

Without waiting for one of them to answer, she grabbed her purse and some folders from one of the teetering piles, then hurried past them and out of the room before either of them could say anything. Rachel had a feeling that Hannah viewed this call back to work as a way to escape them.

Twenty minutes later Rachel and Luke were sitting at an isolated table in the Latte Factory having coffee. Since they passed right by the shop on their way back to headquarters, she'd suggested they stop. Luke had agreed, with a joking remark about her caffeine-deprived body calling out for sustenance.

Now that they were here, she hadn't said a word, nor had she taken one sip of coffee. Instead, she silently stared down at the ceramic mug, which was embellished with the logo of a coffee bean and a mountain and had the words Java Gold written under the picture in gold script. She'd been going over what Hannah had told them in her mind and certain words stuck, begging for explanation.

"You're very quiet. What's on your mind?" Luke asked.

Rachel shrugged, then looked up at him. "Why did Hannah say *the fire that killed my mother?*"

"What?" Obviously that hadn't been the answer he'd expected. "Well, didn't it kill her mother?"

She frowned and nodded. "Yes, but most people would have said *the fire my mother died in.*"

Luke stared at her. "You think she has something to do with this, don't you?"

Rachel sipped her coffee and grimaced when she realized she hadn't added cream or sugar. Once she'd added them, she sipped it again. The warm liquid slid down her throat, helping to take the chill off the uneasy feeling she'd had ever since she'd seen Hannah's coffee cup.

"Not necessarily," she finally said. "I just think it's strange how she put it."

A deep sigh escaped him. "Semantics, Rach. We can't start suspecting everyone whose grammar doesn't meet your expectations. We don't have enough jail space."

She made a face at him, then spun her coffee mug and watched the liquid swirl close to overflowing. "I know. Still…"

Rachel knew Luke was beginning to get impatient. "Sometimes you're like a dog with a bone. Once you get your teeth into something, right or wrong, you just won't let go." He stood. "We have work to do and analyzing someone's grammar is not going to solve our case."

Before she could say another word, he turned on his heel and strode to the restroom.

Rachel watched him go. Maybe he was right. Her time here was running short. Soon, she'd have to get back to her job in Atlanta. Maybe she was just getting so desperate, she was reaching for anything, any little clue.

Her professional instincts had never let her down. But, then again, as she'd learned when the man she'd trusted to always be there for her walked away, there was a first time for everything.

When she got to the mall that evening after work, Rachel found that her heart wasn't into buying clothes. She purchased some undergarments and went back to Luke's house. Once there, the memories of Maggie seemed to press down on her like a lead weight. She had to get out and opted for a walk on the beach just beyond the sand dunes bordering Luke's property.

Rachel found a spot where a dune formed a cutout, plopped down in front of it and leaned back to study the movement of the restless ocean. The sand still held the heat from the day and helped dispel the chill of her haunting memories. Beside her, sea oats stirred slightly in the light breeze coming off the water. Just above the watery horizon, a sliver of the blazing orange sun dipped lower on the horizon. Above it, fingers of lavender, pink and fuchsia shot across the darkening sky. A lone gull flew overhead, searching for his night's roost.

Fatigue gnawed at every part of her body. She was exhausted, mentally and physically. The confrontation with Hannah today had revived all her own memories of the fire that had stolen her life. She recalled the terror of waking up to a burning bedroom, the fear of not getting out, the horror of trying to get to Maggie and not being able to, the awful moment when they'd told her her baby had disappeared. But worst of all, she remembered the moment, many months later, when all hope of ever seeing Maggie alive again had finally left her.

God, how she'd needed Luke back then, to hold her, to tell her not to give up, to reassure her that he loved her. But he hadn't. He'd turned his back and walked out of her life, leaving her to contend with the grief alone. It had damn near killed her, but she'd survived, and she'd survive this, too.

She raised her face to the wind and breathed deeply of the salt air. Smiling, she dug her fingers into the sand and then let it pour through them back to the beach. Her mind absorbed the serenity like a sponge soaking up water. Perhaps she just needed to separate herself from everything for a while. This was the most peaceful Rachel had felt in weeks.

She leaned back, closed her eyes and let the rhythmic pounding of the waves on the sandy shore wash over her, bringing with it the strength to face tomorrow and all the tomorrows to follow.

Luke stood just beyond the edge of the dune looking at his ex-wife. When he'd gotten home and seen her car but found no trace of her inside the house, he'd known where to look for her. He used to tease her about having been a mermaid in another life because when she was troubled, she inevitably went to the sea. And he knew she'd been troubled today. Otherwise, she never would have gone after Hannah like a wolf stalking its prey.

He understood. He could feel her desperation, her need for logical answers, because the same compelling need ate away at his own gut.

Luke shifted his position to see her better. From this new angle, the moonlight turned her hair to silver and her skin to an almost ghostly hue. His heart twisted. She looked so vulnerable.

Instinctively, he felt certain she would not want anyone to see this side of her and he started to turn back to the house. Then a moment later, she lifted her chin, and he saw the Rachel he knew so well, strong, confident and ready to face whatever life threw at her. Relief flowed over him. He stepped into her line of vision.

"Hey. You up for company?"

Rachel opened her eyes slowly, then smiled up at him and patted the sand beside her. "Pull up a piece of beach and make yourself at home."

Luke flopped down next to her, stretched his legs in front of him and leaned back on his elbows. He gazed out over the silver-streaked water. Lost in their own thoughts, neither of them spoke for a long time. A hermit crab skittered by and Rachel let out a little yelp and drew her feet closer to her.

"You okay?" Luke's question had nothing to do with the crab, and they both knew it.

"Yeah. I just needed some time to catch up with things."

He nodded and sighed. "I know what you mean."

"Do you?" Rachel glanced at him. "You always seem so in control, so sure of yourself."

He laughed derisively. "Don't believe everything you see."

Silence again.

"Luke?"

"Hmm?"

"If Maggie and I had died in the fire, would you have forgotten us?"

He swung around and cupped her face in the palm of his hand. "I may have done many things in my life that I'm not proud of, but that's not one of them. Nothing could make me forget either of you. *Nothing.*"

For a long time neither of them said anything. They just sat there with their gazes locked. Rachel saw sincerity in his eyes. She saw honesty. She saw... Could it be...love?

Emotions she'd been burying since she arrived in Orange Grove bubbled to the surface. To hell with everything. She loved Luke, and if this brief time was all she was destined to have with him, then so be it. She would ask nothing more of him than to give her the only thing he could.

Rachel leaned toward him. "Hold me," she whispered just before her lips met his in a brief, soft kiss. "Please."

He adjusted his position, then pulled her into his arms and cradled her against his chest. Rachel snuggled in against him, aligning her body with his, fitting it to all the curves and valleys so that they appeared to be one person. She wrapped her arms around his waist and threw one leg over his thigh. She felt his lower body begin to awaken.

"Ah, Rach, I'm not sure this is a good—"

She tipped her face up to his, then placed her fingers over his mouth. "Kiss me, Luke."

Slowly, deliberately, he lowered his lips to hers. At first the kiss was soft, hesitant, but in seconds it became hungry, searching, demanding. Her mouth opened beneath his like a flower seeking sustenance from the sun.

Their tongues engaged in an age-old duel of desire aching to be quenched. Rachel pressed closer, feeling bonded by his heat.

"Maybe we should go back to the house," he whispered against her lips.

"No. I need to stay near the ocean." She leaned back and looked up and down the deserted beach. "We're alone."

He sighed and settled back on the sand, then twisted so that she lay beneath him. He eased his hand under her T-shirt and smiled when she gasped. Slowly, he skimmed her flesh.

Just as she felt she could stand it no longer, his hand closed over her breast. With exquisite gentleness, he kneaded the tender flesh. She could feel her nipple swell and press into his palm. She could feel the sand beneath her, shifting and conforming to her body. She could feel it abrading her bare skin as he slipped her shirt from her body.

Then she felt the cool ocean breeze caressing her bare thighs. She lifted her hips to help him divest her of her jeans and panties. His weight left her body.

He stood above her like a mythical creature. His gaze bore into her nakedness as he slowly removed his own clothes. The moonlight painted him silver, outlining his muscular body.

Her own body cried out for him. She raised her arms, inviting him back.

A moment later he was in her. Then she felt nothing but the rhythm of their bodies, the thrill of him inside her…and the sad realization that this might be the last time.

Chapter 12

Eyes closed, Rachel rolled over and reached for Luke only to find his side of the bed empty. She opened her eyes and sat up. Where had he gone? Had he decided that what happened the night before on the beach was a mistake? A tiny spark of the same panic she'd felt a lifetime ago began to swell inside her. She recalled all too vividly waking up and finding that plain white envelope propped against her bedside lamp and the cryptic explanation it had contained.

Rachel,
I can't stay anymore. You'll be better off without me.
All my love, Luke

Tears began to gather. Slowly, she turned toward the night table, expecting to find another white envelope. Not only was there no envelope, but she suddenly smelled the fragrant aroma of cinnamon French toast and frying bacon—the same breakfast Luke had often cooked for her and Maggie on Sunday mornings. She smiled wide, then threw back the blankets and padded to the bathroom.

Twenty minutes later, showered and dressed, Rachel walked into the kitchen. Standing at the stove in khaki shorts and bare feet, Luke wielded a spatula in one hand and balanced a plate with a pile of golden-brown toast in the other.

"Morning," she said shyly, not really sure what to expect after last night.

Luke set down the plate and swung his arm wide. "Come here, you."

Rachel hurried into his open arm. It closed around her and hugged her to his side. He kissed her head. "Morning, sunshine."

Rachel inhaled deeply of the aromas filling the kitchen. "You're going to spoil me, not to mention that I'll have to buy a completely new wardrobe when I go home." She looked up at him and could have bitten off her tongue when she saw a cloud pass over his face. "But in the meantime, I'm going to enjoy every obscene calorie." She stood on tiptoe and kissed him soundly.

"Then let's get to it," he said, his good mood restored.

Minutes later she sat side by side with Luke in the breakfast nook. As she wallowed in French toast dripping in warm maple syrup, crisp bacon and fresh-squeezed orange juice, she scanned her notes from the interview with Hannah the day before. Then she noted something she'd missed. She left the table and retrieved her briefcase. Opening it, she took out the Henderson firefighters' report of the Daniels fire.

She could feel Luke's gaze on her as she read it carefully. Then she looked up. "Hannah told us that her mother smoked. This report says a neighbor told her Charlene Daniels didn't smoke."

Luke shrugged. "Maybe she hid the habit from everyone, church friends, neighbors." He plucked the report from her hand and laid it behind them on the counter. "Can we have a quiet breakfast without talking shop? I promise, as soon as we're done, you can tell me all about your theories. Right now, I just want to eat and look at you."

She started to protest, then he kissed her lightly and smiled. Her stomach did a pleasant little somersault. "Okay. Sorry."

Kissing her again, Luke palmed her face. "You're forgiven. Now, eat. All the good food I've been feeding you is finally starting to show, but we still have a ways to go."

She laughed out loud, then picked up her fork and began eating again.

The room fell silent, and Rachel realized they had nothing to talk about except the case and subjects neither of them wanted to broach. The rich smell of brewing coffee filled the room. She glanced longingly toward the corner of the kitchen where the coffeemaker gurgled and churned, the noise the only sound that filled the silence. The coffeemaker gave a last belch and the red light came on, indicating the brew was done.

"Coffee?" she asked, standing and grabbing her cup.

"Please."

As she filled the two cups, Rachel thought about what she'd been able to talk to Luke about, aside from the case, since coming back here. From some of their conversations she knew he thought about Maggie as much as she did and that he hadn't forgotten her. Beyond that, they hadn't talked once about their personal challenges, the challenges that would ultimately make it impossible for them to find any future together. She still didn't trust him not to run again, and she knew he was still unable to share himself fully with her.

She turned back toward the table and stopped, staring at his broad, muscular, bare back. Perhaps now was the time to initiate a conversation about all the things they avoided, but somehow, she couldn't find the words to begin. Eventually she would. She had to…no matter what the outcome. But not right now…

Setting his filled cup in front of him and taking her place at the table, she picked up her fork and forced the rest of her breakfast down.

Rachel finished eating and stared at Luke. "Will you help me do something?"

"Sure," he said, taking his last bit of bacon and then leaning back. "What did you have in mind?"

She swallowed, then hesitated. Preparing herself for an argument, she dived in. "I want to go to Henderson and speak to anyone who knew the Daniels family before the fire."

He laughed, then looked at their empty plates. "I guess we're done."

"Yes, we are, and you said we would discuss the case when we were. So, will you go to Henderson with me to talk to some of the Daniels' neighbors?"

Luke considered her proposal for all of a half a minute, then sighed. "Okay. We'll leave as soon as we get this mess cleaned up." He gestured at the dirty dishes that were all that remained of their breakfast.

His easy agreement shocked her. She was sure he had passed off her misgivings about Hannah as an overactive imagination that was finding proof where there was none, and she had been even more certain he'd squash her idea of going to Henderson.

She studied him. "That was way too easy. What's the catch?"

He leaned forward, pushed his plate back, then rested his forearms on the table. "If we don't find anything, we concentrate on Jackson."

Frowning, Rachel thought about his condition. When had he stopped believing in her abilities? He'd told her more times than she could count that he thought she was the best profiler in the state. Now, suddenly he doubted her. That hurt. Except…

Despite her best efforts, he kept insisting that Jackson had something to do with the arsons. Was it *his* emotions coming into play again? Was Luke pointing the finger at an innocent man simply because the guy made a pass at his ex-wife?

Rachel opened her mouth to tell him once again that he was wrong about Jackson, but he stopped her with a raised hand.

"That's the deal, Rach. Take it or leave it."

She hesitated. That he'd agreed to go to Henderson was a huge step in what she saw as the right direction. When they got back, she'd fix the Jackson problem.

"I'll take it."

Henderson was a carbon copy of many other small, southern towns. As they passed down Main Street, Rachel read aloud the names on the storefronts, which seemed to have been pulled from centuries past.

"Al's Barber Shop, McKinley's Grocery, Thompson's Car Repairs, Harriet's Diner."

Plain and to the point, Luke thought. What you see on the sign is what you get inside. Somehow, that brought a sense of order. Right now he needed that.

What had happened on the beach, and then having Rachel in his bed all night, had thrown his emotions into turmoil. Was she thinking about remaining in Orange Grove? Maybe even starting over with him? It sure didn't seem that way after her earlier remark about going home. So why was she suddenly so affectionate, so willing to share his bed?

He shook himself. He wanted her here with him, but he'd be better off just enjoying it while he had it and stop analyzing every move she made. Making plans for a future that could never be would only make it harder when she left. If she left. He couldn't blame her if she didn't stay.

Since she had only a few more days of her leave of absence remaining, he'd know soon enough if she planned to stay or not.

Right now, he needed to concentrate on putting Rachel's suspicions about Hannah to rest. While the fire could well be related, he just couldn't see Hannah as an arsonist. She was dedicated to helping people. "Well, where do you want to start? Maybe the firehouse?"

"No. Turn in there." Rachel pointed at Harriet's Diner. "In a small town, everyone hangs out at the local eatery. It's a hive of gossip. Maybe we'll find something out."

The diner was empty except for one waitress and a cook. The waitress, fairly new to the area, had no idea who the Daniels were. However, the cook, who had come to Henderson the year of the fire, was able to point them in the direction of the neighborhood where he thought the family had lived.

Two delicious cheeseburgers, a huge plate of French fries and some of the best coffee Rachel had drank in ages later, she and Luke thanked the waitress and the cook and went back to Luke's car.

"So," Luke said, starting the car, "we know the *approximate* location. Do you plan on knocking on all the doors until you find someone who knew the Daniels family?"

Rachel turned sideways in the seat, clicked her seat belt into place and nodded. "Yup."

Using the directions the cook had scribbled on a napkin, they found the neighborhood where Hannah and her mother had lived. Unfortunately, that's all they found. Rachel was beginning to feel frustrated, and she itched to wipe the I-told-you-so smile off Luke's face. They'd already talked to five households and none had any information beyond what she and Luke already knew.

Disappointment began to grow in her. She'd been so sure there were answers to be found here.

They stood on the road in front of the last house they visited and looked up and down the sparsely populated lane.

"What now?" Luke asked, leaning one hip against the fender of his SUV.

"We go to the next house." She pointed at a small, barn-red cottage set among a grove of live oak trees and nestled in behind a hedge of blooming hibiscus bushes whose deep red flowers made it look as if someone had poured blood over the foliage. "Then that one." She indicted a new house on the other side of the cottage.

"Not ready to say uncle, are you?"

She glared at Luke. "No." Opening the car door, she slid into the passenger seat, hooked her seat belt and waited for him to join her.

After he'd gotten in and slammed the door with uncalled-for gusto, he started the car. An instant blast of cool air hit her in the face. She closed her eyes and leaned her head back to allow the chilly AC to wash over her. When the car didn't move, she opened her eyes and looked at Luke. He was gripping the steering wheel and staring out the windshield.

"Well, let's go," she said impatiently.

"Rach," he finally said and turned toward her, "you can be wrong once in a while, you know."

She knew he was referring to her pride. She also knew that it was the one thing about her he had never been able to understand. But right now, she didn't have the time or the patience to get into a discussion about how women were forced to prove themselves more than men. Besides, this was not pride. This was gut instinct telling her that something about Hannah didn't ring true and that her suspicions were as right today as they had been when she sat in the social worker's office. For that reason alone Rachel refused to give up.

"I'm not wrong this time," she said.

He sighed and put the car in gear. "No, you never are," he mumbled.

With his muffled tone she couldn't tell if he was being sarcastic or complimentary. Either way, she didn't have time to find out right now.

At the driveway that led to the red cottage, he swung the car in and parked it in the shade of one of the majestic oak trees. As they walked toward the house, Rachel looked at the home next door and the stumps in the yard and wondered why they'd seen fit to cut down the oak trees that had surrounded it.

As Rachel went to the door and knocked, Luke hung back. When no one answered, she knocked again. They waited.

"Looks like no one's home," Luke called just as the inner, wooden door swung open.

Behind the screen stood an old lady, no more than five feet tall, wearing a flowered apron. Her hair was as white as snow, and her cheery smile seemed to light up the overcast day. "Hello. Can I help you?"

"Hello. I'm Rachel Sutherland and this is Detective Sutherland of the Orange Grove Police Department. We'd like to ask you some questions about a fire that occurred around here five years ago."

Luke seemed to come alert and moved to stand beside her. But rather than looking at the old woman, he stared at Rachel. Before she could ask what was wrong, the old lady swung open the screen door.

"Sure thing. Come in. I'm Sophie Aimes." She waved them toward a room off the short, dark hall. "You must mean the Daniels' fire, next door. Terrible, terrible thing." She clucked her tongue.

Luke followed Rachel into a small living room that, though worn and in need of redecorating, reflected the cheery woman who had led them into it. White lace doilies covered the arms of a faded brown sofa. Brightly embroidered pillows lined the back of the couch and rested in the one chair across from the sofa. Beside the overstuffed chair, a basket overflowed with a tangle of colored threads and an embroidery hoop that held what appeared to be the beginning of another throw pillow with a partially completed cardinal as the focal point.

"You two take a seat, and I'll get us something cold to drink, then we'll talk." Leaving them no room for argument, Sophie hustled through a swinging door at the back of the room.

Rachel chose to sit in the chair, while Luke took a seat on the sofa and leaned back against the wall of pillows. He stared at Rachel. "Why did you do that?"

She started. "What?"

"Introduce yourself that way."

Her brow furrowed. "What way?"

"As Rachel Sutherland."

Her eyes widened. "I did not."

"Rach, I know I'm not as young as I used to be, but my hearing is still excellent."

Before Luke could press the point, Sophie reappeared with a tray holding a cut-glass pitcher of iced tea, three glasses, a dish of lemon slices and a tray of cookies. He hurried to relieve her of the burden.

"Thank you. Such a nice, well-mannered man." She flashed Luke an appreciative grin. "Put it on the coffee table, dear, then we can all reach it." She glanced at Rachel. "I'm afraid I'm going to have to ask you to sit beside the nice detective, my dear. My sciatica can't take sitting on that lumpy sofa." She rubbed her hip with a liver-spotted hand and smiled.

Rachel quickly moved to sit on the sofa beside Luke. Since it was more a love seat than an actual sofa, their thighs touched. Luke noted with a smile that Rachel made no move to sever the contact.

Sophie dropped into her chair and sighed. "It's just plain hell to get old." She tapped her forehead. "The memory's as sharp as ever, but the body is going to hell in a handbasket."

Luke liked this lady. She didn't mince words, just like his gran. And like Gran, he felt she would set them straight on the details of the Daniels' fire in short order.

Rachel hitched forward, notebook on her lap. "Mrs.—"

"Sophie, dear. Please call me Sophie. Mrs. Aimes sounds so damn old, and the last thing I need at my age is to feel any older than I do."

"All right. Sophie, can you tell us about the fire?"

Sophie fixed her tea and motioned for them to do likewise. Luke watched Rachel add two slices of lemon to kill the sweetness of the traditional Southern presweetened iced tea.

"Well," Sophie began, "it was in May right after lunch that I heard the fire trucks going by. Then I realized they were stopping, so I ran to my porch and was horrified to see that the Daniels' house—" she pointed toward the new house "—was a mass of flames." She shook her head and clucked her tongue. "It was terrible, just terrible."

She offered them each a peanut-butter cookie. Both Luke and Rachel declined. The old woman replaced the plate, then sighed and leaned back, balancing her glass of tea on the arm of the chair.

"It wasn't as though those two women didn't have enough tragedy in their lives already." Sophie pulled out a lace-trimmed handkerchief and wiped at a stray tear that had trickled down her wizened cheek.

Rachel made a note on her pad, then asked, "Tragedy?"

"Oh my, yes. You see, Hannah was a product of rape. Her grandfather raped Charlene... That's Hannah's momma...when she was just thirteen. He claimed he didn't, but we all knew better. The man was just no good." Sophie waved her hand. "But that's a story for another day. Charlene raised Hannah mostly on her own."

Luke leaned forward. "The fire, Sophie?" he asked, trying to keep the old woman on track.

"No," Rachel stopped him. "Go on, Sophie. I want to hear this."

"Well, I always thought that the reason Hannah was never quite right was because Charlene's daddy fathered her child. If you know what I mean." Sophie gave them both an intense look, tapped her temple, then shrugged.

Not right? Now, that really didn't sound like the Hannah he knew. She had a college degree. Had to, to be a social worker. He mulled that over, then Sophie started talking again, and he shoved it to the back of his mind to talk to Rachel about later.

"'Course, Charlene wasn't all that right either, so it might just run in the family. But that Hannah was the sweetest thing, even if she wasn't right." Sophie paused and turned to face the mantel. "That's her when she was just a little tyke," she said, pointing to a framed photo of a beautiful little blond girl with an infectious smile.

Rachel's heart lurched. Hannah's childhood photo reminded her of Maggie.

Sophie turned back to them. "She'd come over here and help me with the housework, and I'd pay her, then she'd rush off to the store to buy herself something pretty. One time, she put money into one of those gumball machines in McKinley's Grocery and won herself a ring. Pretty thing it was, green stone and gold band. It turned her finger green, but she wore it anyway." She laughed. "Charlene called it trashy and tried to get her to throw it away, but Hannah refused. Never saw her after that without that ring on her finger."

Rachel glanced at Luke.

"Because Charlene gave birth to Hannah at such an early age, her and her momma used to pass themselves off to people who didn't know them as sisters. I think it was kind of a game they liked to play. They looked that young and very much alike. Charlene could have never denied her daughter. No sir." Sophie bit into a cookie and chewed thoughtfully.

Rachel again scribbled some notes on her pad.

"Was Hannah religious?" Rachel held her pen poised over the notebook to write down Sophie's answer.

The old woman shook her head, and the white cap of hair did a crazy dance in response to her strong denial. "No. Charlene tried to get her to go to church, but once she was old enough to say no, Hannah would have none of it. Now, Charlene was almost...what's that word for being really crazy about something?"

"Fanatical?" Luke offered.

"Yup. That's it. Fanatical. Wouldn't miss a Sunday in church."

Rachel sipped her tea, made a face, then set it back on the tray. "That does go along with them finding a Bible under the body."

"Now, that's just another thing that the coroner and the newspapers got all screwed up," Sophie said, shaking a finger at Rachel. "Those damn reporters got the whole story wrong. 'Course, that idiot Ralph Clark didn't help any either. Man never should have gotten the coroner's job. Didn't know his ass from his elbow." She leaned forward and wagged her finger for emphasis. "Not that I voted for the old coot. Do you know he didn't even want to come here that day? Nope. Was at a barbecue at his son's. Couldn't wait to get out of here and get back to feeding his face after he checked out the body. Damn fool."

Luke exchanged glances with Rachel. It was just as she'd suspected. The coroner had done a sloppy job. And, obviously, Sophie did not suffer fools lightly.

"You said they screwed things up. Didn't they find a Bible under the body?" He felt Rachel hold her breath.

"Oh, yes, they found it all right. But the whole write-up in the papers was wrong. They said she smoked, and she didn't. Charlene wouldn't have smoked. Hannah had a touch of asthma. Why the girl was right sick for a few weeks before the fire. Charlene took Hannah to see the doctor, but they couldn't figure out what was wrong. Now, why would someone with asthma smoke?"

Letting out the breath she'd been holding, Rachel frowned at Sophie. "I'm afraid I don't understand."

They all waited while Sophie refilled her iced tea, took a sip, then leaned back again.

"I don't understand either, dear." She thought for a minute. "Here's another thing that was strange. Charlene wouldn't have been caught dead wearing that cheap ring that Hannah loved so much. That's why I told you about it. When they carried that body past me, her hand slipped out, and I saw that ring, plain as day, right there on her poor little blackened finger. The papers said that Charlene died in the fire, but I'd stake my next social security check on it that Hannah died, not Charlene."

Chapter 13

An hour later, Luke and Rachel sat in his car, both stunned by what Sophie had related to them.

"You suppose Sophie's right, that it was Hannah that died in the fire and not Charlene?" Rachel stared down at her notepad, still processing all the elderly woman had told them.

"She's pretty sharp for her age, but we're gonna need more proof if we expect to get this into court." Luke took a peanut-butter cookie from the Ziploc bag Sophie had insisted they take with them. Instantly, the smell of peanuts filled the car's interior. He stared at the cookie for a moment, then put it back and rezipped the bag.

Was he thinking what she was? That peanut-butter cookies had been Maggie's favorites? How Rachel missed baking cookies for Maggie, brushing her long, silky hair and reading her stories. Rachel blinked back the threatening tears and then rolled down her window to let out the smell of the fresh-baked cookies.

"The sad part is," Luke went on, "she told the authorities, and they talked to the coroner, believed his half-baked conclusions and did nothing more to check it out." He shrugged. "Sounds like a small town. Probably passed it off as the ravings of a senile old woman." Then he laughed. "I wouldn't have wanted to be the one who dismissed her."

Rachel didn't laugh. She was too busy being stunned at Luke's agreement. "You agree that Hannah or Charlene, or whoever the hell she is, is a viable suspect?"

He sighed. "The kind of stuff that Sophie just told us certainly makes me wonder enough to explore it further." He looked away from her, then back. "Rach, I'm sorry I fought you on considering Hannah as a suspect. I know how damn good you are at what you do. If you weren't, A.J. never would have brought you here to help out."

"So why did you?" she asked, hoping to open the secret vault that was Luke's hidden emotions.

He wrapped his fist tighter around the steering wheel. "I don't know. Maybe it was just that I wanted to get past that damn pride of yours."

Rachel put her hand over his, then snatched it away when she realized what she'd done. He grabbed it back and held it. She allowed it, sensing that, right now, he needed that contact. "It's not pride this time, Luke. This time, it's personal. Don't you know I would have backed off on Hannah if I had the least suspicion I was heading in the wrong direction? Solving this one is way too important to me. I don't have time for dead ends."

She wanted to tell him that she'd realized in the last few days that her pride had already robbed her of too much. Pride had kept her from going after him when he left her and fighting for their love. Pride was keeping her from throwing herself in his arms now and asking him to start over. Her pride may have kept her from lots of things she'd wanted, but she would not let it color her judgment when she was so close to catching the arsonist—and by doing so, maybe, just maybe, bringing Maggie's remains home and finally laying her child to rest.

"I know. I should have known you wouldn't make unjustified assumptions with this case, but..." Luke caressed the back of her hand with his fingers, then lifted it and kissed the palm and closed her fingers over it. "Save that for later when we have time to talk. Right now, I suggest we get back to Orange Grove and let A.J. know we're going to need an exhumation order for the body of Charlene Daniels."

Supper was eaten in almost total silence that night as Luke and Rachel cast glances at the phone, waiting for A.J. to call with the news that they had the order of exhumation. Rachel couldn't channel her thoughts away from what Sophie had told them and what this exhumation might reveal.

"What's taking so long?" she asked, dropping her fork onto the plate of food she'd barely touched. Even the enticing aroma of the pasta and marinara sauce that Luke had made held no appeal for her nervous stomach.

The clatter roused Luke out of his thoughts. He looked at her. "It's only been a couple of hours. Be thankful we're in the same jurisdiction. Otherwise it would take much longer to go through channels."

She threw him an impatient frown. Standing, she walked to the phone, picked up the receiver and listened for the dial tone. Dropping it back into the cradle, she grimaced. "It's working."

"Just like it was when you checked it a few minutes ago?"

Luke rose, slung his arm around her shoulders. "Relax. A.J.'s on it. Come on." He guided her into the family room and, taking her shoulders, gently seated her on the sofa. "Let's watch some senseless sitcom. Maybe that'll take our minds off it for a while."

He'd been touching her so naturally, just as if they were still married and he still had that right. And what really shocked her was she didn't mind. In a strange way, it helped her endure this endless wait.

She sat rigidly on the sofa and absently watched him press buttons on the remote. "I thought you said the order wouldn't take long."

He continued to surf the channels. "It doesn't, once A.J. gets to a judge and convinces him we need it."

"We do need it." She grabbed Luke's free hand. "I know we're on the right track. I can feel it here." She balled her fist and placed it firmly against her stomach. "I suspected Hannah—or Charlene—before, but ever since we left Sophie's, I'm sure it's her."

He clicked the off button on the remote, then put it on the coffee table and swung around to face her. "Speaking of Sophie, there's a question you never answered for me."

Rachel frowned and dropped his hand. Was he doubting again? Had he changed his mind about Hannah's mother?

"Why did you use your married name when you introduced yourself to Sophie today?"

Stunned by the question she hadn't expected to be hit with again, Rachel stared at her clenched hands and searched for an explanation that would satisfy him. That wouldn't be easy because, in truth, she didn't have a clue as to why she'd used her married name.

The room grew oppressively silent. The *ticktock* of the clock on the mantel echoed around the room like gunshots. Her pulse throbbed in her temple.

He leaned forward to see her better. "Rach?"

"I don't know," she finally said. "It just…slipped out."

She couldn't tell him that she wished with every fiber of her being that it was true, that she *was* Mrs. Luke Sutherland again, that she could turn time backward and their daughter could be alive and they could be the happy family they used to be. What was the sense? It could never be, and there was no point in thinking otherwise. It would just mean heartache for both of them.

As Luke opened his mouth to question her further, the phone rang. Though both of them had been anxiously awaiting A.J.'s call, they jumped. Luke answered it. Rachel trained all her attention on his expressionless face.

He hung up. "A.J.'s got the order. We're to meet him at the cemetery in Henderson tomorrow morning at eight."

As the backhoe made its first slice into the grave site, Rachel cringed and stepped closer to Luke's side. The perfume wafting to her from flowers left on nearby graves made her stomach heave. Ever since her mother's funeral, cemeteries had not been high on Rachel's list of favorite places to visit, and disturbing the grave of the deceased seemed sacrilegious to her, despite the necessity.

However, when Luke had been in his protect-Rachel mode and given her the chance this morning to stay behind at headquarters, she'd refused. She'd made up her mind long ago not to shy away from any aspect of this investigation. She wanted this arsonist more than she'd ever wanted one before, and she was going to get her. And when they had her in custody, Rachel *would* find out what she'd done with Maggie.

She shivered at the idea of her sweet baby being in a place like this, but it tore her apart to think that Maggie was lying somewhere like a piece of discarded trash.

Luke must have detected her unease and took her hand and squeezed it. Grateful for his presence and his strength, she looked up at him and smiled her thanks.

"So, tell me, what else have you got besides the belief that the body here is Hannah Daniels and not her mother?" A.J. said, pulling his jacket collar up against the brisk breeze that had suddenly swept across the open expanse of grass and grave markers. Thankful for an excuse to turn away from the mesmerizing motion of the bulldozer digging up a scoop of earth, depositing it on a pile, then going back to repeat the motion, Rachel turned her back on the grave and faced A.J.

"We've pinned it down to the arsonist being a woman. When Luke and I interviewed Hannah about the fire her mother died in, she lied about several facts having to do with this fire. And, all the victims have had child abuse charges filed against them at some time or other—and Hannah handled every case."

"*All* the victims?" A.J. asked, leveling an inquiring gaze at her.

"All but one," Luke corrected. "Rachel has never had any charges brought against her. We still haven't figured out the connection to us."

A.J. nodded. "I was sure of that. I just wanted to make sure both of you knew it."

Rachel nodded to affirm that she understood and had no doubts about her exclusion from the abuse connection, then thanked him silently with her eyes.

He grinned, then peeked around Rachel at the grave site. "They should be hitting something soon."

Rachel glanced over her shoulder. Diesel fumes stung her nose as the backhoe chugged about its task and took bite after bite from the musty earth. Then she heard the hollow sound of the big metal teeth scraping across something.

"We got it," the driver yelled down.

Two men stepped forward with ropes and waited for another man with a shovel to clear away enough dirt from around the casket so they could secure it to be removed from the grave. Once cleared, the rope was tied in place and the backhoe driver lifted the casket gently from the hole and placed it beside the grave.

It was dirty and the obviously cheap metal had begun to rust. The top had collapsed in places. As two attendants from the medical examiner's office lifted it into the back of a van for its trip back to Orange Grove for a postmortem autopsy, Rachel turned away.

She stared after the disappearing van and felt as if her insides had been lacerated. The full measure of the certainty of Maggie's death hit her. She had never realized that she had held a faint hope way in the back of her mind that Maggie was still alive. But the events of the last few days had finally brought the truth home to her.

If what Sophie said proved to be true and the woman they knew as Hannah was really Charlene, and she had killed her own daughter, she would not have hesitated to kill Maggie.

Luke had gone for coffee and carried two containers into the task force room. He stopped dead when he saw Rachel, arms folded on the table, her head resting on them and her body shaking with deep, wracking sobs.

He set the cups down and hurried to her. Squatting beside her, he pulled her into his arms. "Rach, honey, what's wrong?"

As she continued to cry against his shoulder, he could do no more than wait, hold her and feel more helpless than he ever had in his life.

Finally, she raised a tear-streaked face to look into his eyes. "I want my baby back."

Luke's heart twisted in his chest and moisture filled his eyes. Rachel's pain washed over him, and it was all he could do to keep from crying out. "So do I, honey. My God, so do I. But we can't have her back, Rach. Maggie's…gone."

Violently, she shook her head. "No, not…that way. I want…her back to put to rest. I want a place to…lay flowers. I want to…talk to her, to tell her…her mommy will always love her and that I'm…I'm so sorry I let her down." The sobs broke out anew.

Rachel blamed herself for Maggie's death?

Her words hit Luke full force. He had to work to get his mind wrapped around the fact that, although none of it was her fault, she blamed herself. He could understand Rachel feeling as if she'd failed Maggie. After all, this was a woman whose pride didn't allow her to take a loss well, to make mistakes. And this time, it wasn't just a case she couldn't solve. What she perceived as her failure had hit her in her very core.

For once Luke could relate to what Rachel was experiencing. He knew that feeling all too well. He'd been living with the guilt twisting his guts into knots for two very long years.

Helplessly, he held her closer and stroked her back. "It wasn't your fault, Rachel. It wasn't anyone's fault."

This time his own words roared to life inside his head. Did he believe what he'd just said? Was it *no one's* fault?

Her sobs had subsided to an occasional hiccup. "I should have known she was in danger." She cupped his cheek and looked deep into his eyes. "Mothers always know things like that. Always."

Luke shook his head. "Not always. Sometimes, we just can't know. Sometimes, things happen that we have no control over."

The more he talked to Rachel, the more he felt the guilt that had been burning inside him for so long start to ease. It would never be totally gone. Because he would never completely forgive himself. But at least now he was able to see that he had no power over what happened that night. Rachel had been home, and she hadn't known. If he'd been there, he might not have known either.

For the first time in two years, Luke felt as if he could begin to embrace life again and plan for a future, if Rachel could ever trust him again. But right now, this wasn't about him.

This was about Rachel. He would not let her go through the tortures of the damned that he had by allowing her to go on thinking she was responsible for Maggie's death.

Rachel took the handkerchief Luke gave her and blew her nose. "Today, at the cemetery, all I could think of was how horrible it was that we were disturbing the final resting place of another human being, but then…" She hiccuped. "Then I thought about our poor baby."

Luke swallowed back his tears. He could feel Rachel's pain as she tore these memories from her soul. "Rach, I can't stand to see you like this. What can I do to make this better?"

Rachel raised her watery eyes to meet his gaze. Tears ran down her face and dripped unnoticed off her chin and onto her blouse, leaving dark spots on the baby-blue material. Rachel took a deep shuddering breath.

She clutched the front of his shirt in her shaking hands. "Help me bring our baby home. Help me put her to rest properly."

Hauling her into his arms, he buried his face in her hair and allowed the tears to slip down his cheeks. "Whatever it takes, we'll bring Maggie home—together." He pulled her from the chair. "Come on. Let's go home."

With his arm around her, he guided her from the task force room, intentionally leaving her briefcase and reports spread out over the table. He paused only long enough to lock the door behind them.

Rachel slid into bed that night, mentally exhausted from the emotional roller coaster she'd ridden all day. She could hear Luke in the kitchen finishing the cleanup from supper. Though she'd offered to help, when he'd insisted she go to bed instead, she'd been grateful.

The feel of the cool percale sheets soothed her aching muscles and cooled her heated body. By morning, she knew, the effects of the exhumation and its aftermath would have faded some. Tomorrow would be better, she told herself as the sounds of clattering dishes being loaded into the dishwasher faded away.

The shriek of fire engines' sirens pierced the night. Rachel and Luke bolted upright in bed almost simultaneously.

"What the hell?" Luke's voice was hoarse with sleep.

She reached out for him. His flesh was warm beneath her fingers.

Before she could say anything, she smelled the acrid odor of smoke and heard the crackle of fire beyond the bedroom door. Luke threw aside the covers and bolted toward the door.

"Don't open it," Rachel called. "Check it for heat."

Luke laid his palm against the door and pulled it back sharply. "It's hot. We can't go that way." He turned and looked around. As he strode to the window, he grabbed her robe off the chair and tossed it to her. "Put that on," he instructed.

Rachel climbed from the bed, pushed her arms into the sleeves and belted the robe while Luke pried the window open and pushed the screen from the frame. She could hear the sound of the fire trucks stopping outside and see the red lights flashing off the walls.

"Come on." Luke ripped the drapes from the window and threw them aside. "You go first," he said, grabbing her arm and pushing her toward the window, then he guided her over the windowsill.

Rachel dropped to the ground a mere few feet below her. She turned to look for him, but he'd gone back inside.

"Luke!" Her scream cut through the night like a knife. She clawed at the stucco house in an attempt to get back inside.

Suddenly, someone grabbed her arm and dragged her away. "He has to do this, Rachel." She turned to see A.J. standing beside her.

"But he'll die in there." She pulled at A.J.'s grasp, but he held her fast.

"Rachel."

Rachel spun toward the sound of her name. In the bedroom window was Hannah Daniels. "He's mine now," Hannah said and began laughing.

Suddenly, the night was filled with the roar of the house erupting in a violent explosion. Windows shattered, scattering glass everywhere. Pieces of burning wood that resembled giant matchsticks shot into the black night. Orange, red and yellow flames curled their hungry fingers around everything. Large, ugly clouds of black smoke surged skyward.

"Luke!" The wretched scream came from Rachel's soul and echoed over and over through her head. "Luke!"

"Rachel!"

He was alive. "He's alive. I heard him. Someone has to go after him," she pleaded, tugging on A.J.'s shirtfront.

"Rachel!"

A.J. was shaking her. But no, it wasn't A.J., it was…

She opened her eyes and found herself staring into Luke's stricken face.

"Honey, are you okay? It was a dream." He pulled her close and held her so tight she had to fight for air.

Relief flooded her. Luke was okay. But a shiver followed quickly behind the relief. How long would he be okay? Was Hannah going to come after him, too, now that she knew they'd been husband and wife?

Chapter 14

The next morning, Rachel filled Sam in on what she and Luke had found out in Henderson. They spent the two hours meticulously poring over the reports and photos covering the tables in the task force room. Rachel had no idea what they were looking for, but she hoped there was something they had missed that would point to Charlene, as she'd come to think of her despite having no word yet on the results of the autopsy, as their arsonist.

Rachel finished reading the Henderson fire report for the fifth time, then read the very brief coroner's report again. *Death due to smoke inhalation.* Every time she read those hastily scrawled words, she saw red. Because someone hadn't done his job, Hannah Daniels' mother may have gotten away with murdering the child she was supposed to love and protect. They never would have found out if Charlene hadn't continued her arson spree and one old lady hadn't paid close attention to detail.

Sam came to stand beside Rachel. "Break time," she announced, rubbing her lower back. "If I have to bend over those tables again today, my back is going to stay that way."

Sam handed her a cup of steaming coffee and sat down. "So why do you supposed she's doing this?"

Rachel sipped the strong coffee appreciatively, then took a deep breath and hitched her backside onto the table. Balancing the disposable cup on her thigh, she thought for a moment. Despite the AC humming softly in the background, she could feel beads of moisture gathering on her forehead. She wiped them away with the back of her hand.

"Until we get the autopsy report, we won't be sure how or why Charlene killed Hannah, or if, indeed, she did," Rachel finally said.

"But you've already made up your mind that Charlene is good for this, right?" Sam blew into the coffee to cool it, but kept her gaze on Rachel.

"Yes, I have. She did it. As for why, I think it was a punishment of some kind. There's no doubt in my mind that the others were killed because of the child abuse allegations. Sophie told us that Charlene was very religious. I think the fires were her warped way of cleansing their sins. A baptism in fire, if you will, and maybe she hoped it would absolve her in some way of the sin of murdering her own child."

Just saying the words made Rachel's blood come to a boil. She would sell her soul to have her child back, and this woman had methodically planned to take her own child's life.

Sam shook her head and crossed her legs. "And I thought I had problems." A frown knitted her smooth forehead.

"Problems?" Rachel asked, grateful for a momentary distraction from their present conversation.

Sam stared down into her cup for a long time. Then, seeming to come to a decision, she raised her head and stared at Rachel. "There's this guy at the firehouse. He's made it his mission to make my life as miserable as possible."

"Harassment?"

"No. He's very careful to stay just the other side of that. In fact, aside from my gut telling me so, I have no proof that it's even him that's doing the things that have happened." She shook her head. "I'm probably just imagining things."

Rachel laughed. "Sam, I know a few people who might imagine they were being harassed. You're not one of them." She sipped her coffee again. "So what's he done?"

"It started out short-sheeting my bed, then tying all the sleeves on my uniforms in knots." Sam shrugged. "It's stuff like that. Harmless pranks. Cleaned my helmet so I look like a probie." When Rachel tried to suppress a smile, Sam looked indignant. "Hey, I've been on the force too long to look like a greenhorn in a shiny, new helmet. Nothing I can bring anyone up on charges for but enough to be damn annoying."

"Have you talked to Chief Robertson about it?"

Sam snorted. "Like he'd help. He's a few months from retirement. He's not going to make waves now, and I'm not sure I want him to."

Rachel slipped off the table and threw her empty coffee cup in a trash can. "Well, until he either does something that you can prove or you decide to report it, I guess you'll have to grin and bear his little-boy antics. But keep in mind, you know as well as I do that being a woman in a man's world is no picnic."

Sam nodded and stood. "Yeah, I know."

Rachel put her hand on Sam's shoulder and looked her in the eye. "My guess is that it's going to get worse before it gets better, so watch your back. And if you need me, I'm always available."

"Thanks. I will."

As Rachel turned back to the reports, Detective Montoya came into the task force room. "Sorry I'm late, Rachel. Tox called with a report on your Bible stain, and I went down to pick it up." He handed her the report.

"Thanks. Can you help Sam go over this stuff again?" She motioned toward the array of reports and photos on the tables. "We're looking for any connection to Hannah Daniels that we may have missed the last time."

He nodded and joined Sam at one of the tables. The low murmur of their voices carried to Rachel as Sam filled Montoya in on what she and Luke had learned in Henderson.

Rachel sat down and studied the toxicology report. Her gaze went straight to the results of the test, bypassing all the rest of the report. The stain they'd found on the Bible was coffee. Crap! She read the explanation of the findings, then frowned.

"Either of you ever hear of a brand of coffee called Java Gold?" she asked Montoya and Sam.

Sam shook her head. "Nope."

"I have," Montoya said. "It's expensive sh—uh, expensive stuff." He threw Rachel an apologetic glance. "Last I heard, it sells for something like a hundred bucks a pound."

Sam whistled. "At that price I could easily become a tea drinker." Then she stopped. "Why do you want to know?" she asked Rachel.

Rachel stood and walked over to them. "The tox report says that's what the stain was on the Bible."

"I know tox is good, but I find it hard to believe that they can nail it down to a specific brand." Sam looked skeptical.

Montoya took the report from Rachel and studied it. "Don't underestimate Tommy Nichols. He's been in tox since God was a baby, and he's as diligent as a worker bee and three times as efficient. Besides, this one isn't that hard to nail down." He handed the report back to Rachel.

"Why?" she asked, looking at the report to see if there was something she hadn't read.

"This coffee is grown on an island off the coast of Papua New Guinea. There's a bat that lives only on that island and eats only figs. The natives have found that if they fertilize the coffee with the droppings of the bat, it enhances the taste of the coffee. Because the bat is so rare, the droppings are hard to find and therefore so is this particular coffee."

"Yuck!" Sam curled her nose. "Tea is sounding better all the time."

Rachel frowned at Sam's outburst, then turned back to the young Cuban detective and listened with renewed interest. "And you learned all this how?"

He flushed, then shook his head. "Before I decided to become a cop, I was studying to be an agricultural engineer. My sophomore thesis was on foreign imports."

Sam slapped his shoulder. "Damn, Montoya. I'm impressed." Then she frowned. "But it's a pretty big jump from agricultural engineer to cop."

The corner of his mouth turned up slightly. "Not when your father is murdered two rooms away from your bedroom." Montoya turned away and busied himself stacking the reports they'd gone over already.

"Crap. Me and my big mouth. I'm sorry, Juan," Sam said, patting Montoya's shoulder awkwardly.

Montoya glanced at her, shrugged, then looked away. "Why? You didn't kill him, and I don't think I would have made a good engineer anyway. Besides, they got the bastard, and he won't be killing anybody else. The state introduced him to Old Sparky a while back." His voice, though showing satisfaction, still held the bitterness of his father being taken from him so violently.

Rachel sliced her finger across her throat, signaling Sam to let it drop. The red-faced young woman picked up a stack of reports they hadn't gone over yet and took a seat at an empty table and immediately immersed herself in studying them.

Before Rachel could start reading the tox report again, Luke came in. "What's up?" he asked, placing a warm hand on Rachel's shoulder. She had to physically stop herself from laying her cheek against it.

"We got the tox report back on the Bible." She waved the sheets of paper at him, then filled him in on what Montoya had told them. "It shouldn't be too hard to find out where this came from. How many places can sell Java Gold in a town the size of Orange Grove?"

"Don't count on it. It can probably be bought over the Internet," Luke said.

"Let's check and see if Java Gold has a list of places on their site." Sam booted up her laptop, connected the phone cord to the wall jack and went online.

Using one of the popular search engines, she found the site quickly. Slowly, it began to load. Before the entire site was visible, the logo came into view—a mountain with a coffee bean superimposed over it.

"Says here," Sam said, running her fingernail over the words on the screen, "it's not sold privately."

Rachel continued to stare at the logo for a moment before it came to her why it looked so familiar.

"I know who sells this," she said. Grabbing her briefcase, she turned to Luke as she headed toward the door. "Let's go pay a visit to our friend Nina at the Latte Factory."

Rachel leaned back against the car seat, her gaze fixed on traffic. "This might be a wild-goose chase."

Luke glanced at her. "Why?"

"Charlene is a social worker. Why would she spend this kind of money on coffee?"

A secretive smile turned up the corners of Luke's mouth.

"What?" Rachel asked, leaning forward to read his expression better.

"You never asked me why I was late getting to headquarters today."

"So, I'm asking now. Why were you late?"

He turned down the AC, then said, "I was checking up on

Charlene. It seems that before Hannah died, she took out a hefty insurance policy on her daughter. She then invested a good piece of the money and has been building a tidy nest egg ever since." He took his gaze off the road long enough to check Rachel's openmouthed surprise. "She moved to Orange Grove a month after Hannah died and bought herself a very nice beach house in the Palms." He placed his finger under Rachel's chin and closed her mouth. "Our Charlene can buy as much of this coffee as she wants."

When he saw the smile of triumph cover Rachel's face, Luke felt satisfaction flood him. They were very close to having enough evidence on Charlene to make an arrest. As soon as the autopsy report came back and confirmed that the body was indeed Hannah's, they could go after her. Unfortunately, they still hadn't made the connection to the fire that had taken their daughter from them.

The Latte Factory was enjoying the quiet time just before the arrival of the lunch crowd. When Luke and Rachel stepped through the door, the aromatic smell of freshly ground coffee beans assaulted them. The bell above the door tinkled softly, alerting the young girl behind the counter to the arrival of a customer.

"Detective Sutherland!" Nina smiled broadly at Luke, then she turned to Rachel. "Hi again."

"Rachel Suth—Lansing," Rachel said, catching herself before she made the same mistake she had at Sophie's. "I don't think we ever exchanged names the last time we talked."

"No, we didn't. I think we were more worried about that slimeball that Detective Sutherland finally got rid of for me." She threw a beaming grin in Luke's direction, then looked back to Rachel. "I'm Nina. What can I get for you?"

"Three coffees and a few minutes of your time to answer a couple of questions," Luke told her.

"You got it." Nina waved toward the tables. "Just find a seat, and I'll get the coffees."

Moments later, the three of them were seated at one of the tables adding cream and sugar to their coffee. As they stirred their respective drinks, Rachel looked down at the logo on her cup. Mountains and a coffee bean.

"So what're the questions?" The artificial light glinted off the earring peeking through the long brown tresses caressing Nina's shoulders as she looked from Rachel to Luke.

"Do you serve Java Gold here?"

Nina smirked. "Yeah. My boss thought it would be a good come-on for the elite residents of the city. Yuppie stuff, you know?" She made a rude noise. "A lot he knows. We only have three customers who buy it."

Rachel could feel the excitement building in her. "Do you recall who the three people are?"

Nina laughed. "When someone pays ten bucks for a cup of coffee, you tend to remember them. There's a guy who claims to be a friend of Burt Reynolds. Like I believe that. There's another guy who has a seventy-five-foot sailboat he's always trying to get me to go on for a sunset cruise." She laughed. The sound had a distinctive sarcastic flavor. "Somehow I don't think that all he wants is to watch the sun set."

Luke and Rachel exchanged glances that said this girl was a sharp cookie that no one was going to fool easily.

"And the third one?" Luke prompted.

Rachel held her breath. *Please God, let the third person be Charlene.*

"The third one's a woman." Nina frowned thoughtfully. "I don't know anything about her. She comes in about three times a week, buys her coffee, drinks it and then leaves." Nina went silent, then her eyes brightened, and she sat straighter. "Oh, and she carries a Bible with her."

Luke stirred in his chair. From his expression, Rachel could tell that he was getting as excited as she already was. They were so close, she could taste victory.

"What does this woman look like?" Under the table Rachel crossed her fingers.

"Hmm." Nina thought for a moment. "Blond, kind of pretty. It's hard to guess her age. She could be in her late twenties, or she could be in her early to mid thirties." Suddenly, Nina turned to Rachel. "I think she was here that day you came in when Jackson was doing his leering thing. That was on a Tuesday, right?"

Rachel thought for a second. It was the day after she'd arrived back in Orange Grove, which was a Monday. She'd come in here the day she'd walked the fire scene with Luke. "Yes, why?"

"She comes in on Tuesdays, Thursdays and Fridays. Like clockwork."

"Would you know her if you saw her again?" Rachel asked.

Nina laughed. "Like I said before, when someone pays that much for a cup of coffee, you don't forget them." She glanced at her watch, then at the door where three businessmen were coming into the shop. "I have to get going. The lunch crowd is arriving. If you need anything else, give me a call. I'm here Monday through Friday. Today I'll be here from six until eight tonight." She pulled out her guest check pad from her apron pocket and scribbled a series of numbers across it. "I take all the overtime I can get." She handed Luke the slip of paper. "That's my home phone number."

Nina stood and hurried off toward the three businessmen who were now settled at a nearby table reading menus.

"What now?" Rachel asked when they were on their way back to headquarters.

That she was asking him where to go from here surprised Luke. He turned to look at his ex-wife. She was massaging her temples with her forefingers. Lines of strain etched her creamy skin. She'd attempted to hide the dark circles beneath her eyes under makeup, but they were still visible enough to testify to her lack of sleep.

"We wait for the results of the autopsy." Luke looked back at the road, grateful for the distraction of heavy noon-hour traffic. Seeing Rachel so stressed out and worried was nearly killing him, but knowing he couldn't stop her was even harder.

She turned sideways on the seat. "But don't we have enough to go after her now?"

"Probably, but do you want to *probably* nail her, or nail her beyond a reasonable doubt?" He didn't expect an answer, but he saw her hands tighten into fists in her lap.

"There's only one thing I want more and that's impossible." Rachel turned her face toward the side window, but he could see the sunlight glint off the lone tear that rolled down her cheek.

Back at headquarters, Montoya approached them as soon as they walked in the task force room. In his hand were the two notes that Rachel had received and one of the DCS victims' files.

"I think you might want to see this."

Rachel dropped her briefcase in a chair, then moved to the detective's side. He handed her the papers he'd been holding. "What am I looking at?" she asked, glancing from one sheet to the other.

Montoya pointed at the word *leeve* in the note Rachel had found on her car's windshield, then at the one she'd found in the Bible placed in her briefcase after the condo fire, and then at the same word in one of the DCS reports Hannah had made out. It was spelled the same way—*leeve.* The handwriting, while not as hurried as it had been on Rachel's notes, was nearly the same.

The detective tapped the paper. "My bet is that a handwriting expert would say the same person wrote both of these notes."

Chapter 15

Luke came into the kitchen and threw his car keys on the counter. Rachel was sitting in the breakfast nook staring blankly at the sliding glass doors. In front of her lay the newspaper, still folded exactly as the paperboy had left it in the driveway, and a cup of coffee full to the top. No steam was rising from the cup. Luke had sent her home early, hoping she would relax and get some rest. Obviously, from the look of the untouched paper and cold coffee, she hadn't.

He flung himself tiredly into the chair next to hers. "Montoya nailed it. It took the handwriting expert all of thirty minutes to determine those notes and the DCS reports were written by the same person—Hannah Daniels. Or rather, Charlene. It's just his opinion at this point, nothing official, but it's a start."

Sadness clouding her eyes, Rachel pushed aside the newspaper and leaned tiredly on the table. "All that proves is she's a lousy speller, and she wanted me out of town because she was afraid I'd connect her to the arsons. Getting rid of me could be for any reason, including that she has the hots for you. But we still have to connect her to our apartment fire and Maggie's disappearance."

Luke concentrated on the knot in the pine table, unable to face the disappointment he knew had to be clouding Rachel's eyes. "The fact that she was the social worker on the victims' cases is circumstantial. But the autopsy results will provide us with the evidence we need to go after her. Hopefully, once we get her in custody, we can get her to admit to the arsons."

"But we don't have enough to go after her now?" The urgency in Rachel's voice cut through the room.

"No, we don't." Luke knew where her need for an end to this stemmed from. She wanted to know where their daughter was. "I want to bring—" He stopped and swallowed hard. "I want to bring Maggie home, too, and I promised you I would. So let me do it."

"But—"

Luke grabbed her hand and kissed it. "Honey, I know it's frustrating, but we have to let the wheels of justice turn at their own speed." He reached across the table and caressed her cheek. "You've done your job, Rach. Now, let me do mine."

Rachel tore her hand from his and glared at him. "Dammit, Luke, don't patronize me. And don't shut me out of this." Her voice revealed the level of her frustration. "We have evidence that connects all the fires, including ours." She ticked them off on her fingers. "Chloroform, the Bibles, the fires set at night, the coffee stain—"

"And the child abuse?" He cut in, his voice harsher than he'd intended. "Where's *your* connection to that?" When she continued to glare at him, he sighed and walked to the refrigerator. "I'm not patronizing you, and I'm not shutting you out, Rachel."

Flinging open the door, he pulled out a can of beer, popped the top, sat again and then took a long drink of the icy liquid. As much as they both believed Charlene was the arsonist and as much as they wanted to see her behind bars, going in too soon could mean the difference between her conviction and her walking free. Rachel knew that as well as he did. Prove the homicide first, then prove the arson. They had to prove Charlene had killed her daughter to connect her to the other victims. The results of the autopsy would do that. If Rachel wasn't letting her emotions rule her head, she'd see that, too.

"You have to understand that even with the high-profile rush A.J. put on the autopsy, the results won't be back for at least another day. Until then, we've done all we can except wait." He took another drink. "Charlene isn't going anywhere. I have two men outside her house."

Rachel threw him a deprecating look, then stood. "I'm going for a walk on the beach."

Silently, Luke watched her leave. The mother in Rachel was thinking for her right now, and he knew that when she had time to work it out and start thinking as a profiler and arson investigator, she'd be fine. Until then, he'd leave her to herself.

But he couldn't stop thinking about her, seeing the impatience written on her face, the frustration and disappointment in her eyes. That she was hurting tore him to pieces. She'd done so well until now, kept her emotions out of it. If he let her go this way, he was terrified of what it would do to her.

Then he remembered the fire at A.J.'s, and the notes.

Rachel sat cross-legged on the beach, just beyond where the waves climbed the sand and stopped before slipping back into the ocean again. But tonight, even though she could smell the salty air, the nocturnal beauty around her failed to soothe and replenish her. Tonight she was only aware of her nerve-shredding frustration with the justice system.

She knew, and so did Luke if he'd only admit it, that they had enough to go after Charlene. Conversely, she also knew he was right. Most of what they had was circumstantial. Better they wait and build the best case against her that they could. But that didn't make the waiting any easier. Nor did it ease her frustration. She picked up a small, fragile seashell and snapped it between her fingers.

She'd waited two years to get Maggie back, to give her the burial she deserved. Now that they were so very close, waiting one minute longer ground her nerves raw.

What makes you think if they arrest Charlene that she'll even admit to any wrongdoing? What makes you think she'll tell you what she did with Maggie?

The unbidden questions popped into Rachel's mind. The idea that this might not end it, that she still might not be able to bring Maggie home and lay her to rest, brought Rachel sharp pain. Surely Charlene wouldn't be that cruel.

She murdered her own daughter, Rachel. Do you think she cares about hurting you by not telling you where Maggie is? Do you think she cares that not knowing Maggie's whereabouts eats at your insides like an insidious disease?

Rachel buried her face in her hands. No tears came, just an overwhelming feeling of defeat. Would she ever know the answers? Would she ever be allowed real closure?

Suddenly her head came up abruptly. Her grief had made her selfish, made her forget. This wasn't just her fight. This was also the fight of all the children left without the mothers Charlene thought had abused them and then had burned to death. They needed closure, too, and if she couldn't get Maggie back, then she'd at least get closure for all of them.

Wasn't that why she'd come here to begin with?

No, it wasn't, she admitted, not entirely. She'd come partly for them, partly for Maggie and partly to lay her own ghosts to rest. She'd come back to face the fire monster again, to regain her confidence as an arson investigator and a top-notch profiler and to find the arsonist killing mothers and leaving babies orphaned. All that was left for her to do was to be patient and wait for her hard work and Luke's to bear fruit.

A soft noise behind her drew her attention. She turned abruptly. Silhouetted against the sky was a man's figure, tall, imposing and rugged. Déjà vu.

"Feeling better?" Luke dropped to the sand beside her.

She nodded. "I just had to think a bit. Get things straight in my mind." She gazed out over the water, then faced him. "I'm sorry about that little scene back at the house. I know we have to take this a step at a time. I know I have to let you do your job. It's just that it's—"

He put his fingers over her lips. "I know. The waiting is hard."

She smiled weakly. "*Intolerable* is a better word. But I can handle it."

He slid his hand around to cup her cheek. For a long moment, he stared at her, as if trying to come to a conclusion, then he kissed her lightly, like a butterfly brushing her lips. "I need to say something, and I want you to listen and not go crazy before I'm done."

His voice sounded ominous, and she knew before he spoke one word that this was not good. A knot of dread gathered in her stomach.

"You only have a couple of days before your leave of absence from your job is up. I want you to go back to Atlanta early. I want you away from this. When it's done, I'll call you."

Pulling free of his touch, Rachel sprang to her feet. "What? My God, I can't go back now, not now! How can you even ask me to?" Her voice rose and echoed around the deserted sand dunes. "We had this settled."

He stood and reached out to her. She backed away. "Rach, Charlene's already tried to hurt you—twice. Now you're even more stressed out. I want you to go home. Let me take care of this."

"What difference do you think a few days is going to

make? Am I supposed to get out of the way, forget all that's happened? You may have been able to forget, but I sure as hell didn't. Not for a minute."

"I never forgot, Rach." His voice had grown soft, each word distinct.

She knew she'd hit a nerve, but she pushed ahead. "You could have fooled me. I wasn't the one who walked out on our marriage. I wasn't the one who turned my back on what little we had left after Maggie was gone. You left me to bear the pain of losing my child alone. You're the coward, Luke, not me. You're the one who ran away, not me. And I'll be damned if I'm going to start now."

Rachel could see that each word hit him like a baseball bat to the gut. She didn't care. This had stayed hidden inside her for too long. She and Luke had been dancing around it for days. It was time it was thrust into the open.

Suddenly, she realized he hadn't said a word to deny the accusations she had thrown at him. My God, she was right. All this time she'd hoped she'd judged him wrong, but she hadn't.

She spun on her heel and trudged across the sand.

"Where are you going?" Luke's voice came from a distance.

"To pack my things and move to a motel," she called back as she kept walking toward the house. "I'll let A.J. know where to get in touch with me."

Luke slipped into the house and headed for the path of light spilling into the hall from Rachel's room. He stepped into the doorway. Rachel was shoving clothes hurriedly into one of his suitcases. He took one step inside the room.

"Rachel—"

Stopping her motions abruptly, she raised her hand. "No. I don't want to hear your excuses." She lowered her gaze and continued throwing her few belongings into the open suitcase. "I'll bring your suitcase to headquarters tomornow." She snapped the locks closed, then lifted the luggage from the bed.

As she made her way toward the door, and he stood by helplessly, Rachel ignored him. Suddenly, she stopped. She looked at the ceiling, her shoulders slumped slightly. "Tell me something," she said without turning around. "Why *did* you walk out on our marriage?"

He took a deep fortifying breath. He knew she'd ask this question eventually. And he knew, when she did, he'd have to answer if he ever hoped to mend things between them. "Because I couldn't handle the guilt of not being there when Maggie disappeared, and you nearly died in the fire. Because maybe, if I'd been home, it wouldn't have happened."

She turned very slowly. Her expression was incredulous. "Is this the same man who held me and assured me that it was no one's fault, that I shouldn't blame myself?"

He nodded. "Yes, and I meant every word. It was not your fault any more than I've come to understand it was mine." He took a step toward her. She backed away. "Rachel, I was so wrong to walk away. I should have stayed. I thought you were strong enough to get through it without me. I didn't know…" He swallowed hard. "Can't we try again?"

She stared at him for a long time. Tears glistened in her eyes. "No. No, we can't."

He extended his hand, his bleeding heart making him unashamed to beg, "I love you. I've never stopped loving you."

"I love you, too, Luke." Shaking her head as if to remove his declaration of love, Rachel backed slowly away from him. "But it's not enough."

He took another step toward her. "But, if we love each other, why can't we try again?"

Her watery gaze met his. When she spoke, her voice was choked and just above a whisper. "Because I can forgive you for thinking it was your fault. I can even forgive you for not having the strength to come to me, to share your grief and help me support us. But when you did that, you took my trust with you. I can never be sure you won't walk away again when the going gets rough. I can never be sure you'll be there for me to lean on when life closes in on me, and I need a shoulder to cry on, because, when it comes to losing a child, no one is strong enough, Luke. Not me and not you. I was going through the same pain and heartache as you were, but you never stuck around to find that out." She stopped and looked at her hands then back to him. "But mostly, what I can't forgive is, when you walked away, you destroyed the little we had left. You destroyed us."

Luke chugged his fifth beer and stared into the darkened living room.

He'd followed Rachel to the hotel then discreetly watched to be sure she checked in and made it safely into a room. He'd surveyed the neighborhood until he was certain no one was around, then come home to his empty house.

He had hoped that getting drunk would take the edge off the laceration of Rachel leaving, fill the emptiness she'd left behind, obliterate the visions of a future without her. Unfortunately, the only thing that happened was the intensification of a blinding headache. He crushed the empty can and added it to the growing pile on the table.

"You've made a hell of a mess of your life, Sutherland," he mumbled into the darkness. "But you're not going to fix it by drowning your sorrows in a beer can." He sat up and rubbed his throbbing temples.

But how did he fix it? How did he show Rachel that she could lean on him, that he'd never leave her again, that they could get back what they'd had and have a future together?

He leaned his head against the back of the chair and closed his eyes against the physical and emotional pain battering his body.

The following morning, after having spent a restless night with little or no sleep, Rachel stood at the motel-room window and watched a sailboat glide smoothly up the Intracoastal Waterway. Behind her, the morning TV news anchor warned of a storm front approaching their area, but she only heard it on the periphery of her consciousness. She had her own storm to weather.

She thought about the accusations she'd hurled at Luke the night before. Did she really not trust him? Deep inside she knew that the circumstances had been those that most marriages would never have to weather. But the bottom line was still that he'd walked away. He'd left, instead of fighting for their family, or what was left of it.

All that said, however, she could not deny that, despite his desertion, despite her mistrust, despite everything, she still loved Luke. She could live without him and had for two years, but did she want to? And truth be told, hadn't she failed him, too? Hadn't she exacerbated the problem by allowing him to walk away, by not stopping him, by not understanding *his* pain?

Disheartened and confused, she turned back to the motel room and looked around her. She'd chosen this motel because it was as far across town from Luke as she could get without camping on the banks of the Intracoastal. Now the impersonal atmosphere of it, which echoed the way her life had been without Luke, struck her: bland, colorless, unexciting, mundane.

Did she want to go back to that or was she willing to take a chance on him and hope that they could mend their relationship?

She dropped to the edge of the bed, then buried her face in her hands. Life shouldn't be this complicated.

The phone rang. Her head came up sharply. She stared at

the flashing light on the phone's face that indicated an incoming call. It rang again. Then she realized it couldn't be Luke. A.J. was the only one who had this number. Unexpected disappointment flowed over her.

Sighing with impatience at her inability to settle on how she felt about Luke, she sprawled across the bed, then plucked the receiver from the cradle.

"Hello."

"Rachel," A.J. said, "I thought you'd want to know that the autopsy results are back."

Chapter 16

Rachel had just secured her hair away from her face with a tortoiseshell clip when a knock sounded on the motel-room door. Not expecting anyone, she peered through the peephole. *Luke.* What was he doing here? And how had he found her? Then she knew. Of course, he'd have followed her last night. She took a deep breath and opened the door.

"Morning," Luke said. His face was lined and tired. Dark circles underscored his eyes. "I thought I'd pick you up on my way into headquarters."

He acted as if nothing had happened last night, as if they hadn't thrown hurtful words at each other. As if she hadn't basically told him to go to hell.

It took her all of a few seconds to figure out why he was here, and it wasn't because he thought she needed a ride or that he thought Charlene would attack in broad daylight.

"I have my own car." Rachel pointed at the blue Chevy Malibu rental parked in front of her motel room.

"I know, but—"

She stopped him with a shake of her head. "You figured I wouldn't be able to make it through the autopsy photos, right? That I'd be too much of a mess to drive." He looked taken aback. "I've seen my share of ghastly photos, Luke, you know that."

"Not recently."

"No, but when you've seen one, you've seen them all." In her heart, she knew that wasn't true. Every death claimed her heart. Every lost soul touched her deeply. "But if you really think I'll fall apart, A.J. can bring me back here." She couldn't let him think she couldn't operate without his support.

"These photos won't be the same," he said, his stubborn streak rising to the surface.

No, they wouldn't be the same, she thought. These would be of a young woman killed by her own mother, a woman who just might have also taken and killed Maggie. Contrarily, as determined as she was to prove she could take it, she was also very pleased that Luke understood it would not be easy, that he'd thought enough about her to make sure she would not have to face this alone. That she even felt that way only increased her anger, mostly with herself. When would she learn that words always came easily for Luke? It was in the putting them into action that he fell short.

"You won't have to look at the actual body." He was staring at her, concern written all over his expression.

"I know." That he felt he had to explain a procedure she'd been through a hundred times before rankled her more. He might as well understand now that she was determined to learn all over again, if necessary, to face life without him, and she might as well start now. "Thanks for coming by, but I prefer to drive myself."

Luke watched her collect her things then squeeze past him out the door. He knew without being told that she was making a concentrated effort not to touch him. That she'd refused to ride with him didn't surprise him. He'd fully expected her to slam the door in his face. But that she was taking one more emotional step away from him felt like a knife to his heart.

That the last person she probably wanted to see was him had almost kept him from coming to pick her up, even after A.J. had ordered him to make sure Rachel didn't drive. When he'd fought against it, A.J. had reminded him of her reaction to the arson victims' autopsy photos just a few days earlier. That changed his mind in a split second. If her reaction to these autopsy photos was the same, he didn't want her behind the wheel of a car.

"Rachel," he called, hurrying after her, "don't be pigheaded about this. Let me drive you."

"No," she mouthed through the closed car window, then started the engine and drove off, leaving him staring after her.

Aside from being concerned about the emotional impact the photos might have on Rachel, he'd been glad to have an excuse for time alone with her. He knew, after they'd made the decision to either go after Charlene or gather more information before making an arrest, that they were very close to ending this case and that this might well be one of the last times he saw Rachel before she returned to Atlanta.

Luke climbed in his car and followed her. He'd watch her at the autopsy briefing with A.J. and if he felt she was too shaken to drive, he'd pick her up bodily and put her in his car if he had to.

When Rachel arrived, A.J. was already in the task force room, several folders laid out in front of him. He looked past her at the door, obviously expecting Luke to be on her heels.

"I drove myself," she said, in answer to his unspoken question. "Luke should be along any minute."

"Do you think that was wise?"

Rachel felt her blood pressure hitch up a notch. Friend or no friend, she was sick to death of this watch-over-Rachel mentality he and Luke seemed to have. She sat across from him and leaned on the table. "Let's get something straight. I do not need Luke, you or anyone else babysitting me. I have managed to get through most of my life alone. I think I can keep doing that."

A.J. threw up his hands in surrender. "Sorry. We were just worried about you."

"Well, don't. If I need either of you, I'll let you know."

Taking a deep breath, she swallowed the regret she suddenly felt about her harsh words. For a moment, she wavered between thanking him for caring and assuring him that she'd have to hurt him if he didn't stop hovering. She chose the former.

Lowering her voice, she laid a hand on his arm and smiled. "Thank you, but I'm okay. Really."

The door behind her opened, and Luke strode in looking none too happy with his ex-wife. "They do have speed limits between here and your motel," he growled, then took a seat beside A.J.

Normally, Rachel was a very careful, law-abiding driver, but today, she wanted to put as much distance between herself and Luke as possible. "Really? I didn't notice," she said perversely, and was unreasonably pleased when he glared back at her.

"Yes, *really.*"

A.J. cleared his throat. "Okay, kiddies, if you're done with your game of gotcha, can we get on with this?"

Rachel looked around. "Aren't we going to wait for Sam and Detective Montoya?"

"Sam's on a fire call, and I sent Montoya to DCS to get Hannah's…Charlene's personnel file." A.J. opened the folder closest to him.

Rachel leaned forward. Her adrenaline went into overdrive. "Then you know that the body in the grave was Hannah's and not Charlene's?"

The frown vanished off Luke's face and was replaced by the same intense interest that had captured Rachel's expression.

A.J. didn't answer. He dug into the folder and extracted a photo, then laid it in the middle of the table for both Rachel and Luke to view. It was a skeletal right hand. Discolored by time and the ravages of the fire and devoid of any sign of the flesh that had once covered them, the M.E. had arranged the bones palm down. A corroded ring encircled the middle finger of the hand. Though the metal had become unrecognizable, the green stone in the center had not.

Rachel's breath caught. Sophie's words rang in her head. *One time, she put money into one of those gumball machines in McKinley's Grocery and won herself a ring. Pretty thing it was, green stone and gold band. It turned her finger green, but she wore it anyway... I saw that ring, plain as day, right there on her poor little blackened finger.*

She could feel both men watching her. Intentionally, she picked up the photo and studied it closer, more aware of their expressions than what she was seeing. A.J. laid out several more that showed breaks to several bones, some of which had healed badly. Rachel again picked up each photo and studied it. She placed the photos back on the table, then looked at the men across from her.

"Since I didn't faint or turn some hideous shade of green, can you both concentrate on where we go from here?"

A.J. cleared his throat, averted his gaze and began fumbling with the other contents of the folder.

Luke looked back at the hand photo and pointed to the green stone. His jaw pulsated. "Looks like Sophie pegged it right."

Pleased that she'd made her point, Rachel nodded.

"There's more," A.J. said, pulling a sheet of paper from the folder. "Tox found significant amounts of arsenic in the hair and no residue of smoke in any of the bones or hair. The conclusion is that the she died of arsenic poisoning, not smoke inhalation."

"What about sex and age?" Luke inhaled deeply. Rachel waited for him to exhale.

A.J. scanned the report. "The M.E. puts the sex as female, age twenty-three to twenty-five."

Luke finally exhaled on a long satisfied sigh. Rachel knew why he seemed relieved. The information put this body in the right age bracket to be Hannah and not her mother.

"They also found evidence that she was five to six months pregnant at the time of death."

A baby?

This news hit Rachel right in the gut. Her heart contracted. That Charlene would kill her own grandchild reconfirmed that she would have had no qualms about killing Maggie, too, if it fit her purpose. It shouldn't surprise her. She knew this kind of killer all too well. They set themselves up as judge, jury and executioner and felt no guilt about the punishments they meted out. Still, because this one hit close to home, it was much harder to analyze dispassionately. But she had to. She struggled to hang on to her composure.

What the hell kind of monster were they dealing with? She took a deep breath and pushed Maggie from her mind, concentrating instead on the implications of this new evidence. If she wanted to remain on the case and see it to its conclusion and if she planned to be of any help to Luke and A.J. to reach that conclusion, she had to keep a tight rein on her emotions.

"Well, that explains a lot." Feigning a casualness she was far from feeling, Rachel leaned back. She pushed aside thoughts of anything but the case and allowed all the scattered pieces to fall into place in her mind. "She probably killed

Hannah because she was pregnant with an illegitimate child. Put that together with the religious overtones of the case and I'd say she either killed her as punishment for her *sin* of immorality, or she may have believed she was saving Hannah from repeating the kind of life she'd led. Either way, in her twisted mind, she felt justified."

"That doesn't explain why she killed the other victims." A.J. went to the coffeepot and poured three cups of the thick black liquid. "None of those women were pregnant." He returned to the table and set a cup in front of each of them.

Rachel took a sip. The pungent smell of the strong coffee filled her nose, erasing the smell of death that had taken up residence there since she'd looked at the photos of Hannah's hand and the evidence of many broken limbs. The hot coffee seared its way down her throat and lay in her stomach like a fireball.

"Any woman who would murder her own child would have no compunction about physically abusing her as well." Rachel picked up one of the photos of Hannah's leg bone. "Look at this break. See how the bones haven't knitted right? If Hannah had seen a doctor, the bone would have been reset and healed properly." She tossed the photo on the table. "My guess is that Charlene splinted this herself, if at all, and Hannah never saw a doctor. Hiding the evidence of injuries is a classic sign of abuse.

"After she killed Hannah, something snapped inside her. Sophie said Charlene had strong religious leanings, so I can't see that she had any feelings of guilt about what she'd done as much as she realized that she'd done something unforgivable in the eyes of God. Thus she is seeking to redeem herself with Him by stopping other abusive mothers." She took a deep breath. "The Bible beneath the bodies, the fire set in the form of a cross with the victim at the foot are all indications that she was punishing them, but at the same time positioning them in a way that depicts repentance…theirs and ultimately hers, as well."

She had just finished her explanation when Detective Montoya entered the room. "Here's Hannah Daniels's personnel file. There's a photocopy of the birth certificate in there." He handed a manila folder to Rachel. "It has Hannah's name on it, but forensics says it's been tampered with."

Opening it, Rachel scanned the personal information. "If this is hers, Charlene's birth certificate puts her at thirty-seven when she started working at the DCS." She closed the folder. "Sophie said Charlene gave birth to Hannah when she was fourteen. That would make our corpse twenty-three."

A.J. sighed and sipped from his coffee. "There's something I still don't get. Charlene could have easily gone on with her life after Hannah died. Why did she take Hannah's identity?"

Opening her mouth to give A.J. his answer, Rachel paused when Luke raised his hand to stop her. Montoya slipped into the chair next to her, obviously eager to hear the answer.

"Let me take a shot at this." Luke thought for a moment. "She took Hannah's identity because by doing so, she kept Hannah alive and absolved herself of the murder."

"Bingo," Rachel said, smiling. "It was the only way she knew to placate her conscience." Rachel stood up and faced Luke. "Can we go after her now?"

Luke knew how much Rachel wanted to be in on the arrest, but he hesitated. What if Charlene decided to fight them? She'd already proven beyond a doubt that she had no respect for human life. The thought of anything else happening to Rachel was unbearable.

He stole a glance in her direction and could see the fury building in her eyes.

"This is your case in more ways than one," A.J. said, looking from one of them to the other. "I think you should both have the satisfaction of bringing her in." When Luke made no move to agree, A.J. laid his hand on Luke's arm. "Rachel needs this closure as much as you do."

In the parking lot, Rachel trudged angrily toward her car. Luke hurried to catch up. They almost made it to the car when she whirled on him.

"You know what this means to me, but you were still ready to leave me behind, weren't you?" Hands planted firmly on her hips, she glared at him. "Admit it."

He glared back. "All right. I was considering it, but for your safety."

"What gives you the right to say what I can and can't do? What gives you the right to decide that for me?"

Luke could never recall seeing her this angry before. He decided to tell her the truth. "Because I love you."

For a moment, the wind left her sails. She stared open-mouthed at him, then she recovered, the anger sparkling in her eyes once more. "You're wrong. Love is your excuse, not your right." She turned and headed for her car.

"I changed my mind," he called after her. "Doesn't that count for something?"

"Yes, it does. It says there is a small brain residing above your hairline." She threw him a deprecating look. "I'll meet you at the DCS building."

Luke swore and walked quickly to his car. He looked over his shoulder to see her speed out of the lot. He continued to watch until her taillights disappeared around the corner.

A.J. came into the lot. "Where's Rachel?"

Luke mumbled a series of four-letter words to himself, then said, "Gone. I'm meeting her there."

"I asked you not to let her drive."

Another couple of curse words flew from Luke's mouth.

He spun on his boss. "Since when has anything I have to say had any effect on what Rachel does?"

Luke climbed into the car and slammed the door. Minutes later he was tearing down Oceanside Boulevard toward the DCS building, trying to catch up with Rachel.

Rachel had to consciously slow the car to a reasonable speed. It wouldn't do her or anyone on the road any good if she continued to allow her anger to translate to the foot on the accelerator. It should be enough that, in an effort to keep Luke from breathing down her neck, as if she were some adolescent who needed watching, she'd taken the long way to the DCS. But it wasn't.

She glanced in the rearview mirror to see if Luke had followed her. Behind her, a semi truck that had Green Nature written across the hood changed lanes, leaving the road empty. If Luke was back there, he was out of sight. She relaxed her hold on the steering wheel and heaved a big sigh.

She really had to get a handle on this need to shun their protection. Blowing the whole thing out of proportion seemed silly in retrospect. That they worried about her safety and her sanity should please her. Wasn't she the one who was complaining that Luke had left and hadn't stayed to help her through the loss of Maggie?

You can't have it both ways, Rachel. Either he's there or he's not. And unfortunately, most of the time when she'd really needed him, he was not.

She rubbed her temple with her finger. Her conflicting feelings about Luke were going to make her head explode if she didn't get them under control soon.

If only she didn't love him. How simple that would make her life.

Ten minutes later, she swung her car into a diagonal parking spot at the DCS and rolled down her window as she waited for Luke to arrive. A few minutes later, he pulled in next to her, glared at her and climbed from the car. She jumped out and slammed her own door.

Silently, they walked into the building and up to the red-headed, gum-chewing receptionist. Once more, she was deep into a magazine, but when she looked up this time, she immediately put it down and gave them her full attention.

"Can I help you, Officers?"

Neither of them bothered to tell her Rachel was not an *officer.*

"We're here to see Hannah Daniels," Luke said evenly.

The receptionist lifted the phone to her ear, dialed a number, spoke into the receiver and then replaced it. "She's in her office."

Once more, Luke and Rachel wove their way through the mouse-hole cubicles to the back of the room. When they walked into Charlene's office without knocking, they found it empty. Luke walked over to the desk and slid a couple of the drawers open.

"Women always keep their purse in their desk drawer. Hers is gone, and my bet is so is she."

Immediately, they both headed for the front of the building and hurried out to the sidewalk. They looked in all directions for any sign of their suspect. Nothing.

"Dammit!" Luke pulled out his cell phone and called headquarters. "A.J., Daniels made a run for it," he said onto the phone. "Put out an APB on her." He glanced at Rachel. "She slipped the two cops watching her. You have any idea what kind of car she drives?"

Rachel shook her head, then thought about the suspicious green sedan she'd seen at A.J.'s condo the day before it was set aflame. "Wait. It might be a late-model, green sedan. Not sure about the make."

"Check with the DMV and see if they have a late model, green sedan registered to Hannah Daniels." Luke folded the phone and stashed it back in his pocket, then turned to Rachel. "You go back to headquarters."

"Where are you going?" She followed him as he made his way to his car.

"I'm going to check her house." He opened the car door, but Rachel slammed it closed, narrowly missing catching his fingers in the door.

"I'm coming with you."

"No. Rachel, don't fight me on this. I need you back at headquarters in case they find her. You can go with A.J. to pick her up." He got into his car without another word and drove off, his tires screeching on the hot pavement.

She stood next to the empty parking space, staring after him, her anger rising to near boiling. He hadn't fooled her for a minute. He'd finally found a way to keep her out of the action. Since she had no idea where Charlene lived, she had no choice but to do as he asked and go back to headquarters.

Feeling about as helpless as she'd ever felt in her life, Rachel got into her car and started it. As she pulled out of the lot and onto the side street, she gave it a little more gas than necessary. Her tires spun then caught and the loud squeal echoed down the street, making people turn their heads to look at her. She smiled weakly and kept her gaze straight ahead. When she reached the corner, she flipped on her directional and automatically glanced in the rearview mirror.

Instead of the panorama of the palm-lined street she'd expected, the entire mirror was filled with the image of Charlene Daniels pointing a gun at the back of Rachel's head.

Chapter 17

By the time the shock of looking in her rearview mirror and seeing Charlene holding a gun had subsided, fear, icy and menacing, gripped Rachel. The cold metal gun barrel pressed against the base of her skull assured her that a wrong move could cost her her life. Sweat that had nothing to do with the warm Florida day trickled down between her shoulder blades.

Fighting to stay as calm as possible, Rachel glanced in the mirror again. "Hello…Charlene, isn't it?"

Rachel took a bit of satisfaction from the surprised expression and the slight widening of the woman's eyes. Evidently, she'd figured out that they were onto her, but not that they'd figured out her true identity.

"So you know." Despite the flat statement of fact, her lips twisted in a chilling grin. "You're too damn smart for your own good. But we'll soon fix that. I can't have you interfering in what God has chosen me to do."

Rachel tightened her grip on the steering wheel to keep her

hands from shaking. Why hadn't she just swallowed her pride and gone with Luke when he'd showed up at the motel? No, that would have been too simple. She had to assert herself, show him she didn't need him. The truth was, she did need him, and for more than just getting her out of this situation. She needed him in her life.

She glanced in the mirror at the gun pointing at her head. A vivid reminder that if she didn't get out of this, there was a good chance she'd have no future of any kind, with or without the man she loved. *Think, Rachel. Think.*

What had she learned as a firefighter that she could use now? Frantically, she searched her mind. Damn! It had been so long ago, so long since she'd had to employ anything from her academy days.

Think, dammit! You've faced tight situations before. Think!

Anxiety choked off her breathing. Forcing herself to think it through, she went over the things she'd been taught to do when facing a fire.

Calm down. Breathe. Collect your thoughts.

Breathing evenly and purposefully, Rachel went over what she would do if Charlene were a building jumper and not holding a gun to her head.

Talk to her. Distract her. Divide her attention.

"I'm curious about something," Rachel said as casually as she could manage while adrenaline pumped through her body at an alarming rate. "Why did you take Hannah's identity when you could have just as easily kept your own? Did God tell you to do that?"

In response, the gun barrel bit into the tender flesh at the base of Rachel's neck. She flinched and tried to pull away.

"Less conversation and more driving." A pause. "Turn right up here."

So much for talking. Rachel made the turn, then noticed

her briefcase lying beside her on the passenger seat. Her cell phone. If she could just get to it. Call Luke—

A burst of sarcastic laughter came from right behind her. "Do I look stupid?" Charlene hissed close to Rachel's ear. The feel of her hot breath made Rachel cringe. Charlene reached over the seat and, grabbing the handle of the briefcase, hauled it into the back seat. "Where you're going, you won't be needing this."

The sound of the locks popping open on the briefcase bit into the silence. Then Rachel heard the window being lowered. Glancing at her side mirror, she saw Charlene toss something out of the car. Rachel recognized it immediately. Her cell phone. Her heart sank as she realized her only hope was now lying on the side of the road. Now, no one would know where she was. Renewed anxiety tied knots in her nerves.

They rode in tense silence for several minutes before Charlene spoke again. "Turn in here and park behind the building."

Rachel pulled into the driveway in front of the old brick building that had once been the Orange Grove High School but had been closed and falling into decay for nearly ten years while the city fathers tried to agree on what to do with it.

As Rachel stared up at the deteriorating brick facade, reality slammed into her gut. She was going to die. Either by gunshot or fire, she would die, and she was staring at her coffin. Fear and bitter bile bubbled up from her belly and threatened to erupt. She swallowed repeatedly and willed herself to hide her fear, but she couldn't take her gaze off the building.

Charlene had planned well. This building was the perfect place for a fire. People died in abandoned-building fires every day all over the country. No one would care if this one went up in flames, and until they found her charred remains, no one would know she was in it.

Cold terror wrapped a clammy hand around her heart. She didn't want to die. She still had so much to do, a child to find and bury, a man to tell she loved him. She couldn't die yet.

Gripping the steering wheel so tight that pain shot up her arms, Rachel forced even breaths from her lungs. Putting on a calm front was getting more difficult with each passing minute, but Rachel gritted her teeth and kept up the masquerade. She would not squirm. She would not give Charlene that satisfaction.

Carefully, Rachel guided the car to the rear of the building, then stopped. Before the vehicle had come to a complete standstill, Charlene jumped out and pointed the gun through the driver's window at Rachel. She wiped her sweaty palms on her jeans and waited for what would come next.

"Get out," Charlene snarled, jerking the barrel of the gun to enforce her order.

Slowly, Rachel emerged from the car, keeping her hands raised so as not to give Charlene any reason to shoot. She kept one eye on Charlene and one on the gun that reminded her of the .40-caliber Glock that Luke carried as his off-duty firearm.

Luke. My God, would she ever get to see him again? Would they ever be able to repair the broken pieces of their relationship?

She tried to fill her mind with his face and shut out the menacing sight of the gun pointing at her heart. Her knees threatened to buckle, but she forced them to remain stiff.

Come on, Rach. You can do this.

Luke's voice rushed through her, imbuing her with welcome strength. With renewed purpose, she glared at Charlene, refusing to give her the power she obviously wanted. This bitch may have terrorized other women, but she wasn't going to terrorize Rachel Sutherland.

"Inside," Charlene directed, pushing her roughly to set Rachel in motion.

Obediently, she headed toward the back door of the school.

The entire building screamed its abandonment, reminding Rachel just how alone she was right now, that she had only herself and her abilities to call on to escape. Once-white paint peeled off the wooden door in large, tissue-thin slices. The paint flecks peppering the cracked concrete steps resembled a light dusting of snowflakes. The rusted carriage lantern beside the door held the remnants of a broken bulb, probably smashed out by the kids who had vandalized the playground equipment until the cops removed it as a safety precaution. The bricks were pockmarked and broken, and where the mortar had started to disintegrate, some were missing, leaving gaping holes scattered over the building's wall. A rusted fire escape hung haphazardly from one side.

As Rachel reached the top of the short flight of stairs, Charlene poked her in the back with the gun to hurry her along. A padlock, obviously having been cut by bolt cutters, hung from the strap that had secured the door. Charlene had prepared well.

The door creaked open on corroded hinges. Inside, the building smelled of dust, mold and disuse. Torn books and papers littered the long, dark hallway that stretched out in front of Rachel. As if someone had decorated the place in preparation for some macabre celebration, cobwebs hung from light fixtures, doorways and the railing of the staircase stretching up to the second floor. Dirty yellow water stains streaked the walls where the rain had seeped through the roof.

"Up the stairs," Charlene ordered from behind. Her voice echoed hollowly around the corridor that had once been filled with children's laughter. "Don't try anything cute. I can shoot a lot faster than you can turn around and come after me."

Rachel doubted that, but if she took the chance and lost, she wouldn't be any good to anyone dead. Her heart pounding heavily in her throat, she obediently climbed the stairs. Dust motes rose around her like an eerie fog. At the top, Charlene directed her into the first classroom to their left.

Aside from the dust covering everything, the grime filtering the meager light coming through the tall windows and the absence of any furniture except a large teacher's desk, the room was as empty as Rachel's life had been for the past two years. A homework assignment for the next day, instructing the students to read page forty-nine in an English textbook, was still visible on the blackboard.

Rachel wondered if she would have any *next days* to look forward to. Instantly Luke's voice intruded on her thoughts. *Stop it. You can't start thinking like that or you'll never get through this.*

"Over there." Charlene pointed at an exposed pipe that protruded vertically from ceiling to floor.

As they passed the teacher's desk, Charlene placed something on it. Rachel was tempted to turn to see what it was, but the butt of the gun being jammed against her back encouraged her to keep moving.

When they reached the pipe, Rachel understood what Charlene was going to do and that to do it, she would have to juggle the gun and whatever she planned on using to tie Rachel to the pipe. Her nerves tightened. Her senses on alert, she watched Charlene's gun hand closely, waiting.

From the pocket of her flowered dress Charlene pulled something that Rachel immediately identified as the Flexi-Cuffs the police used. Charlene grinned at Rachel's look of surprise. "Having access to police headquarters can be very helpful. Put your hands out, arms around the pipe."

Extending her hands in front of her on either side of the pipe, Rachel continued to keep her wary gaze on the gun. Charlene positioned the plastic strip under Rachel's wrists and threaded the end through the opening. When she started to pull it tight, the gun dipped to the side. Rachel slipped her hands from the band and lunged for the gun.

Charlene sidestepped, then brought her knee up sharply into Rachel's stomach. Air gushed from her. She doubled over, clutching her middle. A knifelike pain streaked through her abdomen. Sour bile rose in her throat. Rachel crumpled to the floor with a *thud.* Gasping, she rolled to her back and found herself looking into the barrel of the gun.

"Not a smart move. I had other plans for you, but I can shoot you right now. Bottom line? You're going to die, and it makes no difference to me how it happens. Now, get up and put your hands around the pipe."

Fighting the pain in her stomach, Rachel used the pipe to pull herself to her feet. It shifted slightly under her weight. Once more upright, she leaned her head against the pipe while Charlene attached the cuffs.

The futility of her circumstances brought her close to tears. She forced them back. Crying wasn't going to help. If only Luke were here. Automatically, her hand went to the Oriental pendant on the chain around her neck. She rubbed her thumb over it. Like a mantra, she repeated Luke's name over and over in her mind. The cool metal slowly warmed under her touch.

While she fought the pain that still radiated through her stomach, Rachel stole secretive glances at the other woman. Charlene Daniels possessed an amazingly youthful face and Rachel could see why she'd had no problem passing herself off as her twenty-three-year-old daughter. She was, in a word, stunning. But the lack of emotion in her cold, blue eyes sent shivers racing down Rachel's spine, reminding her of the monster this woman truly was.

Charlene went to the desk and unloaded the contents of a cloth tote bag: a roll of duct tape, a charcoal lighter and matches. Rachel stared at the charcoal lighter. Her mouth went dry.

Approaching Rachel, Charlene ripped off a piece of duct tape, but before she could place it across Rachel's mouth, Rachel turned her head away. Swinging her head back, Rachel looked Charlene in the eye. "I've got a personal interest in this. The least you can do before you kill me is answer a question for me." Charlene stepped back. "What did you do with my daughter?"

Smiling, Charlene sat on the corner of the desk. "Your daughter? She was never your daughter. From the moment I first saw her walking with you in the supermarket, God told me who she was. That blond hair and blue eyes, that face so sweet, so innocent. It was my Hannah." She smiled maniacally. "They told me she died in a fire, but I knew they lied. My Hannah wouldn't leave me. I knew, if I was patient, God would show me where she was, and he did." Charlene's smile disappeared. Her expression turned hard and menacing. "You shouldn't have taken her away from me, Rachel. That was wrong, and now you have to be punished."

Rachel felt a chill chase over her. The woman had totally lost her grip on reality. No wonder she and Luke hadn't been able to link Charlene to their fire. It had nothing to do with the abuse factor that had prompted her to kill the other women. She'd wanted Maggie, and was willing to kill Rachel to get her.

Uncontrollable anger boiled up in Rachel. "Where is she?"

Charlene wagged her finger at Rachel. "Now, you see, that's another reason why you have to die. I just knew that you'd try to take her again, and… Well, that's impossible."

"Where…is…she?" Rachel bit out the words one at a time. Despite the pain, she pulled at the cuffs restraining her. She wanted to launch herself at Charlene and strangle the life out of her.

"Where is she?"

"She's God's child now."

Jagged rage tore through Rachel. "You bastard!" She strained against the cuffs, trying to get loose. The pipe moved and the plastic cut into her flesh. But that pain was nothing compared to the agony in her heart.

It was one thing to assume Maggie was dead. It was another to have it confirmed by her killer. Tears burned at the back of Rachel's eyes, but she blinked them away and allowed her anger to consume her grief.

Frantically, she fought to free herself. Her bindings cut deeper into her flesh, but the pain never got past the one dominating thought in her mind…to rip out Charlene's throat.

Charlene laughed, then her face sobered. Her eyes turned colder, the glow in them crazier. Her jaw worked spasmodically. "No, you have that wrong. Hannah was the bastard. Hannah's brat was the bastard. I am God's handmaiden. I will save the children. I will cleanse the abusers by baptizing them in fire to burn away their sins."

"You are a crazy, cold-blooded killer," Rachel hissed, hatred imbuing each word. "A cold-blooded killer who stole her daughter's identity to appease God for having taken a life. Well, who's going to forgive you for all the other lives, Charlene? Who? Certainly not God. You've broken His Commandments. He'll never forgive you for that."

Charlene jumped to her feet. Her face twisted with rage. The stunning woman transformed into an ugly monster before Rachel's eyes.

"Shut up, bitch!" she screamed and launched herself at Rachel.

Rachel opened her mouth to ask what connection she had to all the other victims, but before she could, Charlene had slapped a strip of tape over her lips, effectively dashing any hope Rachel had of asking Charlene any more about either her arson spree…or about Maggie.

Helplessly, she watched as Charlene poured charcoal lighter over piles of paper she'd stacked neatly in three different spots. Rachel stood in the fourth spot. The bottom of the cross.

Luke entered A.J.'s office. He looked around, expecting to find Rachel there. Only A.J. sat behind the desk.

"Where is she?"

A.J. glanced up from a legal pad he had half filled with scribbled notes and frowned. "Who?"

“Rachel,” Luke almost shouted, his voice impatient and showing traces of the anger he’d been nursing since their confrontation in the DCS parking lot. “When she found out we were there, Charlene took off from the DCS, so I went to check her house. Rachel was supposed to meet me back here.”

“I haven’t seen her, but she would have had to pass the desk sergeant.” He picked up the phone. “Tony, has Rachel Sutherland passed the desk in the last hour or so?” He listened. “Well, try the task force room.” He listened again, then hung up. “She’s not in the annex, and Tony hasn’t seen her come through the front.”

Luke felt a cold chill creep over him. Where could she have gone? Had she done something stupid? No. Rachel did a lot of things he questioned, but stupid wasn’t in her makeup. Something had happened to her. He felt it in his gut.

“Something’s wrong,” he said to A.J., his voice catching in his throat, his heart thudding in his chest. He cleared away the apprehension and leaned both palms on A.J.’s desk. “We need to find her—*now.*”

“Try the house, then her cell phone.”

Luke pulled his cell from his pocket and punched in the numbers he’d memorized. He waited while the phone at the house rang and rang, his heart thudding painfully, all his thoughts centered on Rachel.

Come on, Rach. Don’t fail me now.

When the answering machine picked up, he cut the connection, then dialed her cell-phone number. Pacing in front of the desk, he listened to the interminable ringing in his ear. No answer. He clicked off, then tried her motel with the same results. Cursing himself for not thinking to leave a message on her cell, he dialed the cell number again.

“Rachel, I need you to call me back right away.” Then, because something inside him urged him to say it, he turned his back on A.J. and whispered into the phone, “I love you.

baby. Don't go back to Atlanta. I want us to try again. I want us to be a family." He wiped his expression clean, folded the phone and swung back to A.J. "No answer."

A.J. put his hand on the desk phone. "What kind of car is Rachel driving? I'll put an APB out on it."

Luke could see the car in his mind's eyes. It was blue. A Chevy? Yes. "A Chevy Malibu, but an APB is going to take too long."

He racked his brains for anywhere else she might be that they hadn't checked. The firehouse. Quickly, he punched in the number. When a voice declared it to be Jensen's Pharmacy, he cursed and cut off the call, then redialed.

"Engine 108," a deep voice said.

"This is Detective Luke Sutherland. Is Rachel Lansing there?"

"I haven't seen her since last week. Want me to tell her you're looking for her?'

"Please." He clicked off without saying goodbye. "Dammit, where can she be?"

"Calm down. She's can't be far. There has to be somewhere we haven't looked." A.J. frowned in thought.

Luke brightened. "Don't the new GM cars come with a locating device installed?"

"Not all models, but it's worth a try." A.J. picked up the receiver and instructed the desk sergeant to connect him to the rental-car company that they'd used to reserve the car for Rachel in Atlanta.

Luke stood next to him, his palms planted on the desktop, his gaze glued to A.J. Inside him, his gut churned. He could smell his own fear. Sweat broke out on his face, despite the AC that A.J. kept on arctic temperatures. The ticking clock above the file cabinet reminded him of the passage of precious time.

"Thanks," A.J. said, scribbling a number across a folder on his desk. He hung up. "Her car has Find Now on it." He dialed the number he'd written on the folder. "This is Chief Branson of the Orange Grove, Florida, police department. I need you to locate a car that was rented to Rachel Suth—" Luke stopped him with a frantic wave of his hand. A.J. stared at Luke for a moment, then nodded. "The car was rented to Rachel Lansing."

More time ticked by while they waited for them to locate Rachel's rental car. Luke's nerves tightened with each tick of the clock. Finally, A.J. raised his head and nodded at Luke.

Again he scribbled something on the folder. "Okay, got it. Thanks." A.J. hung up. He stood and checked the location against the map on the wall behind him. "This makes no sense. She's at the old Orange Grove High School."

"School? What the hell is she doing at a condemned school?" Then it hit him. *Charlene.*

Luke was out the door and hit the parking lot running with A.J. right behind him calling orders over his shoulder to have a patrol car meet them at the school. There was only one reason Rachel would be at a school that had been closed for years, and it had nothing to do with furthering her education.

Either she had followed Charlene there, or...Luke swallowed hard...or Charlene had taken her there. Either way, Luke hoped he was wrong. His gut told him he wasn't, and his heart told him he had to find her, because losing Rachel again, especially this way, would be like losing his soul.

Stop it. You can't start thinking like that or you'll never get through this. He kept repeating that over and over in his head as he gassed the car to top speed and hurtled through traffic toward the school.

Charlene stared at Rachel, then smiled. "You know, this is your own fault. It didn't have to happen this way." Her eerily calm, matter-of-fact tone sent chills down Rachel's spine. "I tried to get you to leave. I warned you with my note, then the condo fire. I could have killed you in that fire, you know. But

I didn't." She thought for a moment. "That was probably a mistake." Then she shrugged. "Oh well, that will be remedied very shortly." She opened the box of matchsticks and took one out.

Rachel stared at Charlene. She'd barely heard what the woman had said over the frantic pounding of her heart. It was one thing to talk bravely. But it was a whole different thing to sit here and look her own mortality in the eye.

It was true what everyone said about seeing your life and all the regrets pass before you when death was breathing down your neck. Rachel thought about her damn pride and how many things she had allowed it to rob her of in her lifetime. She regretted not having made a bigger effort to make friends along the way. Other than Sam, she really had no close friends, people she could turn to and lean on in times of emotional need, people she could laugh with and live life with and love.

Love.

Her pride had stolen love from her as well. She should have gone after Luke when he'd walked out. Instead, she had allowed her foolish pride to take one of the most precious things in her world from her. Why had she not fought for Luke as much as she felt he should have fought for her?

She'd never feel the security of his arms again. She'd never get to taste his lips again, to share his passion. She'd never get to tell him she didn't want to go back to Atlanta. She wanted to stay right here, with him, and start their family again.

Stop it. You can't start thinking like that, or you'll never get through this. Luke's voice echoed in her ears. *I will not let you die. Be strong for me, for yourself, for Maggie.* His voice was as clear as if he was standing beside her.

From deep inside her came renewed resolution. Pride be damned. If she didn't have this gag over her mouth, she'd swallow her almighty pride and beg Charlene for her life. Anything to have another chance at doing everything she'd never done, at winning Luke back and at starting their life over. Maybe even having another baby. But even if Rachel was free to plead with her captor, the twisted look on Charlene's face told Rachel the woman was well past reason.

"Well, I have to get home." Charlene glanced at her watch and spoke as casually as if she were addressing a friend over lunch. "No chloroform this time. I wouldn't want you to miss seeing your salvation." She laughed.

Rachel closed her eyes. But she could not close out the blood-freezing reverberation of the sound of a match being struck.

Chapter 18

The air in the classroom smelled strongly of charcoal lighter. Rachel opened her eyes and realized why. Charlene was gone, but before she left she had not only used the accelerant to ignite the piles of paper she'd positioned at the three points of the cross, but she'd also used it to connect the left and right points. She'd then dribbled a line from the top of the cross to within several feet of where Rachel stood imprisoned on the pipe. Charlene had placed her in the same subservient position at the foot of the cross as her other victims.

Rachel's imminent death approached her like a stalking, enraged animal with hot, searing breath, feeding voraciously off the accelerant and the old wooden floor.

All the fear she'd hidden from Charlene boiled to the surface. Adrenaline surged through her. Her heart thundered in her ears. She had to save herself.

Using every bit of strength she had, she yanked at the strip of plastic around her wrists. It seemed futile. If big, burly prisoners couldn't break free of the cuffs, what chance did she have? Giving up, she looked around her.

Smoke had begun to fill the room and the deadly sound of the crackling blaze had grown to a low roar, blocking off the door with a growing wall of fire. Terror began to subtly contaminate her mind. She envisioned herself burned beyond recognition, until she resembled the photos of the victims she'd seen in A.J.'s office. Bile flooded her mouth. She swallowed hard, realizing for the first time that some of the smoke had already found its way down her throat and raked it raw. Ignoring the pain and fighting the panic building inside her, she tried to organize her scattered thoughts.

Then, Luke's voice whispered in her ear again, *Concentrate. You can do this.*

His voice brought with it an oddly calming effect that slowed her heart rate and helped her focus.

Searching her surroundings for an escape route, Rachel zeroed in on the grimy windows. They were old and tall with small panes divided by wooden slats, the sill no more than two feet off the floor. She had to get to the windows. But as long as she was tied to this damn pipe, she wasn't going anywhere. She had to get free of the pipe.

Urgency renewed her strength. Using all her weight, she planted her feet on the floor and pulled at her bindings. Pain shot through her wrists. The cuffs cut off the blood flow. Her fingers went numb. Still she pulled.

She'd just about decided it was hopeless when ceiling plaster cascaded around her. Small chunks battered her head. She ducked, afraid the ceiling was falling. When it finally stopped, she glanced up cautiously. Right above her was a hole in the plaster that had obviously been eaten away by water seepage. But what really caught her attention was the heavy rust that encased the pipe where it went through the plaster.

Hope bloomed inside her.

Unable to prevent the smoke from going up her nose and into her lungs, she choked and coughed until her eyes overflowed with burning tears. A mixture of old wood and man-made materials had turned the smoke acrid. The room was disintegrating around her.

Floor tiles curled and popped off the floor. An empty bookcase crumbled into charred ruins. The dried wood of the teacher's desk burst into a column of orange flame that stretched its destructive fingers toward the ceiling.

Sweat beads blossomed on Rachel's forehead only to be dried almost instantly by the hot air. Taking a deep breath, she closed her mind to the pain and with renewed effort pulled on the pipe. More plaster fell from the ceiling. Maneuvering to the other side of the pipe, she pulled in a new direction. Again she moved and again she pulled. Warm, slick liquid trickled over her hands. Blood. But she kept pulling.

After working her way around the pipe and hauling on it several times, she heard a crack and instead of plaster falling around her, large pieces of rusty metal hit the floor. The pipe was crumbling. Encouraged, she began again. This time, each pull brought a shower of rust and the pipe began to list sideways.

Elated, she positioned her hands around the pipe and shook it back and forth as hard as she could. More rust. She repeated the motion and finally, like a tree falling under the blows of a lumberjack's ax, the pipe gave way and tumbled to the floor, taking her with it.

Unable to break her fall, she hit the floor hard. Precious air gushed through her nose from her burning lungs. She inhaled sharply and cringed as smoke followed the air down her throat. Clumsily, she crawled the length of the pipe and slipped the cuffs over the end. Once the pipe had been removed, she had no trouble slipping her hands free of the FlexiCuffs and tearing the duct tape from her mouth.

She only had a moment to relish her freedom when the

sound of the encroaching fire drew her attention. It had advanced dangerously while she'd been fighting for freedom. The old building was quickly going up. A wall of flame separated her from the door, and it was creeping ever closer.

Quickly, she pulled her shirt up to cover her nose and mouth and hurried to the windows. Rachel peered out the window to the grass two stories below. The idea of jumping made her stomach heave, but she didn't have a choice. She had to jump. Nor did she have the luxury of hesitation. Once the window gave way, oxygen would rush in and the fire beast would devour it and grow quickly. Breaking the window and then climbing out and jumping was not an option.

She knew what she had to do. Screwing up her courage, she took a step. Then she heard it.

"Rachel!"

For a moment, she'd thought Luke was only in her head, then she heard it again.

"Rachel!"

She ran to the window and saw Luke and A.J. running toward the building. Relief weakened her knees.

"Jump!" Luke called as he ran. "Jump!"

Behind her a *whoosh* of air drew her attention. The fire consuming the desk had reached the ceiling and was spreading quickly. The temperature in the room began to rise noticeably. She had only seconds to get out.

"Rachel?" Luke's voice had become frantic, filled with the same panic she fought to keep at bay inside herself. "Jump. I'll break your fall."

She stared down at him through the window and despite the years of grime, reflections of the angry flames leaped behind her in the dirty glass. The heat filling the room had quickly escalated and was approaching temperatures that could kill in seconds.

She had to have faith in the one man in the world in whom she had lost all trust.

Taking a deep breath, she closed her eyes and threw her body at the window. Wood splintered and glass shattered, and she was airborne.

Luke heard the crash, then, in the next second, Rachel's body plummeted toward him. Holding his breath, he stepped into her path. Her descent seemed to happen in slow motion. Shards of glass rained down on him, but he didn't dare look away from her. Though instinct said otherwise, he deliberately kept his muscles relaxed. Bending his knees, he cushioned himself for the collision and waited for her to land on him.

An instant later, she hit him with bone-jarring force. His arms closed around her. Air whooshed from their lungs. His teeth slammed together. Pain shot through his head and ribs. His ears rang. They slammed onto the grass in a tangle of limbs.

Clinging to her, he gasped for air, afraid to let go, afraid she'd disappear, and he'd lose her again. Evidently Rachel was feeling the same way. She nuzzled her face into his neck and pressed as close as she could. In response, he tightened his arms. She raised her head and looked down at him, then he covered her face with kisses.

Wanting more, he sealed her lips with his. He leaned back, framed her face in his hands, looked at her and grinned with all the delight of a kid on Christmas morning.

"Thank God," he said over and over, his heart bursting with gratitude that she was here and alive. Each word was punctuated with a kiss.

"Are you okay?" A.J.'s terrified voice came from just above them.

Emotions too varied and too many to untangle blocked his throat. Luke could only nod. The muscles in his neck screamed at the movement. Every ache and pain was worth saving Rachel.

"Thank God." A.J. checked toward the road. "You two have to get out of the way. I called the fire company. They should be here any minute."

Just then, a loud roar came from above them. A flame shot out the window where Rachel had stood moments ago.

"Is she still in there?" Luke asked.

Rachel looked at him, her muddled brain refusing to work. Then she shook her head. "No…she got away." Her voice was hoarse and sounded painful. Then, as if she remembered something and using his sore chest for leverage, Rachel pawed her way to her feet. "Come on," she urged, pulling at his hand.

Ignoring his screaming muscles, he levered himself up. "Where?"

"To Charlene's." Rachel pulled him toward his car. "She said she was…going home."

When Luke and Rachel arrived at Charlene's two-story, beige-stucco home in one of the better sections of Orange Grove, the garage door was closed, and there was no car in the driveway. Luke parked his SUV a little bit down the block and turned to Rachel to tell her to wait there for him.

The look of disappointment on her face told him she knew what he was about to say. But he couldn't say it. After what she'd been through, she deserved to be with him. She had earned the right to face Charlene.

"You ready?" he asked.

Her soot-stained face transformed into a wide grin. His heart turned over. She looked as if he'd given her the moon.

"What happened to—" she swallowed hard "*—protect Rachel at all costs?*"

He placed his palm against her blackened cheek. "Lady, you can't be talking about my Rachel. She's one tough broad who doesn't need protecting."

Without warning, she leaned over and kissed him soundly on the lips. "Thanks," she rasped, her smile still in place. "Let's go."

They got out of the car, and he motioned for her to follow

him. He cut through the neighbor's yard and noted, when they crossed in front of Charlene's garage, that the door was not completely down. He dropped to his knees and peeked underneath. Charlene's car was inside.

"She's here," he told Rachel as he stood up. He drew his gun. "Stay right behind me."

He moved through the expertly landscaped flower bed close to the outside front wall and into an alcove that housed the ornate front door. Noiselessly, he turned the knob. The door was unlocked. Making sure the way was clear, he slipped inside. Rachel slipped in behind him.

The house was eerily silent, except for the deep-throated tick of a grandfather clock in the hall. A crystal bowl filled with potpourri on a side table perfumed the air with a flowery scent. Expensive furniture filled the rooms. Revulsion rose up in Luke's throat. Charlene had done well from her daughter's death.

The house was as neat as a pin. Not a thing out of place, not even a magazine on the coffee table. To Luke, it spoke not so much of a good housekeeper as it did of being in control. Everything in its place, the place that Charlene designated for it. Anger rose up in him when he thought about how much he and Rachel missed Maggie, and then how Charlene had seen Hannah and her baby as clutter that she'd simply burned like yesterday's trash.

Slowly and quietly, they padded through the downstairs, a room at a time. As each room showed itself to be empty of humans, Luke's heart sank a little lower. She had to be here. This nightmare had to come to an end to free Rachel of her torment. Determination pumped through him, fueling his need to free them once and for all.

After checking out the last room, they made their way back to the hall.

A muffled noise, like something heavy being dropped on a carpeted floor, drifted down to them from upstairs. Luke started, glanced to the floor above them, laid a finger over his lips and signaled Rachel that they were going upstairs. She nodded.

Staying right behind Luke, Rachel crept up the carpeted stairs and down the hall to the first door. Her heart felt as if it would burst from her body, and her hands began to sweat.

With his gun ready, Luke simultaneously threw the door open and stepped inside. Rachel waited until he motioned for her to follow. They both looked around what appeared to be the master bedroom. It was as neat as the rest of the house and just as empty, except for the three suitcases standing at the end of the bed. Looks like they'd got here just in time. He jerked the closet door open. Nothing. They repeated the process in two more rooms and again found nothing.

When they entered the next room and Luke stopped short, Rachel almost ran into his back. He snared her attention and motioned toward a closet on the far side of the room. A sliver of material protruded from beneath the door. It was the same flower print as the dress Charlene had worn in the school. As they watched, the material disappeared inside the closet.

Luke motioned for Rachel to go to the hinged side of the door. On tiptoe, she followed his instructions. Once she was in position, he pointed at the doorknob with his gun. She grabbed it, turned and yanked it toward her.

"Freeze—" He gasped. The color drained from Luke's face. His eyes grew large. His hands shook. "My God…"

Luke's reaction sent an avalanche of questions pouring through Rachel's mind. Was Charlene dead? Had she committed suicide? Was the scene inside the closet so grotesque that it could even shock a seasoned cop like Luke?

Not knowing what to expect, Rachel peered around the door and into the closet. She sucked in her breath. It was as if she'd stepped backward in time. Sitting on the floor of the closet, Charlene clasped a small, blond child to her. With her face buried against Charlene, Rachel couldn't see the little one's face, but the blond hair instantly brought to mind the childhood picture of Hannah Daniels that Sophie had showed them.

But what made her blood run cold was the gun pointed at the child's head.

"Don't touch me. I'll kill her." She glared at them with crazed eyes.

"Charlene, give us the child," Luke said softly.

"No!" Charlene snapped. "You can't take my baby. I promised Him I would never let her go again. He'll punish me. I'll kill her before I let you take her again."

Again? Rachel searched her profiler's mind for the meaning to that one word, but the mother in her couldn't get past the horrific sight of a gun threatening the life of the innocent child.

Luke squatted in front of them. "No one will punish you, Charlene. Let the little girl go." His voice was soft, reassuring, but Rachel heard the quiver. Keeping his gun trained on Charlene, Luke stretched out his hand. "Give me the gun."

"No." She pressed the gun harder against the child's head. The little girl began to whimper softly. "And you can't have her either." She turned half away from Luke's hand. "She's mine."

Rachel's heart rebounded into her throat. If Luke pushed Charlene too hard, there was no telling what she'd do in her state of mind. Harnessing her rioting emotions and wiping her face clean of any expression that didn't say compassion, she touched his shoulder lightly. "Luke, let me."

At first, she thought he was going to argue with her, but then he nodded and moved aside.

Rachel squatted in front of Charlene and the child. "Charlene, remember that God has work for you to do for Him. How will you do that if you're in prison for hurting your baby?"

Charlene's forehead creased in thought. "But if I let you take her, He'll be angry with me again."

She had to get the child away from this maniac. Keeping

her voice calm, something she was far from feeling inside, Rachel rested her hands on her thighs and dug her nails into her legs to keep from lunging for the child. "How about if we take care of your baby until you do your job? Would that be okay with God?"

Tilting her head as if listening to a voice only she could hear, Charlene stared blankly at Rachel. "He says you won't give her back."

Please, God, work with me, Rachel prayed silently.

Forcing a smile, Rachel imbued her voice with concern. "Oh, but we would. As soon as you finish your work for God, you can have her back."

Though her grip on the whimpering child remained strong, the gun sagged a little and the look in Charlene's eyes told Rachel she was wavering. "How do I know you're not lying just to get my baby?"

A soft sigh of exasperation came from Luke. He shifted his feet impatiently. Charlene became visibly agitated by his actions. Cold dread invaded Rachel's limbs. Now that she'd come this close, Rachel didn't need him spooking Charlene. Furtively, Rachel reached behind her, grabbed his ankle and squeezed. Her tightly coiled nerves relaxed a bit when he immediately stilled.

"Charlene," Rachel said in a soft understanding tone, "I'm a mother, too, and I would never take a baby that wasn't mine. I know how much that would hurt you." The child stirred and her whimpering became marginally louder. Rachel held her breath.

"Shut up!" Charlene cried at the child. The whimpers died to a soft sob. "You're always crying. I can't stand it!" Using the same hand that held the gun, she laid her palm against her head.

As if choreographed, Rachel and Luke sprung at the same time. Luke grabbed the gun, and Rachel hauled the child into her arms and rolled to the side to get her out of harm's way.

Clutching a dirty, ragged, patchwork teddy bear to her chest, the child's blue-eyed gaze met Rachel's for the first time.

Rachel sucked in her breath. Her throat constricted with the threat of tears. She blinked to keep her vision clear. Slowly, the years of pain, loneliness, empty arms, the days and nights of longing evaporated from her memory. Still, she was afraid to believe, afraid that she'd wake up again and find it was all a dream. But, despite being two years older, this child had the same beautiful blue eyes, the same cherubic face, the same riot of blond curls, the same sweet mouth.

Then, never taking her eyes off Rachel, she rubbed her cheek on the teddy bear's head. How many times had Rachel watched Maggie do that same thing just before she drifted off to sleep?

Rachel's heart opened like a flower beneath a healing, warming sun. Hot, silent tears of the purest joy cascaded down her cheeks. But not an ounce of recognition showed from those beautiful blue eyes.

"Maggie?" Rachel croaked, barely above a whisper. "Maggie, baby, it's Mommy, sweetheart."

The sound of a single ring of Luke's metal cuffs being clicked into place on Charlene's wrist intruded on Rachel's thoughts. Out of the corner of her eye, she saw Luke let go of Charlene and turn sharply toward her.

"Maggie?" His voice was full of the tears shining in his eyes. Rachel nodded, then looked back at the little face staring up at her.

The child blinked, but still showed no sign of recognition. Rachel's heart broke. Her baby had forgotten her. Bittersweet pain knifed through her. But she wasn't ready to give up.

She sat up and cradled her in her lap. Softly, she began to sing.

"Hush, little Maggie, don't say a word...." Her throat dried out. She swallowed to moisten it, then continued, *"Momma's gonna buy you a mocking bird."* Rachel choked on a sob. Maggie's head tilted. *"If the mocking bird don't sing..."* Luke's voice joined hers. *"Daddy's gonna buy you a diamond ring."*

Over Maggie's head, Rachel looked at Luke. Tears rolled

down his cheeks. She placed her arm around him, drawing him into the circle of their love. He buried his face against Maggie's hair.

"Maggie," he whispered, his voice hoarse and filled with the same awe Rachel was feeling. "My God, Maggie."

Deep, wrenching sobs tore from him.

Maggie lifted his chin, then wiped the tears away with her small hand. His embrace tightened. The touch of one little girl had reduced him from the big, brave detective to the most important position he'd ever held in his life, Maggie's daddy.

For a long time, they stayed that way, secure in the knowledge that Maggie was alive and that they were together again.

Maggie raised her head from her mother's shoulder and peered behind her. Her blue eyes grew enormous. "Momma, fire!"

Chapter 19

Luke and Rachel sprang to their feet and backed away from the flames blocking the bedroom door. Rachel cuddled Maggie close to her body and retreated to a far corner of the bedroom. Charlene had not only gotten away again, she'd tried to guarantee her escape.

"Damn!" Luke swore, then bit back the other curse words that crossed his mind. How stupid could he be? He should have watched her, but the shock of seeing his daughter alive had shaken his world to its very roots. "Help me!" he yelled to Rachel. He could only pray that Charlene would run into the open arms of A.J. and his backup. But they'd left so fast, there was no way of knowing if A.J. had followed.

Placing Maggie into the corner, safe from the fire, she tried to make her face remain placid. "Stay here, sweetheart. Mommy will be right back." Rachel raced to Luke's side

Thankfully, the fire hadn't had time to grow into anything they couldn't handle alone. It had barely burned the rug across the opening to the bedroom door, but it was growing. Luke grabbed the spread off the bed and threw it to Rachel, then he ripped off the blanket. Working together they quickly smothered the flames.

Throwing the scorched bedding aside, Luke scooped Maggie into his arms, then grabbed Rachel's hand and steered her out the bedroom door. As they hurried down the stairs, heat slammed them in the face and the density of smoke increased.

Rachel's blood chilled. This was much more than the residue of the fire upstairs. Smoke hung against the ceiling. She glanced over her shoulder. Behind them flames spread quickly through the living room. When she turned back, a new fire had roared to life in front of them. They were trapped.

"Stay here," Luke ordered, handing Maggie to her. He raced back up the stairs.

The child buried her face in Rachel's neck and whimpered softly. Rachel kept an eye on the fire and murmured reassurances to Maggie. Periodically, she glanced up the staircase. Her hands trembled. Getting herself out of a fire was one thing, but getting Maggie out was something else entirely. She thanked God that Luke was there to help.

After what seemed like forever, Luke reappeared on the stairs carrying the bedding they'd used to extinguish the fire in the bedroom. He must have wet the blankets down because streams of water ran freely from the material.

"Put this around you." He took Maggie and cloaked himself and his daughter in the bedspread.

Rachel threw the heavy, wet blanket over her own head, leaving only a slit to peer out, then gathered the excess in her hand to keep from tripping over it.

"When I say *go,* run. Don't stop until we're outside." Luke gripped Maggie tight in his arms and pulled the bedspread up around them to cover all but a small portion of his face. "Ready?"

Rachel took a deep breath and nodded.

"Go!"

As if the hounds of hell were chasing her, she ran after Luke. She tried to think of anything except that they were about to run through a wall of flames. She had to make it. They had to make it. They had so much to look forward to now. Fate would not be cruel enough to give her Maggie back only to take her again.

The fire heated the water in the blanket almost instantly. The air grew thick and hard to breathe. Just as she reached the flames, Rachel held her breath, closed the small opening she'd left to see through and pushed her aching muscles to keep moving. Heat intensified, almost to the point of being unbearable, but she kept going. It seemed like forever before she felt the temperature cool and fresh air enter her nostrils.

Rachel peeled the blanket off her and looked frantically around for Luke and Maggie. He must have tripped over the spread because he and Maggie lay near her on the grass with the bedspread wound around them. Maggie was astride his chest laughing. It was the first time Rachel had heard her daughter laugh, and the sound sent ripples of pleasure washing over her. How very much she'd missed Maggie's laughter.

Then she looked at Luke. His eyes were closed, and he wasn't moving. Pleasure turned to fear. Rachel's heart stopped. Please, God, they couldn't have saved Maggie only to lose him. She hurried toward him.

"Luke." Her voice rose. "Luke?"

"We've got to stop meeting like this, woman," he growled from beneath his daughter's body. "Two fires in one day is about all my heart can take."

Rachel put her hand to her forehead and let out a long sigh of relief. When she removed it, she saw a flash of familiar color in the bushes on a neighboring lawn. At the same time, the sound of police sirens rent the air. Ignoring the sirens,

Rachel studied the color as it seemed to move among a thick grouping of trees. Then she suddenly realized why it looked familiar. It was Charlene's dress.

"Watch Maggie," she called to Luke and took off running.

Plowing through the neat ligustrum hedges at the side of the lawn, she jumped a bed of bloodred geraniums with one thought in mind...bring her down. Just as Rachel reached the stand of palms, Charlene stood up and started to inch around them. Rachel launched herself onto the woman.

For the third time that day, air rushed from Rachel's lungs. They rolled over and over across the spongy Saint Augustine grass. Rachel held on to Charlene as if she were a lifeline. Charlene grabbed a handful of Rachel's hair and yanked to get her off. Searing pain cut through Rachel's scalp, but she would not let go. The twisting, turning tangle of female limbs and bodies finally come to rest near the roadside, with Rachel sitting astride Charlene's chest, her arms pinned to her sides by Rachel's legs.

"Get off me," Charlene snarled, squirming and bucking her hips to dislodge Rachel.

"Not in this lifetime, bitch," Rachel growled back, shoving her hair out of her face and glaring down at her captive.

A snort of laughter came from Luke and A.J., who had come to stand beside them.

Something hard dug into Rachel's leg. Fearing it was the gun, Rachel reached for it and found that Charlene still wore one half of the handcuffs Luke had attached to her earlier. She grabbed the second ring and slapped it on Charlene's other wrist. Then she leaned a hand on either side of Charlene's head, and bent close to the woman's ear.

"You have split up my family, kidnapped my daughter and tried to kill me more times than I care to count, so, on behalf of me, my family, all those babies whose mothers you killed and for Hannah and her baby, rot in hell." Then she rolled off her and allowed A.J. to lift Charlene to her feet and lead her to the patrol car.

A small hand tugged at her sleeve. Rachel raised her head to see Maggie standing beside her. She hauled her into her lap, unable to get enough of touching Maggie, making sure she was really there and not another dream Rachel's mind had conjured. "Yes, sweetie?"

"Can we go home now?'

Rachel laughed. "Tell you what. You and I will go home and have a bath. How's that sound?"

"With bubbles?" Maggie asked shyly.

Tears filled Rachel's throat. Maggie had always wanted bubbles in her bathwater. One more confirmation that Maggie remembered her life before Charlene.

"With bubbles." Rachel pushed herself to her feet and turned to tell Luke they were ready to go home, but he wasn't there. Then she saw him walking toward his car.

You and I... Rachel's words rang in Luke's ears and wrenched his heart.

He'd foolishly allowed himself to believe that since they had Maggie back, it would mean they could be a family again, but Rachel's words made it abundantly clear that she did not plan on him being a part of their life. He knew she would never keep Maggie from him, but he didn't want to live the rest of his life as a weekend visitor in either Maggie's life or Rachel's. He wanted them all together as a family. But when she'd moved out to the motel, Rachel had made it very clear that, although she loved him, she couldn't trust him not to walk away again.

So exactly what are you doing now, Sutherland? Proving her right?

He'd reached the car and leaned his forehead against the hot metal and answered his own question. Walking away.

Instead of staying and fighting for his family and Rachel's love, he was tucking his tail between his legs and leaving like a whipped puppy.

"Damn!" He slammed his fist against the car's roof and spun around, determined to go back and face Rachel, to fight for their love and their family. But he never got to take one step.

She was standing behind him, her hands on her hips, looking as mad as he'd ever seen her. Behind her, he could see A.J. holding Maggie and smiling like a Cheshire cat.

"Where do you think you're going?"

"I was just—"

"Walking away," she spat. "Well, guess what?" She stepped closer and wagged a finger in his face. "I'm not going to let you. The last time I did that, I lived to regret it. My damn pride kept me from going after you and making you stay. Not this time. This time you're going to have to walk over me to run away."

Stunned speechless by her tirade, Luke moved back. "I just—"

"No, don't try to feed me a bunch of half-baked excuses. There is no excuse for walking out on people who love you." She swallowed hard, her throat obviously sore, but she forged on. "When Charlene had a gun to my head in the car, do you know who I thought of calling? Not 911, not A.J. You! I wanted to call you, Luke. When I was tied to that damn pipe, who came into my head and helped me get through it? You! Does that sound like a woman who wants you out of her life? Does it?" She took another step toward him. He automatically took a step back.

"I have never had to admit this in my life and to do so now is one of the hardest things I've ever had to say, but..." She looked away, then back at him, her eyes welling with tears. "I need you. Can't you see that? I love you." She picked up his hand and fingered the gold band. "And this tells me you still love me."

"But you don't trust me," he said, hope rising in him like a spring thaw. Again she stepped toward him. His back hit the side of the car. Physically and literally, he was done retreating. Done running away, but he needed to hear her say the words.

"If I didn't trust you, would I have jumped out a second-story window into your arms? Would I have allowed you to carry our precious baby through a wall of fire?" Her voice cracked. "Would I be here now begging you not to leave us? Would I—"

He yanked her into his arms and covered her mouth with his. "Shut up, woman," he growled against her lips a long time later. "I'm not going anywhere but home with my wife and child."

Rachel let out a whoop of joy and threw her arms around his neck. He swept her from the ground and twirled her around, then settled her to her feet. He looked down into her lovely face. Soot and all, she was still the most beautiful thing he'd ever seen.

He wiped a smudge of dirt from her nose, then framed her face with his palms. "I'm not sure I'll ever stop protecting you, but two things you can count on. I'll never leave you again, and I sure as hell will never stop loving you."

Epilogue

One Year Later…

Luke threw his key ring on the hall table as he walked toward the voices coming from the family room. The sound never failed to bring warmth to his soul. This last year his life had become better than it had been in a very long time, and coming home to a house filled with love and laughter was the best part of it.

Thanks to A.J., Maggie had gotten some superior psychological help and was adjusting to life with her family very well. Her nightmares had stopped weeks ago, and she smiled and laughed more often.

"I'm home, family," he called, entering the big friendly room he and Rachel had done over to accommodate their growing family.

"Daddy!" Maggie hurled herself into his arms as he came through the door. She spread butterfly kisses across his cheeks and forehead.

"Hey, Magpie." He carried her forward and glanced around the room. The coffee table was buried under papers and folders. Sam sat on the floor at one end. Rachel, who had been sitting on the sofa, bounded to her feet and kissed him.

He carried Maggie to the corner of the room, where, snuggled down in his cradle fast asleep, was Austin James Sutherland, their three-month-old son, better known as Jay. Beside him was a ragged, patchwork teddy bear. Luke looked at the bear then to Rachel. The psychologist told them that when Maggie gave up the bear that had been her constant companion and security blanket for the two years with Charlene and the year since she'd come back to them, she would need only the love of her family to complete her rehabilitation.

"Tell Daddy what you did today," Rachel urged, snuggling into Luke's arm and grinning up at him.

"I gave Jay my teddy. I'm not a baby anymore, so I don't need it."

Luke hugged her close. "Good for you, sweetie. I'm sure Jay will take very good care of him." Jay stirred. Rachel laid her finger over her lips, then steered them away from him. "What's all this?" Luke asked, sitting on the sofa and placing Maggie on his lap, then motioning to the littered table.

"Mommy's starting a club," Maggie told him importantly.

"A club?" He looked from Rachel to Sam, who was grinning like she'd just won the state's largest lottery. "What kind of club?"

Sam turned to Rachel. "It was your idea. You tell him."

"Well," his wife began, her face wreathed in smiles, "the County Fire Commissioners have asked us to organize a specialized group to investigate arsons, state wide. It's going to be called Fire Investigation Special Team, or F.I.S.T." She hesitated, then looked at Sam.

Sam nodded. "Go ahead."

Rachel took a deep breath. "We want you to be a part of it."

Luke was so pleased to see Rachel back in her element, he would have agreed to anything for any reason to keep her smiling. But deep inside, he knew that he would say yes because, if he was with her, he could do the one thing he'd sworn to himself he would never stop doing—protecting his family. "I would be honored."

* * * * *

“OH, NO!”

The reaction slipped out before Emma Valentine could stop it, for there stood the very man she most wanted to avoid seeing again.

He didn’t look any happier to see her.

“Well, come on, get on board,” he said gruffly. “I won’t bite.” One eyebrow rose. “Though I might nibble a little,” he added, mostly to amuse himself.

But she wasn’t paying any attention to what he was saying. She was staring at him, taking in the royal blue uniform he was wearing, with gold braid and glistening badges decorating the sleeves, epaulettes and an upright collar. Ribbons and medals covered the breast of the short, fitted jacket. A gold-encrusted sabre hung at his side. And suddenly it was clear to her who this man really was.

She gulped wordlessly. Reaching out, he took her elbow

and pulled her aboard. The doors slid closed. And finally she found her tongue.

"You…you're the prince."

He nodded, barely glancing at her. "Yes. Of course."

She raised a hand and covered her mouth for a moment. "I should have known."

"Of course you should have. I don't know why you didn't." He punched the ground-floor button to get the elevator moving again, then turned to look down at her. "A relatively bright five-year-old child would have tumbled to the truth right away."

Her shock faded as her indignation at his tone asserted itself. He might be the prince, but he was still just as annoying as he had been earlier that day.

"A relatively bright five-year-old child without a bump on the head from a badly thrown water polo ball, maybe," she said defensively. She wasn't feeling woozy any longer and she wasn't about to let him bully her, no matter how royal he was. "I was unconscious half the time."

"And just clueless the other half, I guess," he said, looking bemused.

The arrogance of the man was really galling.

"I suppose you think your 'royalness' is so obvious it sort of shimmers around you for all to see?" she challenged. "Or better yet, oozes from your pores like…like sweat on a hot day?"

"Something like that," he acknowledged calmly. "Most people tumble to it pretty quickly. In fact, it's hard to hide even when I want to avoid dealing with it."

"Poor baby," she said, still resenting his manner. "I guess that works better with injured people who are half asleep." Looking at him, she felt a strange emotion she couldn't identify. It was as though she wanted to prove something to him, but she wasn't sure what. "And anyway, you know you did your best to fool me," she added.

His brows knit together as though he really didn't know what she was talking about. "I didn't do a thing."

"You told me your name was Monty."

"It is." He shrugged. "I have a lot of names. Some of them are too rude to be spoken to my face, I'm sure." He glanced at her sideways, his hand on the hilt of his sabre. "Perhaps you're contemplating one of those right now."

You bet I am.

That was what she would like to say. But it suddenly occurred to her that she was supposed to be working for this man. If she wanted to keep the job of coronation chef, maybe she'd better keep her opinions to herself. So she clamped her mouth shut, took a deep breath and looked away, trying hard to calm down.

The elevator ground to a halt and the doors slid open laboriously. She moved to step forward, hoping to make her escape, but his hand shot out again and caught her elbow.

"Wait a minute. *You're* a woman," he said, as though that thought had just presented itself to him.

"That's a rare ability for insight you have there, Your Highness," she snapped before she could stop herself. And then she winced. She was going to have to do better than that if she was going to keep this relationship on an even keel.

But he was ignoring her dig. Nodding, he stared at her with a speculative gleam in his golden eyes. "I've been looking for a woman, but you'll do."

She blanched, stiffening. "I'll do for what?"

He made a head gesture in a direction she knew was opposite of where she was going and his grip tightened on her elbow.

"Come with me," he said abruptly, making it an order.

She dug in her heels, thinking fast. She didn't much like orders. "Wait! I can't. I have to get to the kitchen."

"Not yet. I need you."

"You what?" Her breathless gasp of surprise was soft, but she knew he'd heard it.

"I need you," he said firmly. "Oh, don't look so shocked. I'm not planning to throw you into the hay and have my way with you. I need you for something a bit more mundane than that."

She felt color rushing into her cheeks and she silently begged it to stop. Here she was, formless and stodgy in her chef's whites. No makeup, no stiletto heels. Hardly the picture of the femmes fatales he was undoubtedly used to. The likelihood that he would have any carnal interest in her was remote at best. To have him think she was hysterically defending her virtue was humiliating.

"Well, what if I don't want to go with you?" she said in hopes of deflecting his attention from her blush.

"Too bad."

"What?"

Amusement sparkled in his eyes. He was certainly enjoying this. And that only made her more determined to resist him.

"I'm the prince, remember? And we're in the castle. My orders take precedence. It's that old pesky divine rights thing."

Her jaw jutted out. Despite her embarrassment, she couldn't let that pass.

"Over my free will? Never!"

Exasperation filled his face.

"Hey, call out the historians. Someone will write a book about you and your courageous principles." His eyes glittered sardonically. "But in the meantime, Emma Valentine, you're coming with me."

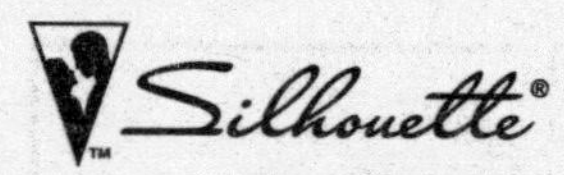

INTIMATE MOMENTS®

COMING NEXT MONTH

#1431 CAVANAUGH WATCH—Marie Ferrarella
Cavanaugh Justice
An intense attraction threatens to blur the boundaries between business and pleasure when a prosecutor falls hard for the bodyguard assigned to protect her.

#1432 THE REBEL KING—Kathleen Creighton
Capturing the Crown
When a rebel leader is revealed as the true heir to the throne, bounty hunter Rhia de Hayes will stop at nothing to retain the fleeing prince. But what will Rhia do when she falls for the future king?

#1433 LUCKY'S WOMAN—Linda Winstead Jones
Last Chance Heroes
A psychic and a detective team up to pose as a happy couple in hopes of luring a serial killer—and in turn discover that the bonds that tie them together are much deeper than they'd expected.

#1434 HEAT OF THE MOMENT—Diana Duncan
Forever in a Day
When a stalker begins upping the odds, Kate Chabeau is reunited with her ex-love, SWAT bomb tech Liam O'Rourke, and is forced to face her deepest fears and trust the only man she's ever loved.

SIMCNM0806